Advance Praise for *Murder...S*

In her debut novel, *Murder...Suicide...Whatever...*, Gwen Freeman
has created an entertaining and engaging heroine in Fifi Cutter, an
insurance claims adjuster who not-so-effortlessly juggles sleuthing
with her colorful—if not particularly helpful—extended family.
Droll, cynical and sharp-witted, Fifi may be small in stature but
comes up big when peeling back the surprising layers in this well-
crafted mystery.
  —Kathleen Tracy, *Unkindness of Ravens*

I fell in love with her heroine, Fifi Cutter—couldn't put the book
down. Fifi's acerbic wit, rapidfire dialogue, and off-the-wall
situations will win you over.
  —Sheila Lowe, *Poison Pen*

Intricate plot twists keep the action moving, while you're laughing
too hard to figure out whodunit. It's like Carl Hiaasen moved to
LA and became a hip young black woman.
  —James Phillippi, *Airstream*

There is a sly sophistication lurking behind the laughter created
by Fifi Cutter, the scrappy heroine of *Murder...Suicide...Whatever...*,
the witty debut novel of Gwen Freeman. This first in her mystery
series may be set in the guise of a traditional locked-door, but Ms.
Freeman wrestles a generation of self-absorbed Los Angelinos flat
to the mat before they know the match has begun.
  —Robert Fate, *Baby Shark* and *Baby's Shark's Beaumont Blues*

Fifi Cutter has outrageous 'tude. She is the most entertaining
amateur sleuth since Stephanie Plum. Fifi and her mismatched
sibling fumble their way through the investigation of an apparent
heart attack victim—
a guy found in a locked room. Although Ms. Freeman begins from
a standard whodunit set-up, this is not your Aunt Mabel's mystery.
  —Bruce Cook, *Phillipine Fever*

A bouncy, fun, witty whirlwind of a mystery, with enough twists
and turns to keep you guessing right up to the last page.
  —David Hosp, *Innocence* and *Dark Harbor*

MURDER...
SUICIDE...
WHATEVER...

GWEN FREEMAN

CAPITAL CRIME PRESS
FORT COLLINS, COLORADO

Copyright © 2007 by Gwen Freeman

First edition published in the United States by Capital Crime Press. Printed in Canada. Cover art by Gwen Freeman. Cover design by Nick Zelinger.

Capital Crime Press is a registered trademark.

Library of Congress Catalog Card Number: 2006936523
ISBN-13: 978-0-9776276-1-5
ISBN-10: 0-9776276-1-6

www.capitalcrimepress.com

For my peeps with whom I roll

Chapter 1

"Uncle Ted was murdered," said Bosco.

I blocked the doorway with my body. "We don't have an Uncle Ted."

"Okay, it was a courtesy title," Bosco amended. "But he's dead."

"Sorry to hear that. It still doesn't explain what you're doing on my front porch, with…" I counted silently, "six pieces of matching Gucci luggage."

"I told you, I'm here to investigate his death." Bosco lowered his voice, as if the Pakistani cab driver who was hovering behind him could understand what he was saying.

"Investigate? What do you mean, investigate? Like a reporter? All of a sudden you're a reporter? When did you get that job? You've never had a job. And even if you did get a job, why in hell would you assume you could stay with me while you're doing it?"

"You're my sister…" he began.

"Half-sister," I interrupted. The cabbie had picked up on my tone of voice and was starting to look anxious.

"All right, half-sister. Now, would you mind just paying the nice gentleman, so we can continue this discussion inside?" Bosco moved forward.

"Forty-eight dollars!" The cabbie waved his arms.

I ducked behind the door and yelled through the crack.

"Yes, I would mind, I don't have forty-eight bucks to throw away."

"Fifty-three bucks," Bosco corrected me. "You have to tip the guy, Fifi."

The cabbie raised his voice. "You pay me! You pay me!" A neighbor, walking by with a wiener dog on a leash, turned to look.

"Bosco Dorff, you get right back in that cab," I ordered.

"And go where?"

"I don't care. Go anywhere. Go back to New York."

"I'm not going back to New York. It's almost November. They're expecting snow."

"Then go stay with Mother in the Valley."

"Mom and I are not speaking, as you well know."

"I'm not speaking to you either. You ruined my graduation from college? Remember that?"

"Oh come on, I didn't ruin it." Bosco put a hand on the door and pushed, forcing it open a few more inches. "And that was eight years ago. Give it a rest."

"Five years ago." I propped my shoulder against the door. "It was only five years ago. And I'll never live down the humiliation. Not in a hundred years. You hit on my Spanish professor, and you stole the limousine." Memories of that un-avenged insult gave me extra strength. The door closed an inch.

"Miss Gomez wanted to go to the beach, Fifi. What was I supposed to do? She had bazongas out to here."

"Get back in the cab. Get back in that cab right now." I leaned harder, putting some bootie into it. Bosco pushed back. The cabbie abandoned English and screeched at the top of his lungs in some Pakistani dialect. Two more neighbors paused on the sidewalk to enjoy the show.

"Be reasonable, Fifi. You owe it to Aunt Angela."

"Who the hell is Aunt Angela?"

"Uncle Ted's widow."

"I don't remember Uncle Ted. I don't remember Aunt Angela. I don't owe anyone anything."

"Just let me in."

"It's really not convenient."

"Fifi, I need a place to stay. I'm your brother."

"Half-brother."

"Family is family, Fifi. Anyway, your dad left you this huge house and you live by yourself. And you're probably lonely. You don't date a lot, do you? It'll be good for you to have some company."

"I like living alone, and I get plenty of dates." The first part of that statement was mostly accurate. The second part, not really. I'm short and skinny. I'm ethnically ambiguous. I have a big nose and hair that sticks out like a windsock in a hurricane. Black eyebrows that make me look like I'm perpetually annoyed, which, by the way, is close to the truth.

"You're a mooch," I told him. "You always think you can get by on your looks."

"Well, I'm a handsome guy, Feef."

"I'm not paying for your taxi." I braced my knees to get better leverage.

"I said I'd pay you back." Bosco countered my knees with his shoulder. He had eighty pounds on me. I couldn't hold out much longer. I was going to have to let him in. But not without a fight.

"Pay me with what? You don't have any money, and you don't have a job."

"I do have a job, Fifi. Uncle Ted's firm retained me to investigate his death. It was a very mysterious death. That's what I've been trying to tell you." He gave a final shove, and the door swung wide.

The cabby's audience had grown to include seven neighbors: the original woman with the dachshund, two elderly gay men, three youngish women, and a hard-body marathon type who had paused in his jog to see what the commotion was about. "They no pay, they no pay, I drive alla way from LAX—teeny, windy roads alla way up here. I no get lost! I good driver! They no pay!"

The phalanx of neighbors glared in my direction.

I stalked off to the kitchen, got my purse from the counter, and counted out fifty-three dollars in crumpled fives and ones. The taxi driver didn't seem impressed with his tip, but he left, allowing the mini-crowd to disperse. Bosco gave me a big hug, like that would make up for everything. I stared past him, at the pile of luggage. "You can stay for three days. Three days, that's it."

"Fifi, it's going to take longer than three days. At least I hope it is—I'm getting paid by the hour. That's two hundred dollars an hour. Can you give me a hand with the bags? I hurt my back in Vail last week."

"You don't ski."

"Of course I don't ski. I like the indoor sports. And Jenna, this really hot girl I met..."

"I don't want to hear about it," I muttered, grabbing the medium-sized bag. He followed me in, empty-handed.

"Shit," he remarked looking around. "You don't have much in the way of furniture, do you?"

"Sore subject," I warned him. "Mother cleaned me out."

Bosco gave me an inquiring look as I struggled with the suit bag.

"Pop left me the house," I explained, "but according to our Mutual Mother, he did not leave me the contents."

"What's that got to do with Mom? They were divorced."

"Not exactly. Pop bought the house after he and Mother separated, just two months before he died." I cleared my throat. If Mother was a sore subject, Pop dying was the sorest subject ever. "An aneurysm they said. Mother was super-pissed. She had been really looking forward to taking him for everything he had."

"She couldn't take the house, though?"

"Just everything in it."

"That's so Mom." Bosco snort-laughed.

"It's not funny, Bosco."

He patted me on the head as he looked around the spacious, darkly paneled living room, and up at the box beam ceiling. The house was a stone-and-shingle Craftsman, perched at the top of Mt. Washington, a canyon-creased old LA neighborhood, one hill over the freeway from Dodger Stadium. I couldn't even afford the property taxes. I should have put it on the market and sold out. That would have been the smart thing to do.

"Damn, she really did take everything. There's really nothing left here at all." Bosco gestured.

"There's a desk," I pointed with my chin toward a card table I had set up in the dining room, on which my p.c. precariously sat. "And a table and a chair in the kitchen."

"So where's the TV?" Bosco asked.

"I don't have a TV, Bosco."

Bosco squeaked. "How are we going to watch TV?"

I thought about it. "I guess we're not," I replied.

This news kept Bosco silent for fifteen seconds. "Don't you think you ought to buy a TV? I could go with you, make sure you got a real good deal."

"Bosco, look. I work freelance out of my house. I'm an independent insurance adjustor. I handle car dents and fall downs. I don't make a ton of money."

"I thought you had a good job with a big insurance company?"

"It didn't work out. We had different goals."

"You got fired?"

I nodded.

"Race related?" he asked. "If it was, you could sue."

"I'd like to say so, but from what I got at the exit interview, they hated everything about me. Except this one guy. He liked me okay, and sends me a few jobs. Or maybe," I considered, "maybe he doesn't like me. He only sends me crappy jobs in terrible parts of town that he couldn't get his own guys to do, not even for extra doughnuts. But the thing is, I have bills to pay, like electricity and water. And my property taxes come due in three weeks. I'm going to owe like twenty-two hundred dollars. I sleep on a futon, and you're going to be sleeping on a pool raft."

"Fifi, I can't sleep on a pool raft. My back." Bosco gave me his patented dimples-forward smile.

That damn smile.

*   *   *

I spent the rest of the afternoon working at my desk, comparing pictures and witness reports of accident scenes with repair estimates and writing up reports. Found one charge for a door-ding repair where the accident photos clearly showed a rear-ender.

I also got two telephone calls. One wrong number and one for Bosco. He was pretty quick, giving out this number, I thought as I yelled up the stairs for him to come down and take the call.

"Don't you have a cell phone?" I groused.

Bosco placed his hand over the mouthpiece. "If you will excuse me, I'll take this in the other room. Very important call concerning the investigation." Oh sure. Like I wanted to listen in. Like I cared about some dead guy who wasn't really my uncle.

Around seven, Bosco came into the dining room.

"When's dinner? This detecting is hard work."

"Who was that on the phone?" I asked. "If you're hungry, look in the refrigerator."

"Nobody you know. I did look in the refrigerator and there's nothing to eat."

"Fine, I don't care who was on the phone. If you have some money, we can go get cheap Chinese."

"I don't have a lot of money," Bosco admitted—big surprise. "But I do have a credit card."

I eyed him suspiciously.

"It's my Dad's," he explained. "He let me use it for the trip."

I was happy to believe that. Mr. Dorff was unaccountably fond of his only son.

Chapter 2

"We can't go in this thing." Bosco looked with un-disguised contempt at the peeling, not very clean Ford flat-bed in the driveway, which someone in the distant past had painted orange. Not a subtle sienna or a pale peach. Bright orange. It was the un-coolest car in LA.

"Only wheels I got," I said. "It belongs to a business acquaintance of Lloyd's, some guy who owns a construction company. He's out in the Middle East now or something. It's just a loaner."

Lloyd Tuttle was the man Mother had married with unseemly haste four months ago in a lovely backyard ceremony, to which Bosco had not been invited. Lloyd made big money, belonged to two country clubs and played golf. Which meant he had lots of useful friends.

"What do you call it, Truck L'Orange?" Bosco asked as he got in.

I ignored him. *God, he thinks he's so funny.*

We slipped down the hill into Chinatown and took a table at my favorite dive, the Golden Turtle Palace. The room was bathed in bright fluorescent lights. The no-longer-white walls were dotted with faded posters of Oriental beauties in one-piece swimsuits.

The service at the Golden Turtle is so fast you hardly have time to sit down at all. I ordered the sesame noodles and tofu with baby corn. I'm partial to bland, beige foods in manageable portions. Bosco ordered won-ton soup, steamed rice, Szech-wan beef and slippery shrimp. He's partial to excess.

When the waiter had taken the menus and delivered the tea, Bosco smiled fondly at me and asked, "Has it really been five years since we last saw each other? Amazing. My baby sister is all grown up."

"And my grown-up brother is still a baby." I saluted him with my tea cup.

The food arrived twelve minutes later and the smile became a grin. "It's great to see you."

"What?" I asked, my eyes narrowing.

Bosco dropped the grin and leaned forward. "I have a little favor to ask you."

"Another little favor," I corrected him. "I am already doing you a favor. In fact, I am doing you a big favor by letting you stay at my house. A huge favor. A gigundus favor."

"And I appreciate it," he hastened to assure me. "It's just that I was thinking tomorrow, you know, you'd like to come with me to Uncle Ted's funeral."

"Why would I do that? I'm telling you, I don't remember any Uncle Ted. If you brought him in here right now with the Lakers starting lineup, I wouldn't recognize him. Except he'd be the dead, white one."

"Well, he was a friend of the family. Ted Heffernan. He was the trustee for the money I earned on The Tisdales."

Bosco had been the cute brother in a sitcom for a few years, when he was a kid. Before his dad won the custody battle and spirited him away to New York.

"Oh, that guy. Why didn't you say so? Buddy of your dad's, right?"

"Yeah, he was dad's insurance broker. Dad figured that if I didn't have a trustee, Mom would end up spending all the money."

I chopsticked a baby corn. "Well, he was married to her for several months, so he must have known her pretty well. But I was five years old when you left, and I'm telling you right now that I am really not the least bit interested in going with you to a funeral. Funerals remind me of death. I don't like thinking about death. I haven't come to terms with it, okay? I don't want you to even mention the word. If you mention the word, I'll keep thinking about it. It's like that thing where they tell you not to think of a hippopotamus, but then once they say 'hippopotamus,' all you can think of is 'hippopotamus.' Death is like that."

"There's a particular reason I want you to go," Bosco persisted, unmoved by my existential angst. "There's this guy. Eddie Waller. He's the one who hired me to investigate Uncle Ted's death."

"He hired you? I thought you said the firm hired you. Not that I believe anyone would really hire you." A tofu square slipped from my grasp and dropped on my lap. I discreetly allowed it to plop to the floor.

"Well, Eddie's part of the firm. He's a broker."

"How do you know him, and why is he hiring you to investigate a murder?"

"Uncle Ted got me a summer job at the firm a few years ago. I was majoring in business at the time, so he thought it might be useful. Eddie and I stayed in touch. When he called to tell me about Uncle Ted, he asked me, you know, how'd I'd been and what I was doing. I happened to mention about how I almost joined the FBI."

I laughed. "You didn't 'almost join the FBI.' The FBI wouldn't have you on a plate with wasabe and pickled ginger. I don't even think you ever got an undergraduate degree, but, if you did, it would be in New Age Dream Therapy or Appalachian Musical Traditions. The FBI doesn't have a lot of use for that type of expertise."

"I most certainly did get my undergraduate degree. Sociology. In fact, I have taken several postgraduate classes. And for your information, I dated an FBI agent. She was a stone babe, and smart, too. She encouraged me to seriously consider a career with law enforcement. I felt that if I could develop my natural intuitive instincts, I could be of great assistance in profiling serial killers."

I squeezed my eyes shut. He was still there when I opened them.

"It was just that I ultimately realized I am not cut out for the more militaristic nuances of an organization like that."

I concentrated on not dropping any more tofu bits. Had it really been five years since I'd last seen him? Seemed like yesterday.

"Anyway," continued Bosco, "Eddie is under the impression that I have law enforcement experience. So he asked if maybe I could help out."

The waiter zoomed in and whisked away the plates.

"Naturally. And why do you want me to meet this man who obviously has such poor judgment?"

"I told him that my sister was also a private investigator and licensed here in California. I thought maybe he should hire both of us. You know, like a partnership."

A partnership. To solve a murder. With Bosco. The boy who never grew up. Right.

The waiter threw two fortune cookies on the table as he raced by.

"I don't have a private investigator's license, you retard. I have an independent insurance adjustor's license. Not the same thing at all. C'mon, let's go, they don't like you to linger." I took a last sip of tea. "They only have eleven tables, so they need to turn them at least seventeen times in an evening to make any money. Actually, by the time the check comes, we should be half way to the door with our credit card out."

This was a hint. I didn't mean our credit card. I meant his Dad's credit card. Bosco didn't take the hint.

"Okay, an insurance adjustor's license. Same thing. Maybe even better, since Uncle Ted was an insurance broker, and the firm is an insurance brokerage firm."

"Insurance brokers sell insurance. I adjust claims. The two things have nothing..."

"Can you focus, here, Fifi? This is serious stuff. Eddie doesn't imagine things. He is very level headed. He has to be—working in insurance and all. And he was there when they discovered the body. Uncle Ted died right in his office. They found him last Sunday. It was pretty horrible, I mean they figure he had to have been there since he died on Friday night."

"How do they know for sure when he died?" I couldn't help it.

"A bunch of the women who work in the office came in on Saturday and made a banner for him. It was his fifty-ninth birthday, so there was this huge door-sized sheet of paper, with a big 59 on it and a picture of a cake and skull and crossbones, you know, with all this glitter and everyone had signed it and everything. See, the idea was, they taped the banner over the door to his office, completely covering the door, and then Uncle Ted would come in on Monday and have to break through it to get into his office."

"Office humor. One of the many reasons I'm glad I work at home."

"I know, but you see, when they were taping this over the door on Saturday, he must have been in there—dead—the whole time. That's the really horrible part."

"I disagree," I said, pretending to consider the situation from all angles. "I think that being dead is the horrible part."

I tilted my head as the waiter whizzed back and slammed down the brown plastic tray with the bill, jostling the tea pot, which almost overturned.

Bosco was oblivious. "And the coroner never really gave any cause of death, you know, he just said heart failure. That doesn't tell us what caused the heart failure. 'Heart failure' is what coroners say when they don't really know why the dude died. Eddie says there were a lot of suspicious circumstances, but the cops never really investigated anything. He thinks someone should look into it. He thinks we should look into it. I told him about what a great PI you were and how you caught a whole gang of crooks."

"For the last time, I am not a PI." I unwrapped a fortune cookie and motioned him to silence. "It says 'Do not let others impose on you.'"

"It doesn't say that," Bosco scoffed.

He was right. It really said "Laughter is the best medicine," but that was inapplicable to the situation. At least as far as I was concerned.

"Besides, you did capture that gang, didn't you?" Bosco waved his fortune cookie aside.

I explained that it was not a "gang" in the sense of some street gang, with zip guns and knuckle-dusters. It was a "gang" of loosely connected chiropractors, lawyers, and gypsies who pretended to be hurt in a series of staged accidents.

And I didn't "capture them," as in go out to the 'hood, beat them up, and handcuff them. I simply compared files in the comfort of my cubicle and contacted the fraud units at other companies and matched names and similarities so that the DA was able to put together a case to take to the grand jury. It was, after all, my job. Although, being a lowly claims adjustor, I didn't even get credit for it. My supervisor's supervisor took all the credit, and I got let go.

I spent several minutes explaining all this to Bosco.

"Wow," said Bosco. "You caught a gang of thieves."

"Bosco, what's in it for you if I help this guy?"

"I'm trying to throw some business your way, Fifi. Be a good big brother. Here you are, just starting out—you could use the exposure. Obermeyer & Schlefly is a big firm. And Eddie will pay. I told you, he said he would pay a hundred dollars an hour. Some good coin in the exchequer isn't going to hurt you, is it?"

"You said two hundred dollars an hour," I pointed out.

"Did I? I meant one hundred. But it's still good money, right?"

"You just want me to do all the work, while you sit around doing nothing."

Bosco looked at me with those deceptively soulful eyes. "Please. For me? Just talk to him."

"Oh, okay. I'll go to the funeral and I'll talk to your guy. But no promises."

By this time both the waiter and maitre d' were buzzing around our table like Africanized bees. Bosco stood up and reached into his wallet, a sight I really enjoyed until he made that face. "Oh goddammit," he said. "I must have left the credit card in my carry-on bag back at the house. Hey, I'll catch the next one."

Chapter 3

The funeral was at 10:30 in Glendale, an enclave just north of downtown LA. Glendale is superficially indistinguishable from the suburbs of Akron, Ohio, but 87 different languages are spoken in the public schools. It has good freeway access from Mt. Washington.

Bosco looked even better than usual, dressed in a super-nice suit, a true charcoal grey, with a light grey shirt, and red, black, and silver tie. I assumed he hadn't paid for it himself. I had donned a beautifully tailored two-piece navy linen ensemble. The jacket was short, with 3/4 sleeves, and the shin-length skirt had a kick pleat. Mother would have almost approved.

The church was light and airy inside, whitewashed walls with a gold modernistic chandelier. The space was big, and it was filling up. Bosco would have walked right down to sit in front, but I jerked his arm and made him sit with me toward the back. We got a good seat on the aisle.

Bosco smiled and nodded at people as they passed, providing me with a running commentary.

A plump, faded blonde who looked to be near sixty supported a pretty young woman in a very short skirt. The skirt was black, but it just didn't say "mourning," since it was halfway up her ass.

"That's Chloe, Uncle Ted's daughter, and her mom. I don't really know the mom. She and Uncle Ted got divorced a really long time ago, when Chloe was just a baby. Chloe's okay. We went out a few times when I was here that summer."

Chloe smiled wanly when she caught Bosco's eye and leaned over me to give him a quick half-hug before following her mother up the aisle.

"That's Aunt Angela," Bosco indicated another blonde. "You know, Uncle Ted's widow."

Angela Heffernan was wearing a lot of makeup, but in colors like "Barely There" and "Pink Whispers," so you couldn't really tell. Her platinum highlights had been meticulously woven in through the golden under-color, swept back to a chignon and fixed with a black velvet bow. She clutched the arm of a short, paunchy man with thick brownish-gray hair, a man who radiated arrogance.

"Robert Schlefly," Bosco informed me as the pair approached. "One of the partners in the insurance firm. Obermeyer & Schlefly."

As Aunt Angela passed us, she, too, recognized Bosco, and leaned over me to give his hand a squeeze.

"So good of you to come," she whispered. "You must visit me while you're out here. Bobby," she said turning to the man at her side, "You remember Bosco, Ted's nephew? He interned for the firm a few summers ago?"

Schlefly flashed teeth that were as big and white as piano keys. He also leaned over me and gave Bosco a two handed "hey buddy" handshake before moving on.

I noticed a brunette walking dispiritedly behind them. She was fortyish and would still have been attractive if not for the defeated slump to her shoulders. Mrs. Schlefly, according to Bosco.

"And that's Obermeyer," Bosco whispered, indicating a gangly, balding man who looked to be seventy. He ignored Bosco and did not lean over me to get to him, so I gave him points.

Bosco continued. "Eddie told me that Aunt Angela and

Uncle Ted were separated. He had gotten his own apartment, but nothing was final."

"So if Ted was murdered, do you think Angela has a motive?"

"Maybe. Eddie told me that Uncle Ted was fooling around with someone at work. He had a daughter with Angela, though—Paige. Looks like they didn't bring her. Probably a good idea. She's just a little kid."

"Wasn't Uncle Ted kind of old to be having children too young to go to his funeral?" I asked.

An overweight, homely woman in a black serge coatdress plodded up the aisle to a place saved for her by Obermeyer. Bosco said her name was Karen Something. She had been Ted Heffernan's assistant. I doubted she was the person Ted was fooling around with.

I noted a striking Hispanic woman wearing a fabulous hunter green shawl-collared jacket over a fitted skirt, sailing down the aisle in Manolo Blahniks which perfectly matched the color of her suit. Nicely done.

"Who's that?"

"That's Corazon Villareal. She was Ted's main competition at the firm. Eddie calls her 'Horchata.'"

"Why?'

"Mexican ice."

"I'm gonna love Eddie, aren't I?"

A man who was almost really good looking—but not quite—caught my attention as he made a show of offering Angela his condolences a little too loudly. Bosco didn't know him.

"He wasn't at the firm the summer I was there. Looks like a friendly guy, though."

The last to enter was yet another blonde, but a very different type from Angela Heffernan—big hair and drug-store cosmetics of the "Poppy Red" and "Midnight Blue" variety. Bosco thought she looked familiar but couldn't put a name to her. There were, he said, a lot of hot chicks around that summer. It seemed to me that this particular hot chick took note of Angela and then sat as far away from her as was possible.

As the organist hit the opening chords, Bosco craned his neck to catch the attention of a particularly repellent individual sitting two rows up. Even from that distance I could tell the suit had been bought at a buy two, get one free sale.

It had to be Eddie Waller, and Bosco confirmed that it was. Eddie looked back and gave Bosco a head-bob. I caught a glimpse of brownish hair, gelled straight back, revealing a sloping forehead and emphasizing a long, sharp nose. He was with his wife and teenage son. I couldn't see the wife very well but the son turned around to stare at us, a miniature version of his father, with acne.

I zoned out for most of the service, sifting through the individuals Bosco had pointed out to me. Did he really think one of them had deliberately killed Ted Heffernan? Or was he just interested in putting me to work so that I could buy a television and he could hang out at my house forever?

After the procession, Bosco and I edged out a side door. Since Uncle Ted had been cremated, there wasn't going to be any graveside service, and we could leave as soon as we linked up with Eddie.

He came out the front with his wife and son. Mrs. Waller, with her arm around the boy, headed for the parking lot, but stopped when Eddie touched her arm. He talked to her, pumping his hands and jerking his head in our direction. She yelled back at Eddie in kind of a low voice, you know—funeral appropriate.

I wasn't close enough to hear what they were saying, but I had a guess. He was informing her for the first time that he wanted to take the car and was telling her that she had to get a ride home from someone else.

Mrs. Waller gave Eddie a light punch to the midsection, spun on her heel and said something over her shoulder. I still couldn't hear her, but it looked like two syllables, first word starting with an "F." She marched over to the fat woman and gesticulated. Karen, the one Bosco had identified as Uncle Ted's assistant, made calming motions with her hands, and the two women walked toward the parking lot together. The boy stood uncertainly, looking over at Eddie, before turning and trotting after his mother.

Eddie came over, stood in front of me and looked me up and down while Bosco introduced us. He frowned. "This is your sister the PI? Isn't she kind of...," he paused, "short for this work?"

"Not at all. Investigation is nine tenths mental and Fifi here, she's a mental giant. And she has great resources to bring to the job. Did we mention that her other brother–half brother–is a homicide cop with LAPD?"

More Bosco hyperbole. I knew that Joseph Cutter, III, my Pop's oldest child (first marriage, 100% black), was in the LAPD. But I had no idea whether he was a homicide cop or a meter maid. I last saw him at Pop's funeral and he was all ticked off because he didn't get anything under Pop's will, which is ridiculous, because Joey Three already has a house.

Eddie stared for another minute before grunting his acquiescence. "Alright already, get outta here. We need someplace we can talk privately," he said. "There's a restaurant on mid-Wilshire, Aldo's." I looked dubious. "I'm buying," he added grudgingly.

Okay, I'd have to drive to mid-Wilshire but at least I'd get lunch out of the deal. Although I had my doubts about any restaurant Eddie would choose. Judging from his clothes, he had all the sophistication of a Jell-O shot.

*   *   *

My doubts were justified. Aldo's was dark-mirrored glass, red Naugahyde booths and black walls. There were no other patrons in the main dining room, but we walked past two middle-aged pale males hunched over the bar, discussing something that gave them no joy.

Eddie asked the fruity little squirt who seated us for the booth in the corner. I understood why Eddie had picked Aldo's: there was no chance of running into anyone from the funeral. Or anyone who cared about good food.

"The thing is," Eddie began directly, "There's something very suspicious about Ted's death. Seemingly healthy guy, heart just quits. Nobody saw it coming. His death becomes a homily to the rest of us to live life to the fullest, love our families, relax." Eddie sighed. "Ted would have hated that."

"I can sympathize." A black-skirted waitress plopped three sloppy water glasses down on the linen-like tablecloth and walked away.

"And," Eddie continued, "toxicology was negative. Ted was just slumped in his chair at his desk. There was a phone within reach, but he didn't phone anyone."

"Not knowing the cause of death is not evidence, Eddie. It's just the lack of evidence," I pointed out and began to peruse the menu, although I could have told you what was on it without looking.

"But I have evidence," Eddie insisted.

The waitress returned.

"MynameisJessieandIwillbeyourservertoday. MayItell-youaboutthespecials?" Plain, sullen, and a mumbler. I really hoped she didn't want to be an actress.

"Nah," said Eddie. "Steak/swordfish combo, fries and a Heineken."

"Salad, Coke," I said.

Bosco cleared his throat and gave Jessie the benefit of his full attention. "I would like the orange roughy, but hold the caper-cream sauce. Just lightly seared." He looked Jessie over with a keen eye. "Are the asparagus fresh or canned?" Jessie's face was a perfect blank.

"If they're fresh, substitute the asparagus for the green beans. If they're both canned, then bring whatever vegetable is fresh. Toast the bread. Do you have a tapenade? No? Well, maybe I'll just use olive oil. Extra virgin. On the side."

Bosco reached over to pat her arm, but Jessie had already fled.

"I didn't order my drink," Bosco protested.

I turned back to Eddie. "What evidence?"

"You heard how we found him?"

Bosco nodded. "Sunday afternoon. The security guard, you, and a secretary working overtime."

"Right. We were spooked. His wife, you know, Angela, called me. She hadn't been able to reach him. She was pretty upset. They were going through this separation thing and she wanted to tell him something about picking the kid up on Monday. He was supposed to be at a marketing event in Laguna Beach. Thing is, when she called to the hotel, they said he hadn't been there at all. So Angela called me."

Eddie shrugged, apparently recognizing the improbability of anyone turning to him for help.

"Did he just blow it off?" I asked.

"We don't know," Eddie replied. "He was originally scheduled to go; and then on Friday, right at the last minute, he told his assistant—that's Karen Odom—to go in his place. Very strange, since we all knew this conference was partly a boondoggle for Ted to get away with Belinda Barrett to a ritzy hotel at the firm's expense."

"Belinda Barrett?" I pictured Miss Poppy Red.

"She's on our staff. She's the one Ted was banging. So, anyway, Angela called me. I had no idea where Ted was. So I...uh...I called Rob Schlefly..." Eddie trailed off.

I deduced that old Eddie had leaped at the opportunity to squeal on Ted to the boss.

"Rob lives in Brentwood. Maybe ten minutes from the office. But he told me to go in. Why did he tell me that? I don't live anywhere close to the office. I live in San Marino."

"I thought you lived in Alhambra," said Bosco.

"Right on the border," Eddie glared. "Anyway, I do not live anywhere close to Century City. Rob insisted I drive all

the way in. Like he didn't want to be the one to find him."
Eddie paused for emphasis.

"That's your evidence?" I jeered.

"I'm telling you, it was like Rob knew something," Eddie insisted. "And how could he, if it was a totally unexpected freak heart thing that had never before been detected? Which is also not very likely. The partners are all insured, and they have to have annual insurance physicals every year."

"That's redundant."

"I know it's redundant. But I am telling you they make the partners undergo annual physicals every year."

"I mean 'annual' and 'every year' is redundant."

"You are completely missing the point!" Eddie raised his voice. "Pay attention. I went up to Ted's office. The door was closed. And there was this huge sheet of white paper taped over the whole door. 'Happy birthday, Ted!' Signed by everyone. Well, not everyone. I mean I didn't sign it. I didn't even know they were doing it. But all the secretaries and Warren and Rob signed it. Monday was his birthday."

I was unmoved. It isn't worse to die a few days before your birthday than a few days after. I mean, it's never a good time.

"I tried the door. But it was locked," Eddie said as the food arrived.

My salad was a pile of limp iceberg lettuce, three watery tomato wedges, and a black olive. I felt better when I noticed that Bosco's orange roughy was smothered in caper-cream sauce. And I would say it was "burned" rather than "lightly seared," accompanied by obviously canned peas. Jessie had brought olive oil on the side, but it was a mocking gesture since the toast was dripping in butter.

Eddie dug into his steak and swordfish, and conversation stalled for a good eleven minutes.

"So, how'd you open the door?" I finally prompted.

"Had to go get the security guard."

"Do you all usually lock the doors to your individual offices when you leave at night?"

"Only Warren, because he keeps all that sensitive information about promotions and salaries." Eddie looked a little guilty when he said that. Tickled my curiosity. "But not the rest of us. That's what was so suspicious."

"I don't think that's so suspicious."

"Of course it's suspicious. Bosco, you think it's suspicious, don't you?"

Bosco's head snapped up from the delicate caper-cream sauce-ectomy he was performing on his orange roughy. Since he hadn't been paying attention, it took him a second to figure out which answer was in his best interest. "Very suspicious," he agreed.

"Okay, Eddie, it was suspicious. Tell me what happened next."

"Ted was there, sitting in his chair, looking dead. I knew he was dead. His face was a horrible green color. Debi, the secretary who was putting in overtime, started to gag so we got out of there and I called 911. Then I called Rob, then Karen. She had just gotten back from church. She said she would come right over, and she got there before the paramedics. We watched them load Ted onto the gurney and take him out."

Eddie's eyes bulged a little at the recollection. For a moment I thought he might not finish his fries.

"Karen followed the paramedics out to the elevators, and I went back into his office. Ted's calendar book was there on his desk."

With a flourish, Eddie produced an expensive black leather rectangle slightly larger than a checkbook. It was a daily. Flipping the pages to that fateful Friday, he pointed out the last entry. "Look there."

I did and saw "Laguna" crossed out and "8:00 appt. w/S." scribbled in. "So?"

Eddie's confidence in me hit a new low. "So he had an appointment for the very evening he was killed!"

I shook my head and ticked off on my fingers the numerous fallacies in Eddie's conclusion. "A, you don't know he was killed. From what you're telling us, everybody else thinks he just died. B, you don't know that's 8:00 at night. It might be 8:00 in the morning."

"If it was for 8:00 AM, he wouldn't have had to cancel Laguna."

"All right. C, you don't know it was an appointment for the office. It could have been personal."

Eddie snorted. "What, a haircut? It had to be something important enough to cancel the Laguna trip. And 'S,' that means Schlefly. "

"Maybe the meeting got cancelled."

Eddie snatched back the calendar and riffled through the pages. "Look," he pointed out, "Every time an appointment is cancelled, he crosses it out."

Eddie thrust the calendar at me, showing me pages where entries such as "Jim-Trilogy Co. 3:30" and "Tennis w/Gursky 6:00" had been neatly crossed out.

"You don't know that he did that every time. There might be plenty of unmarked cancellations in there." I pointed with my fork. "We just don't know it because he didn't cross them out. See, it's a logical fallacy to go from 'he did it several times' to 'he did it all the time.'"

Eddie did not respond well to logic. "You're a jerk, you know that? You didn't even know Ted. I knew Ted, and I am telling you that Ted was very methodical."

I ate the olive. "Even so, the 'S' could be anybody. Susan. Steve. Sarah. Lots of names start with 'S.' Besides, it's a far cry from 'he had an appointment' to 'he had an appointment and the person he had an appointment with killed him.' I think we're missing a big piece of information here, Edster. Why would anyone want to kill Ted?"

"You gotta be kidding. Didn't you know Ted?"

"You just told me I didn't."

Eddie squinted his beady eyes in exasperation. "Everyone wanted to kill Ted."

"I didn't want to kill him. I don't think Bosco here wanted to kill him. Bosco?" Bosco reluctantly shook his head.

"I mean everyone at the firm." Eddie's nostrils flared. "Ted was the kind of person who made enemies. He was dynamic, the life of the party, but he could also be a real dick. And then there was the lawsuit fiasco."

"I love a good lawsuit," I cheered. Pop had been a lawyer, a great lawyer. I had grown up on courtroom lore. "Tell all."

"See, about four years ago, the firm got sued by a receptionist. Dina Mraz. For sexual harassment. She accused Ted. He denied everything, but we all knew there was some basis for it. They had a thing, and they weren't very discreet. If you ask me, I think she was totally into it and just got infuriated when he dumped her. Dumped her for Belinda, actually."

"Then she got fired, 'cause she stank. She was snotty to the clients, and she kept directing calls to the wrong people. But, see, she claimed she got fired because she wouldn't submit to Ted's attentions, which was such a lie because, really, the only reason she wasn't fired for so long was because of his attentions. It went all the way to trial, and about a year ago she won, and won big. A million seven. Punitive damages. Our lawyers appealed, but there really wasn't much to argue. It was just that the jury believed Dina when she said Ted forced himself on her, and they didn't believe Ted when he swore nothing ever happened."

"It is such a bummer when your lies aren't believed and someone else's are." I examined the last tomato wedge and pushed the plate away. "So?"

"About a month ago, the court of appeals shot us down. We've staved off immediate collection by appealing to the California Supreme Court. But it isn't going to do any good. She's going to have her judgment, plus interest, which is really racking up. Pretty soon, it's gonna be payday for Dina."

"I can see why everyone would be extremely vexed at Ted," I said, "whose amorous adventures turned out to be not only immoral, but worse, expensive. What I don't see is what good it does to take him out now. The liability is the firm's."

"Very true. But here's the thing. That yearly physical? It was for key-man insurance. The firm carries it on all of its partners. Especially Ted, who brought in millions in commissions every year. Which is why they all put up with his incessant skirt-chasing in the first place."

"Hence the punitive damages," I remarked, seeing, pretty clearly, the jury's point.

Eddie glowered. "Yeah, but the payoff on that insurance is five million dollars. That would solve all our problems and give Warren and Rob a great big bonus for this year. A bonus they wouldn't have to share with Ted."

Bosco looked up from the remains of his blackened roughy. "What's key-man insurance?"

"A business can get life insurance on the important partners," explained Eddie. "It pays off directly to the firm in case something happens to one of your key men. Or women," he conceded. "Although we don't happen to have any women yet."

Okay, I got why Eddie's antennae were up. Someone might think that having Ted's death pay for his excesses in life was justice both poetic and practical. Still, I had trouble agreeing with a weaselly guy in a suit that any dutiful wife would have talked him out of.

"What's in it for you? You're not a partner, are you?"

"No, but Ted was my friend," Eddie said. "If Schlefly and Obermeyer did this, they shouldn't get away with it. It's just not right."

Eddie was trying hard to sound sincere, but he couldn't pull it off. Not with that face. "Eddie, do you really think the two most senior partners in a very well known insurance firm actually conspired to kill the other partner?"

"Yes, I do. Rob Schlefly has no heart at all and neither does Warren Obermeyer. I owe it to Ted to find out what happened." Eddie stuck out his chin defiantly. I still wasn't buying it and even if I actually had been a PI, there was no way I could work for this guy. I glanced meaningfully over at Bosco, who avoided my eye.

"We'll take the job," Bosco stuck his hand out and Eddie took it.

I kicked Bosco under the table.

"First thing I want you to do." Eddie stabbed the air with his finger. "Come with me to the office, after hours, and help me look through Ted's office. No one's touched it, at least no one was supposed to. Not yet. The cops locked it right after I..."

"Stole Ted's calendar?" I suggested.

"After I placed it in my custody for safekeeping. The cops searched the premises after the paramedics had taken Ted away and all, but I don't think they took anything. I don't think they searched all that well, either. I guess they wouldn't. They didn't think there had been a crime. Anyway, I have a key so we can get in."

"How do you have a key?" I asked. I wouldn't give Eddie a key if I had anything I wanted locked up.

"I have a lot of keys."

"If you had a key, why did you need the security guard to open the door to Ted's office?"

"I didn't want anyone to know I had a key. Christ!" Eddie shook his head at how dense some people were.

"What would we be looking for?"

"A motive. Evidence. Something. I don't know. That's what we have to find out," Eddie replied, irritated.

Bosco crossed his arms. "We're going to need a retainer of two thousand dollars."

I was impressed. Eddie less so. "I'll give you five hundred." He pulled out his checkbook and wrote a check.

I took it. Eddie was unpleasant and I didn't trust him, but I had to admit the work would certainly be more interesting than investigating who really had the red light at the busy intersection.

Not to mention that tax bill. If I couldn't pay my property

taxes, they would take the house and sell it, and I'd end up in a cheap little apartment in North Hollywood. As I had explained to my brother Joe when I confronted him at the graveside, Pop wanted me to have the house.

Chapter 4

"I'm warning you," the voice hissed in my ear. "Don't do it."

I tried to respond, but my tongue got stuck in my throat.

"It's a very bad idea," the voice continued.

"Uh..."

"You let him stay for a few days, you'll never get rid of him. He's a freeloader. He's never had a real job."

"Mother, he's already here, and I already said he could stay," I finally blurted out. It was barely 8:00 on Monday morning, way too early for a full scale Mother-attack.

"He pretends to have family feeling. He doesn't give a rat's ass about any of us, Fifi. He pours on the charm so you'll let him do whatever he wants."

"He hasn't been charming at all," I protested. "And, for your information, Mother, he does have a job. He's working for an insurance firm. It's good money, and he got me some temporary work too."

"You are so gullible, Fifi. You're just like your father, you want to believe the best about everyone. I used to tell him, 'Joe, nice guys finish last.' I must have said that a million times."

"Yeah, I know, Mom, I was right there when you said it. I think I got the message."

Mother responded by giving me fifteen minutes of Shock and Awe about everything else that was wrong with me and hung up.

*   *   *

Later that morning, I had to inspect a three-car accident in Westwood—fairly serious injuries. All three vehicles had been towed to a lot, and I needed to photograph them before they were scrapped to make sure the accident had really happened the way it was reporteu. I figured I might as well stop by the Obermeyer & Schlefly office on the way.

Here's what I was thinking, what if someone *had* killed Ted? Say, an evil research chemist had fed him some untraceable poison or an Asian martial arts master had applied a deadly pressure point to his big toe. Someone like that. Well, maybe I could find out something from the sign-in book. Every office building today requires people to sign in. If somebody had killed Ted, maybe that person signed in. I could look for people whose name started with "S." Okay, it was a long shot but the worst that could happen is that I wasted a little time.

I dressed in a beige pantsuit, for maximum inconspicuousness, waited for traffic to subside, then drove out to Century City.

The insurance brokerage firm of Obermeyer & Schlefly was housed in one of the smaller, older buildings. I parked underground, and took the stairs to the lobby, where the recessed lighting was subdued to the point of gloomy, and the air conditioning was arctic.

I waited until there wasn't anyone else around, and then strode up to the U-shaped mahogany-veneered security console. The bespectacled guard, identified by his nametag as Mr. Ballon, pushed over a large spiral-bound book with a yellow shiny cover. It said "All-Star Security Log" on the front.

"Man, security is such a big deal these days, " I said, picking up the pen. "Does everyone have to sign in?"

"All visitors. People who work here only have to sign in on the weekend."

"Wow, brand new book," I commented. "Looks like it was started this morning." The newness of the book frustrated my great plan to flip back and look at last Friday, the day of Ted's death.

Mr. Ballon shook his head. "Would you believe someone made off with my old one yesterday? Twenty years I've been in security, and no one has ever stolen the book before. I was doing the rounds, and on Sunday, you know, you only have one guy, so you got to leave the desk to do the rounds. Don't blame me, I said; I told them they needed three people at all times. Anyone can get hold of a card key to get in."

I commiserated.

"Truth is," he continued, "they don't want to spend the money. They already cut back on our vacations."

I commiserated again. "And it can be dangerous, too, right?" I said, "I mean, I heard some dude got killed on the fifteenth floor last week."

The old troll shook his head indulgently. "He didn't get killed. He just died. Heart. Anyway, I wasn't on duty then. Or when he was discovered on Sunday, neither. I had Friday day and Sunday night, so I missed the fun at both ends."

I was disappointed, and even more so when, at that moment, our delightful tête-à-tête was interrupted by a horde of grim-faced businessmen and one equally grim-faced woman, marching across the lobby like a detail of storm troopers. They really wanted to get up to the seventh floor, and they didn't want to wait.

I quickly wrote in "Harriet Stowe" under "Your Name" and "Obermeyer & Schlefly" under the heading "Firm, Person or Company Visited."

Mr. Ballon called out "Have a good day, Ms. Stowe," as I slunk off to the elevator bank for floors 11 through 18. Once out of sight, I slipped over to the lobby shop where I called Eddie from a pay phone. He wasn't as excited as I thought he would be about the missing sign-in book.

"You know, Eddie, maybe the book isn't that big a deal standing alone. But I think the timing of the theft is as interesting as anything else. This is now over a week after the murder. If you were going to take it, why not lift it a lot sooner?"

"I don't know," Eddie said. "I can't figure it out."

"Are you sure you didn't tell anyone about maybe you were thinking of hiring me to investigate? I mean, this is the day right after we met. It's the only explanation I can come up with."

He denied it vehemently. "I wouldn't tell anyone here, believe me. I don't want Schlefly and Obermeyer knowing I've hired a private investigator. Are you crazy?"

"Okay, fine." I backed off. "But you know, security in this building is pretty lax. I didn't have to show my driver's license or anything."

"Yeah the old guy's pretty useless, but after hours, you not only need a card key to get into the parking structure—you need it to get the elevator to work. Plus, it'll only stop on the floor your card key's imprinted for. And once you get out on that floor, the doors to Obermeyer & Schlefly are extremely heavy, and you have to have a key. It has to be someone from the office."

I shrugged. The way I figured it if you were a recently laid-off employee, or a family member of an employee, or lucky enough to have pilfered the wallet and key ring of an employee, it wouldn't be all that hard to stroll right in, sign in a fake name, and make off with all of Obermeyer & Schlefly's portable office supplies. Eddie, however, didn't sound like he wanted to listen to other theories.

Walking through the parking garage, I scored a folding chair that the valet guys had just left there while they went off to park cars. No security cameras, I noticed, as I tossed the chair in the back of the Truck L'Orange.

From there I went to check out the totals at the body shop. It was apparent from my observation that the Civic had T-boned the Pontiac, which had spun sideways into the Cabriolet, a perfectly head-shaped hole in the windshield eloquently testifying to the legitimacy of the claimed injury.

Mr. Cabriolet Driver wasn't going to get as much settlement money as his attorney thought, though, because it was also clear that the dumb ass had not been wearing his seat belt. When will they ever learn?

Bosco was already in the kitchen, sitting in the lone chair at the Formica table. I set the new folding chair on the other side.

"Look, I got another chair. Now we can both sit down."

"And a lovely piece of furniture it is."

"Screw you, Bosco, I worked hard to steal this chair. You think it's easy? I coulda got caught."

*   *   *

Before I could sit down, I heard the rumble of the mail truck turning around in my driveway, and went out to the mailbox at the curb. Past-due notices, a "You May Have Already Won" postcard, and greetings from the local politicians—the usual stuff that goes directly to the recycling bin.

And, a check from Jack at Colchester for work I had done last month, $487.03; plus the $232.54 I had in checking, minus $200.00 I had gotten in cash, plus the five hundred dollar retainer, leaving me with $1,024.57, still way short of what I needed for the property taxes. I shoved the check into my pocket before worry could paralyze me and flipped through the rest of the mail.

Hey, I got a letter too—a real letter, hand addressed to me by name. I puzzled over it as I entered the kitchen by the side door, dumping the rest of the day's takings on the worn wooden countertop.

I ripped the envelope, noting that it was sealed with cellophane tape. One page of plain paper. My mouth dropped as I realized that not only was the letter unfriendly, it was positively insulting. No, worse, it was threatening. The words were formed in block letters with a standard issue black Magic Marker. I ran over and smacked Bosco on the head to get him to pay attention.

"Omigod Bosco! I got a death threat! Listen to this." I cleared my throat and began to read, "'We know who you are. We know where you live. Bottom line, here, you are being warned. Keep your big nose...'"

Bosco interrupted with a shriek, "Eeekkkk! They do know who you are!" he exclaimed.

I gave him my best venomous glare, and continued reading, "'...out of our business.'" I gulped for air. "'Or we will cut it off, and stuff it down your throat.'" My voice dried. "'And choke you with it.'" I paused. "'This will slightly improve your looks.' Oh, that is frosty." I gasped, hyperventilating.

Maybe I was overreacting, but not that many people really get a death threat. The worst thing most people ever get in the mail is a Christmas letter.

Bosco led me back to the kitchen, set me down, got me a glass of water from the sink and took the note from my hand.

"You're not going to let this scare you off, are you?" Bosco said anxiously. "I mean, you can't let the team down. We're a team, right?"

I hesitated, feeling very fluttery. But the tax due notice was still affixed to the refrigerator. Also, okay, I couldn't let the team down.

"Alright, alright, I took the job. I won't quit."

"Atta girl," Bosco beamed. "I always said nothing could stop you when you made your mind up. Nobody bullies Fifi. I always said, Fifi's like a rock..."

"Okay, that's enough. I said I'm not going to quit. But you're sticking to me like glue. Like a bodyguard. Where I go, you go. Got it?"

"Got it, " Bosco said, lounging against the counter and looking like a sportswear model. I really hoped I wouldn't be needing a bodyguard.

*   *   *

I was still hoping I wouldn't need a bodyguard when, just as the sun went down, two hooded figures appeared at the end of my driveway. They were wearing Halloween masks. I froze, my nose pressed to the window. Then I remembered. It *was* Halloween. I had forgotten to buy candy.

Wincing, I turned off all the lights and Bosco and I pretended no one was home for the next two hours, as several eggs splattered against the door and a ripe pumpkin met its spectacular end on my sidewalk. The perfect end to a perfect day.

Chapter 5

Twenty minutes later, the phone rang. It was Eddie.

"We need to have that look-see around Ted's office tonight. We can't wait," he explained. "Somebody's gonna claim that office soon. It's a corner. Come here and we'll drive over together."

I promised we would be at his house by ten. He gave me directions. San Marino, my ass.

I dressed in black Capris, black Pumas and a black turtleneck. Bosco had on chinos, a white button-down shirt and a light gray jacket. He said he should look legit so if anyone discovered us in the office, he could talk his way out of it. I said that if anyone discovered us, I could run away and hide. Fundamental difference.

"I wish I knew what exactly we were looking for," I remarked as we got into the Truck. "If they killed him for the insurance, nothing in that office is going to tell us anything. I gotta tell you, Bosco, I don't think Eddie hired us because he felt so much loyalty to Ted. I'm thinking it over, and it occurs to me that this is all about Eddie snaking Ted's clients now that Ted is gone. If Eddie could get some clients of his own, maybe he could finally make partner."

"That hardly explains his fixation on proving that Rob Schlefly or Warren Obermeyer are the killers," Bosco pointed out. "Anyway, what do we care, we are billing him by the hour. You have to keep that in mind, Fifi. Eye on the prize."

We managed to find the address—no thanks to the directions he gave us (seems Eddie had a little problem with "right" and "left"). We arrived at 10:26. The house was diminutive—a tan stucco with aluminum windows and a chain-link fence around the back. Street parking was scarce, so the Truck L'Orange ended up half a block away. When we walked up the sidewalk, Eddie burst out of the door, practically foaming at the mouth.

"Time is of the essence," he barked at us. "They don't let anyone in the building between midnight and 6:00 AM, whether you have a key card or not."

"So we have to be out by midnight? That doesn't give us a lot of time, Eddie."

"No, once you're in, you're in. You just can't get in after midnight. Come on. I parked here in the street." We crammed into the battered brown Jetta, and Eddie took the wheel. The floor was littered with empty paper cups, gum wrappers and a leaky ballpoint pen. I flicked a hamburger wrapper onto the floor.

The drive to Century City only took thirty-two minutes, no traffic at that time of night, but I could imagine days when Eddie spent over an hour in that depressing little car staring at the big, fat butt of an Astro van all the way in.

We didn't talk much. I was pretty nervous. I wasn't sure if this was really breaking and entering since Eddie was with us and he had a right to be on the Obermeyer & Schlefly premises if not in Ted's office. Still, if we got caught it would be very unpleasant.

We took the stairs to the lobby where Eddie signed us in at the security desk. The night guard paid no attention to us.

Eddie flashed his card for the elevator, which beeped in protest but eventually dragged its sorry elevator ass up to the fifteenth floor. He used his key to get into the main office.

"See, that's four systems that have to be overcome," Eddie observed, "making it likely it was somebody who works here."

"Assuming they parked in the building," I said.

"Assuming they parked in the building," I said.

"Have to park in the building. No street parking. You'd get towed."

"Really?" I raised my eyebrows. "Then we should be able to tell who came in and out that night. You can get a readout of all the parking cards used. I believe these systems tell you the exact minute the car goes in or out."

"Hmmm. Well, maybe I'll look into that." Like he couldn't believe I'd had a good idea.

*   *   *

Eddie took us into the Obermeyer & Schlefly office by the back door. It was creepy dark. Low-wattage nightlights barely illuminated a long hallway. We walked about twenty feet straight down the hall. Eddie stopped in front of a door on the left and took out his well-stocked key ring. He fumbled for a minute, turning towards the inadequate glow of the nearest mini-light and squinting until he found the right key.

Ted's office.

We entered and Eddie flicked on the lights. As offices go, this one was nice, but not Uber Executive. The dark cherry furniture all matched, a desk, two armchairs, a bookcase. And the gray-tweed swivel chair of death.

No photographs, not even of his daughters, big Chloe and little Paige. Instead, two abstract paintings hung over the armchairs, maroon and yellow shapes against a dark background, chosen by a decorator to go with the carpet. Ted's ostentatiously framed diplomas and insurance broker's license hung on the wall behind the desk. The east and south walls were floor-to-ceiling windows.

Eddie made for the credenza behind the desk and pulled out yet another key, a tiny thing that opened the built-in filing cabinet. The guy really did have keys to everything. "I'm going to take a look through these. These are his client files, recent stuff he was working on."

I threw Bosco a triumphant smile. I had been right. Eddie was all about muscling in on Ted's clients.

"Fifi, I want you to go through his electronic data, his files, his correspondence. You want to look for anything that would show a pattern, like fraud or something. Mistakes, kickbacks, cover-ups, anything like that."

Eddie gave me Ted's pass code.

"How do you have his pass code?" I asked.

Eddie explained that the pass codes were all the same as the phone extensions, unless the employee took the trouble to change it, and no one over the age of forty ever did, except, of course, Eddie himself, because he was "careful as to security-related issues, and really pretty knowledgeable in the computer field" (his words). In other words (my words), he was a paranoid tech geek.

I plopped myself down in Ted's cushiony swivel chair, trying not to think about what it would be like to die there, and started skimming. This was, at least, something I was actually qualified to do. Each client had its own file. There were a few big companies and hundreds of smaller companies.

Karen Odom appeared to be the real author of almost all of the correspondence and reports, even though Ted's signature was appended. Ted and Karen. Kind of a Beauty and the Beast, Karen being the large, brainy, efficient Beast; Ted, the handsome, glad-handing Beauty.

Nothing really stood out. No deliciously indiscrete e-mails. No files marked "Profit from Embezzlement." Nonetheless, I conscientiously made notes on the data and printed out premium payment schedules.

Bosco stretched out in one of the armchairs, a pillow behind his head.

"Read these," I commanded, tossing the printouts over to him. "Make notes." I didn't really think there would be anything important in a bunch of payment schedules, but it tweaked my nerves that Bosco wasn't helping. We should all do our part.

A few times during the night, Eddie left the room to go photocopy something, the only break in the coma-inducing monotony. The silence was all the more oppressive for not being quite complete.

All offices have a nearly imperceptible, constant, low-grade hum. At night, the hum becomes a presence—an annoying, inescapable presence. I tried to concentrate on the screen, but the time passed slowly, and the hum nearly drove me insane.

It was three minutes after three by the computer clock when Eddie said he was done. I had finished my review forty minutes earlier. Bosco had made a few notes, but had given up just past midnight and was dozing.

The most I could say was that Ted did, indeed, bring in a lot of business for the company.

We wearily collected up our printouts and Xeroxes, but before we could leave, Eddie made us go to his office. It was much smaller than Ted's, and messy. Files piled up, documents spilling everywhere. Cornucopias of paper. I counted five coffee mugs on the desk and two on the floor. The carpet was spotted.

Eddie reached behind his credenza and pulled out a ragged roll of thin white paper. I hoped it wasn't what I knew it would be.

The birthday banner. It was ripped diagonally and crumbled. The glitter fluttered off like tiny moths as Eddie thrust the bundle into my hands.

"Make sure this thing is on the level," he said.

"What are you talking about? You think it's a forgery?" I asked. "The mysterious case of the forged birthday banner?"

"Don't be retarded," Eddie said. "We have to be sure this thing is real, because the time of Ted's death was fixed by the fact that Belinda, Leah and Karen taped it over the door on Saturday. Sealing the body in the office. Schlefly and Obermeyer were at some dinner Friday night. But I was thinking that maybe they wanted to make it seem like Ted died Friday night. You know, because they had this alibi."

I was getting too tired to follow. "What do you mean?"

"See, Belinda, Leah and Karen come and put this up on Saturday, right? So we find it Sunday, and it's not torn down. It's completely intact. Check the edges here, there is no way it could be put up and taken off without some sign of it. This is pretty thin paper. It's almost like tissue paper."

I dutifully examined the edges. Eddie was right. It had been taped all the way around the entire door, and there was no sign of re-taping.

"If you wanted to establish that Ted died Friday, then you would dummy up this banner. After the girls put up the real one on Saturday afternoon, you could come in with this on Saturday night, kill Ted, then take down the real banner and put up the fake banner. Copying everyone's signatures. I mean, as ticked off as we all were at Ted, I really doubt that half the people in the office conspired to kill him, " Eddie crowed. "Belinda was going to throw this away, but I got it from her and saved it. It's been hidden behind there ever since."

"Are you saying you want me to take this to a handwriting analyst?"

"Yeah, you know guys like that, don't you? Bosco said you do a lot of work in insurance fraud."

In fact, I had never had a claim involving a forged document. Such a thing is pretty rare in the bumper-banging end of the business. Still, I was sure I could find one. I told Eddie that I needed samples for the handwriting expert to compare the signatures to.

"Got'ya covered." Eddie handed over a thick pile of miscellaneous paper, memos, letters, pages torn out of spiral notebooks. "Here," he said. "I collected all these. And here, take this, too," he added, piling on the documents he had photocopied. "And these." He piled on a huge stack of velo-bound volumes. "These are the depositions from the

Mraz sexual harassment suit. You should read up on it. In case there's a clue there."

By the time we got back to the car, my arms ached from the weight. And my head hurt. And my eyes burned. And Bosco whined all the way home.

*   *   *

I woke up on the pool raft, stiff and groggy, at eightish. The bright sunshine blasted into the room through the naked window. Maybe I should put up a couple of beach towels. Match my decor.

I stumbled down to the kitchen. No sign of Bosco.

The printouts and Xeroxes from last night, almost a foot of documents, were spread across the counter. Bosco must have looked at them before turning in, probably at the first light of day. I swept them to one side and set the coffee brewing, then padded out in my bare feet to get the paper.

Not there. I scanned the brick walk, then ventured down to the sidewalk, looked right and left. I heard birds chirp and squirrels chitter, so it was morning all right, but there was no Los Angeles Times on the driveway. The badly cracked driveway. I wondered how much a new driveway would cost.

I sighed and padded back to the house, called the automated delivery number and poured my favorite first cup. Having nothing else to read, I reached over and started going through the pile of Ted's client records. I winced at the "Employee Infectious Disease" report submitted by a restaurant franchisee, optimistically intent on renewing its workers compensation policy.

I decided to chart out the claims, to see if I could spot a pattern. A phony claims scheme would likely involve a very small number of adjustors. It is a risky thing to set up. You have to trust the people involved to even broach the subject, and by definition, bent employees aren't very trustworthy.

There were a lot of claims against this one slumlord, but mostly for small amounts: lead poisoning class action (dismissed); rat bites baby (pending); falling light fixture klonks old man ($2,700.00 paid); aliens moved in with crazy tenant (also dismissed). All handled by different adjustors.

The only hit I got was with the biggest client, an outfit called Dobbins/McCray. Looked like it had various subsidiaries in publishing and advertising. All their lines were written through the same insurance company.

Karen Odom had written all of the early correspondence, I noted. I also noted that one adjustor had been assigned to all claims: an Estelle Ng. This wasn't suspicious in itself. Dobbins/McCray was of sufficient significance to warrant a dedicated claims handler.

But Ms. Ng was also the adjustor assigned to some kind of special effects company. I could hardly call this a "pattern," but it was all I had, so I put it down for further investigation. "SXYFX, Inc." I had never heard of the company and mentally pronounced it "Zizafix, Inc."

I soon lost interest, went upstairs and took a shower. Screw Eddie anyway, the cheap peckerwood, stiffing me on my retainer like that. Five hundred lousy bucks.

Plus, he was trying to screw poor Karen Odom. In order to snag Ted's clients, Eddie would certainly have to displace Karen who was, I surmised, politically vulnerable. Let's face it, she was a woman, she was fat and she was ugly. Clearly, Ted had protected her.

Now that Ted was gone, how hard would it be to elbow her out and snatch up all the accounts that had been Ted's, while no one else was paying attention? If Eddie wormed his way in with Ted's clients, all that would be left of Fat Karen was a Twinkie wrapper in the wastebasket.

Admittedly, as Bosco had pointed out, this scenario didn't explain why Eddie wanted so badly to pin a murder charge on Rob Schlefly or Warren Obermeyer. Presumably, that wouldn't do the firm's reputation any good. Still, whatever

Eddie's real plan was, tubing Karen on the way by was perfectly in character.

When I got back down to the kitchen, Bosco was up, awake, seated at the table and drinking the last cup of coffee.

"I got a plan," he said. "Let's go to lunch."

"That's the plan? Go to lunch? I can't afford to keep going out to eat," I protested.

"You didn't even pay for lunch at Aldo's...Eddie did. C'mon, we have to eat."

I gestured toward the refrigerator. He ignored me.

We went to a little taco stand on Figueroa. I had a bean enchilada, no lard. Bosco had three beef burritos, with all the lard. The reformed gang member behind the counter laughed when Bosco asked him to hold the onions.

After we had made ourselves comfortable on the picnic bench farthest from the street, I voiced my concerns about Eddie.

"Eddie's okay," Bosco assured me. "He just comes off a little sharp. He was nice to me when I was working at Obermeyer & Schlefly."

I strongly suspected Eddie of being nice to Bosco to suck up to Uncle Ted, but if Bosco wanted to believe Eddie really liked him, I wasn't being paid to burst bubbles.

"So about this plan," I prompted.

Chapter 6

Bosco's plan was so bad I was speechless.

"I'm speechless," I gasped.

"You have never been speechless." Bosco stuffed half a burrito in his mouth.

"We can't pretend to be grief counselors," I said. "That's ridiculous. It's probably illegal."

"Oh, get out–it's not like impersonating a doctor. And it's not like I don't have training. I have a master's in psychology."

I politely expressed my extreme disbelief. He back-pedaled. "Well, not a masters, but I did take several classes in psychology."

"Undergraduate survey classes, and only because you thought they were easy C's. Your entire college career, and I use the word 'career' very loosely, was geared toward prolonging the gravy train."

Bosco swatted the air, as if brushing away the truth.

"Anyway, bro, I can't do it. I can't lie like you can. I'm not proud of it; it's simply the way that it is. I am a very direct person. If I talk, the truth comes out. That's why so many people hate me." I took a sip of watery root beer.

"I don't think that's why they hate you, Fifi. At least, I don't think that's the whole reason."

I crumpled up the paper cup. "Well, I certainly can't say stuff just to make people feel better."

Bosco looked momentarily concerned.

"That is a handicap," he admitted. "Maybe that explains why you're so rude all the time and don't have any friends."

"I have friends. One friend, anyway."

"That tall girl from your high school? She was pretty good looking. You still see her?"

"Forget it, I'm not introducing you to her."

"Fine, don't."

"I won't."

"Fine."

We ate in silence for a few minutes. Then Bosco started up again. "I still say it's a great plan. I just have to teach you a little bit about verbal flexibility, a wonderful, useful skill. My God, Fifi, you can't be a private investigator if you don't have any ability to throw up a little protective screening."

"I'm not a private investigator."

"All you have to do is say you're a grief counselor, and ask questions, and look concerned, like you care. What's so hard?"

I tossed the paper cup into a blue trash barrel decorating the middle of the patio.

"I just can't do it."

It went on like that, all the way home. Me telling him he was an irresponsible cretin. Him telling me I was an unimaginative coward. I guess both of us were right. But Bosco called Eddie as soon as we got home and told Eddie that I had dreamed the whole thing up. He was preserving deniability in case Eddie didn't like the idea, but Eddie loved it. Eddie said I was a genius.

I could live with that.

*　　*　　*

Eddie spent the next day working on Obermeyer & Schlefly to spring for our services. They finally agreed to pay $1,200 for three days of grief counseling. I thought it was a particularly neat touch. Getting us to spy on his bosses and getting them to pay for our time doing it.

Still, I felt uneasy and took it out on Bosco the whole way to the Obermeyer & Schlefly office Thursday morning.

"A lot of those people know you at Obermeyer & Schlefly," I fretted as we caromed up the entrance ramp to the 10 freeway. I had debated surface streets (it was right in the thick of rush hour), but decided to take a chance.

Of course, we didn't go two exits before there was a rear-ender fender-bender on the shoulder. The accident wasn't anything, but the spectator slowing had caused a standstill backup of one mile. My stomach knotted up, and I slammed on the brakes.

"Sure they know me. That's how Eddie convinced Schlefly to hire us."

"Meaning, they know you aren't a grief counselor."

"They don't know what I did since I left. Besides Eddie, Uncle Ted was the only one I kept up with, and I doubt even Uncle Ted could have told you that I didn't major in psychology. Or get a masters in it, even. I could be very good in my field. I could be operating a very successful chain of clinics, speaking at AMA meetings, getting called as an expert witness in court. How could they possibly know it isn't true?"

"Bosco, the standard isn't whether the other person could possibly know that what you are saying isn't true."

"Then what is the standard?"

"How should I know? But what if someone decides to Google you? Or check with whatever licensing board you need a license from? I live here in Los Angeles; I have a reputation to protect."

Bosco legitimately scoffed. I tried again.

"We could get sued."

"Big deal. You don't have any money. You don't even have any furniture. You don't even have a TV for them to take."

"I have a house," I argued.

"Yeah, but when you go into bankruptcy, you can protect your house. They can't get your house."

This being one of those situations where I had no idea if what he was saying was true, I lapsed into silence.

It took us a full fifty-eight minutes to get to Century City. Christ.

We parked in the Obermeyer & Schlefly reserved parking. I had previously given Eddie the license plate number, make and model of Truck L'Orange so we could park there and not get towed. Nonetheless, a parking attendant came over and rudely questioned our right to Space No. 32, looking askance at the truck. Yet another Angelino who believed that people should not be judged by the color of their skin, but by the cost of their car.

We arrived at Obermeyer & Schlefly right at nine, with no time to reconsider.

The reception area, which we had missed the previous night by going in the back, was dominated by two bold assemblages—a bunch of pointy metal things welded together and painted rainbow colors. A high, curved reception desk faced the entrance. It was pretty impressive.

The receptionist was a tall, large-boned, fake-tanned woman, dressed in a Kelly-green wool suit with gold buttons and black trim. She greeted us kindly, even enthusiastically. Her hair was teased pretty high and shellacked into an exaggerated flip. Her peach-tinted finger-nails were so long I wondered how she managed to punch the little buttons on the switchboard.

But she did, swiftly and with great delicacy, keeping her fingers curved back like a Balinese dancer. I thought she kind of looked like a transvestite. I mentioned this in an undertone to Bosco, who responded that of course she was a transvestite.

"What?" I whispered back, "They wanted to make sure that Ted would keep his hands off the receptionist?"

Her name was Mandy, which showed a sense of humor. She cheerfully invited us to have a seat while she paged Eddie.

He did not keep us waiting too long, hopping nervously into the lobby area. We had a brief conference with him in the corridor, and he showed us the "Memo to All" announcing that "Grief Counseling" would be available Thursday, Friday and again on Monday. All at the firm's expense. Sign on up.

Lots of people had. After all, for the staff it was a paid break from work. But Eddie said several of the brokers had also signed up, including Karen Odom and Corazon Villareal.

"Corazon is one of the top producers. She makes a ton of money, but Warren and Rob spend a lot of effort trying to keep as much of the profit as they can," Eddie explained as we walked down the hall. "They only made Ted a full partner two years ago. Corazon is still waiting, and I think she's getting impatient. If they don't make her a partner soon, she's going to jump ship. It's just stupidity and greed. If you don't pay your good people, you can't keep them. Corazon brings in more business than both those old bastards combined."

Of course, as soon as these words were out of Eddie's mouth, we turned the corner and practically ran into Warren Obermeyer and Rob Schlefly. Eddie paled, but I don't think they heard his observations. The phoniness of their smiles was just the usual phoniness.

"Bosco, it's so good to see you again," said Rob.

"Hi, Mr. Schlefly, hello, Mr. Obermeyer," Bosco nodded. Schlefly nodded back. Obermeyer just stood there, like his Depends were getting full. Bosco turned to me. "This is my business partner, Fifi Cutter. She also happens to be my sister."

"Fifi?" repeated Obermeyer, as if he couldn't trust the accuracy of his hearing. He bent his tall frame toward me as if getting a good look would explain the bizarre name. I stepped back.

"Well," said Rob, "welcome to Obermeyer & Schlefly. Eddie will show you the room we have set aside for your use, and if you need anything, our receptionist Mandy will be able to assist you." The words were polite, but Schlefly, I felt, was one of those men who constantly simmer with suppressed irritation, always impatient to get on to the next thing. Men to avoid.

As they walked off, I heard Schlefly say "Bottom line, Warren, remember the bottom line. We've got to do more to…"

Bottom line. An idea began to percolate. "Hey, Eddie does Schlefly say 'bottom line' a lot?"

"Oh, yeah. Bottom line this, bottom line that. It's one of his phrases. He says it all the time."

"The note," I whispered to Bosco. "It said 'bottom line.'"

"You think Schlefly wrote it? Fifi, a lot of people say 'bottom line.' It's a cliché."

"It's an old cliché. Very last century. People don't say it any more."

"Older people do."

"My point. Schlefly is older."

We reached the doorway to a small conference room, paneled in dark wood, insipid landscapes on two of the walls. A floor-to-ceiling window looked out over Avenue of the Stars. The glass-topped oval conference table and four chairs were too big for the space. I felt claustrophobic.

Eddie ushered us in and gave us the sign-up sheet. There was a name filled in for each time slot, I saw with dread. Three hours without a break until lunch? What if we had to go to the bathroom?

We didn't have long to worry about it. There was a knock on the door, and a plump woman with eighties hair—mouse brown, frosted, and limply layered—came into the room. This was a woman, I might add, who shouldn't have been wearing her skirt so short. Bosco glanced down at her name and smoothly invited her to sit.

"Leah, you just make yourself comfortable. We're here to help."

"I thought I should take the first slot," Leah explained, with an odd mixture of apology and self-importance. "I was his secretary." She paused a moment to allow that fact to sink in.

Bosco leaped right into the sympathy pile with both feet, spouting off about the nature of life and death, friendship, grief, all that kind of stuff. Maybe it was good he was able to throw himself into his role, but we were supposed to be listening, not talking. Here we had a veritable Wikipedia of potentially relevant information, and Bosco wouldn't shut up.

I interrupted Bosco's recitation of some interminable poem about how life is a journey, and death is hopping on a boat and sailing away out to sea. "So when did you start working for Mr. Heffernan?"

"Just two years ago," Leah admitted. "It seems like we were together forever, though; you know how it is when you click with someone? That bond of sympathy? It's like you've always known them."

I had no idea what she was talking about. "Did you come to Obermeyer to work with Mr. Heffernan, or were you already working with someone else here?"

She looked a little put off by the briskness of the question, but she answered. "No, I was working at first for Mr. Schlefly. You know, he's like the second most senior partner. Really, he's the one who runs the firm now. Mr. Obermeyer is mostly retired; he hardly ever comes in. It was really hard, working for Mr. Schlefly. I had to type a lot, you know, and then it was like all these personal and social things, which I don't really consider my job. I am a trained professional, thank you very much."

Bosco oiled in with a soothing, "Of course you are," and after a little prodding, we got Leah wound up again, and she explained that by "mutual agreement," she had been transferred from Mr. Schlefly to Mr. Heffernan.

It was clear to me that Schlefly had punted her. I wondered if getting the secretarial cast-off of the second-most senior partner could cause friction to the point of murder. I thought the answer to that question would depend entirely on how bad the secretary was, but any such motive would, in this case, run the other way. If secretarial-assignment-rage had triggered tragic homicide, Ted would have offed Schlefly; Schlefly wouldn't have offed Ted.

And, really, wouldn't it be far simpler to off Leah?

We talked at great length about how particularly horrible Leah felt about the whole birthday-banner-on-the-door thing, certainly a touch of the macabre that might have troubled a stronger soul.

"It was all my idea," she confessed, tearing up a little. "It was his fifty-ninth birthday, you know, so I got my niece, she's a really good artist, to draw this cake with a big skull and crossbones on a sheet of tissue paper, and it said 'Black Monday' in really big letters, and I got everyone to sign it." Leah looked up through her bangs. "It was supposed to be funny," she whispered.

We established that Leah, Belinda Barrett, and Karen Odom had taped up the birthday banner on Saturday afternoon. Karen and Belinda had come straight from the convention in Laguna to help, arriving at the office around two. Actually, they were about twenty minutes late, which Leah did not appreciate, thank you very much.

"Seems like a lot of trouble, coming all the way in on a Saturday, when you could just do it Monday morning."

"That's what I said," Leah huffed, "But Belinda and Karen were going to be there anyway, because they were coming back from Laguna and Karen left her car here that Friday."

"You should have just let them do it, then," I objected. "It didn't take three of you." I tactfully refrained from making a joke about how many office workers does it take to screw in a light bulb, but Leah took offense anyway.

"Thank you very much," she drew herself up, "but this

was my idea! I mean, I'm not one to grab all the credit, but really, I was the one who thought of it. And it was my niece who drew the pictures, and glued all the glitter on, and all. I was certainly going to be there to put it up."

Again, Bosco calmed her down and said it had been a great idea, and she was great to have thought of it, and everything was great.

I tried to bring her around to the night in question, without blowing our cover by being too obvious. But Leah did not respond to gently nuanced conversational leads. As the minutes sped by, I finally just asked her whether Mr. Heffernan had an appointment for that Friday night. Leah answered, more or less.

"Well, you know, I don't think so, because Ted didn't usually have meetings really late like that, but I can't say he never did, because sometimes the client just can't make it during the regular business day. If it's an important client, you try to be accommodating. But if so, Ted would ask me to be there, you know, to get coffee and copy stuff if they needed it, and do stuff like that, and, I mean, if you're asking me did I know of anything, I certainly didn't. He didn't ask me to stay. But if it was really late on Friday, I don't think I would agree to stay. I mean, Friday night. Right when you're looking forward to the weekend. That would be quite an imposition, thank you very much."

"Do you think you would know about it, though?" I probed.

Leah thought about this for a few seconds, the longest consideration she had given to any answer yet, and then said, "If he told me, I would know. But if he didn't tell me, then I wouldn't."

There was a knock at the door. Our first half hour session was mercifully up.

Chapter 7

The next person to take up our time was a cheerful young slacker dude who worked in the mailroom and who really hadn't known Ted Heffernan and appeared to think that we were there to discuss the problems he was having with his girlfriend, who was expecting their second child. I told him to get a vasectomy and get married.

I was getting pretty good at this counseling stuff.

* * *

At 11:30 Karen Odom walked in, the last slot before lunch. My stomach was rumbling, and the coffee, although still hot in the silver thermos, was undrinkably bitter. I smiled wanly.

As we had noticed at the funeral, she was a brutally plain woman, with a beefy, shapeless body. Up close was no treat, either: small, keen, dark eyes in a slab-like face, with a thin mouth and a broad nose. Her graying hair was cut short, just this side of dykey. As if to compensate, her gabardine suit was tastefully tailored, and her low-heeled, spectator pumps gleamed. She sported baroque pearl earrings and a truly honking-huge diamond on her right hand in an old-fashioned setting.

"Hello, Bosco, it's good to see you again. Karen Odom." She shook both of our hands and continued. "I don't know if you remember me," she spoke to Bosco, "but I remember you very well. I was so delighted when Eddie told me that you had finally finished your academic pursuits and had decided on a career helping others." The hint of irony in her voice garnered my respect. Karen might be ugly, but she was perceptive and obviously had an excellent memory.

Karen sat directly across from us and did the take-control-at-the-onset-of-the-meeting thing, sitting up very straight and placing her hands on the table in front of her as if she owned it. "I don't really need grief counseling. Eddie asked some of the more senior people to sign up in order to make the staff members feel comfortable," she explained, setting the agenda. "Of course, I was very close to Ted; I worked with him hand-in-glove for almost twenty years. And I will certainly suffer from his loss, perhaps more than anyone here. But I'm just not really the grief counseling type." She smiled a really sweet smile and shook her head.

Bosco reached over the table into her space and patted her hand. He has no shame at all. "You know, Karen, we so appreciate that. There are some people who are just strong." He clenched his fist close to his chest to symbolize "strong." Karen looked dubious.

"And yet," Bosco went on, "there are others who need a little help. Maybe you can help us with our work today and tell us about some of the others and the impact of Ted's death on the office? What Ted meant to the people here."

Karen crossed her arms. Bosco had just re-set the agenda.

"Ted meant money in the door. Job security," she answered cautiously.

"Is that really all, Karen? I mean, I knew him, not as well as you did, but enough to know that he had real personality. He was something, wasn't he?" Bosco's voice was as warm as sand in the sun.

Karen uncrossed her arms. "Well, sure, I'm going to miss him. I didn't mean I wouldn't miss him," she conceded. "As far as bosses go, he was as good as they get, if you have to have a boss. He didn't micromanage. He rarely got upset. He was realistic in his demands. Kept everyone informed of everything they needed to know to do their job."

"You were okay working for him, then?" I asked.

"Sure. Ted was the rainmaker," explained Karen. "He was the one they made partner. But I expect I will make partner eventually, too. Ted supported that. Very much."

She looked pensively into her now uncertain future. "In that way, Ted was very good to me. He was free with sharing access to his clients." She qualified: "At least where I was concerned. He trusted me, and I greatly appreciated that trust. He was a great guy in so many ways. But he was…"

We weren't to know what else Ted was. Karen glanced at Bosco and finished out the sentence in corporate speak. "His loss will be felt by all, even as we rise up to meet this challenge."

It was time for some basic factual questions.

"He sent you in his place to the Laguna convention, didn't he?" I asked.

"Yes, he did. He asked me Friday morning if I could go." She sighed. "How sad; if he had gone, he would have been sleeping with someone when the heart attack happened. Maybe Belinda could have done something."

Ah, the practical view of marital infidelity.

"Belinda?" I ventured.

"Yes," Karen was unembarrassed. "Belinda Barrett is an account assistant. She would hardly rate a trip to the convention. But she and Ted were an on-again, off-again item, and since his wife had thrown him out, Ted made it on again."

"There wasn't really a business purpose to the trip?"

"Oh, there certainly was—relationships to be cultivated, status in the brokerage community to be maintained. Networking. And I do think Belinda was pretty good at the cocktail circuit chatter. Of course, nothing like Ted, but…," she looked directly at me, "better than I am. Don't misunderstand that as false modesty. I give excellent service to my clients. But the glad-handing part of it does not come naturally to me."

"Still, Ted asked you to go," I observed, impressed by her clear-sighted honesty.

"Yes," Karen agreed, "but only because something came up at the last minute, and he couldn't make it."

"Did he say what it was that had come up?"

Karen shook her head. "No, I didn't ask. He just called Belinda and me into his office and told us both at the same time that he couldn't go, and I had to substitute for him. I presume he did it that way because he thought she couldn't yell at him for standing her up if we were both there."

"What time was this?" I asked.

Karen's dark eyes narrowed as she considered the relevance of the question to the level of her grief, which, after all, we were supposed to be ministering to.

Bosco patted her hand again and said, "Sometimes talking over all the details, you know, actually getting a time line of the last minutes, is cathartic. It's one of the tools we use, a version of the LaPorte method so popular in France. I actually studied under LaPorte for a semester. Very interesting stuff."

Karen looked skeptical but answered the question. "Just before noon. I really didn't have a lot of time. We were supposed to leave by three in order to make sure we registered in time for the opening remarks."

"Did you and Belinda go down to Laguna together?"

"Yes, I went home to pack but came back here and met up with her. We drove down in her car and got to the hotel sometime after five–maybe even closer to six, I don't really remember. We made it to the reception with no trouble." Karen looked uncomfortable at the memory and began twisting at the diamond ring, slipping it on and off of her plump finger.

Bosco pressed his lips together and looked very much as if he were sharing her pain. Encouraged, Karen continued.

"Ted gave me my first job. He was young, but already a mover and a shaker, and I followed him from firm to firm. He moved around a lot, especially in the early years, always trading up. We started at Dell & Carson. Actually, Obermeyer was there, too, for a while. Then Ollie Dell died, and Obermeyer split off and started Obermeyer & Schlefly, with most of Ollie's clients. I followed Ted to the Olympus Group, and after that, we changed jobs about every two or three years. Then he met up with Obermeyer again, and they made an offer. We've been here at Obermeyer & Schlefly for six and a half years, and I am telling you, that's a record."

"He finally found a home?" Bosco asked.

Karen gave a rueful smile. "Until something better came along. This place was good at first, money rolling in, and Ted could intimidate Warren and Rob into giving him a huge bonus every year by threatening to leave."

I caught the reference to "good at first." Meaning, not so good lately.

"What will you do now?" I asked.

Bosco hurriedly interjected, "Don't feel guilty because you're worrying about yourself, that's perfectly natural."

"I don't feel guilty," Karen assured us. "To answer your question, I have reason to believe that some of Ted's clients may stay with me. Not all, of course, but there are people in today's world who appreciate solid, reliable work and sound judgment more than a game of golf and a whiskey and soda."

Whoa, I thought, Eddie might be in for a bit of competition from a source he hadn't considered. And maybe stiff competition, too, since Eddie had neither social skills nor competence.

"Strange deal about that birthday banner, huh?" I asked.

"Yeah," Karen grimaced. "Not something I would normally have had anything to do with, believe me. Leah and Belinda thought it was so funny."

"But you helped put it up?"

"Ah, no, not really," Karen made a deprecating gesture, "I just came up with Belinda to get some papers I needed to review. I left them to it. It wouldn't take more than two people to tape up a banner over a door, even if one of them is Leah." Karen and I shared an amused glance as she rose to go.

After the door closed behind her, I turned to Bosco. "Do you really think she was fooled?"

"Of course, why would she be suspicious? Only a guilty person would be suspicious."

"I think anyone with a brain would be suspicious, and Karen most definitely has a brain."

*　*　*

Mandy was next, after a terrible lunch of pressed-turkey sandwiches and chips. Large boned and broad shouldered, she sat down with exaggerated delicacy. Looking at her face—the coarse, masculine features overlaid with heavy make up—I was reminded of that optical illusion where if you look at it one way it's a vase, and if you look at it the other way, it's two profiles.

She dabbed her eyes. "Excuse me. I'm so fragile right now. You see, I had a major life experience a few years ago." She paused as if we were supposed to ask her what that life experience was. Neither of us did but she told us anyway.

In horrifyingly clinical detail. By the time they had finally regulated her hormone levels and she had recovered from the second breast augmentation surgery, the half hour was almost up. Bosco's smile had become frozen, and his eyes had glazed over, so I stepped in.

"Did you work closely with Ted?"

"In a way, I work closely with everyone here because I take all the calls. So I always know what's going on with people."

"Really? What was going on with Ted?"

Mandy gave an arch smile, took out her compact, and ostentatiously refreshed her lipstick. "Oh that Ted, he was a one."

"You mean a one for the ladies?"

"Mustn't gossip," Mandy's theatrically clasped her hands and looked up at the ceiling. She was thoroughly enjoying herself.

"It's not gossip when you're in therapy," I played along. "It's part of the counseling process."

Mandy fanned her face. "Ted Heffernan was such a—how shall I say it?—such a studly man. I've been here three years, and in that time to my personal knowledge, he slept with four different women. Not including his wife. You know about Belinda?" She cocked an eyebrow. We nodded. "There were others, too. He treated them all like dirt. But he must have been the Barry Bonds of the bedroom, they kept coming back for more."

"Like who?" I asked.

"Like Dina Mraz." Mandy fluttered her inch-long lashes. "Dina called him the very day he died. And he took her call, too. After the lawsuit and the trial and everything. How'dya like that?" She sat back in a satisfied manner and looked at her watch. "Whoops, time's up. I have to get back to the front desk. The switchboard is a cruel, cruel taskmaster."

With that, and a wave, she was gone.

*   *   *

For the rest of the day, we had a series of secretaries, most over forty, some over fifty, fat, thin, tall, short, smart, dull, white, black, prune-faced and doll-faced. There were Kathys, Nancys, Lindas, at least two Debbies–except one was a Debi–and a Susan. The output of corporate America rests soundly in the hands of just such ordinary and good women as these, I reflected, chatty and honest and, whatever their limitations may be, pretty observant of the people around them, especially those who had the power to make them miserable.

I learned that Ted was superficially liked by superficial people and somewhat hated by the more discerning, and that Karen did most of his actual work, with a tactful talent for making Ted believe that her ideas were, in fact, his ideas.

Belinda was more pitied than despised. Dina Mraz was despised and not pitied at all. The big difference was that Belinda was competent, and always did her own work, and Dina was a screw-up, always leaving others to fill in for her.

Ted was blamed for the Dina lawsuit mess, but not very much, and more for bad taste than immorality. The universal view of the secretaries was that the portly Rob Schlefly was in no position to criticize Ted on that score.

Obermeyer, as Leah had said, was retired in all but name and no longer showed up regularly. Corazon Villareal was respected.

Eddie was, among the secretaries, the worst draw.

They all knew Leah was hopeless and had all helped Ted out at one time or another.

Just the usual office politics, I thought.

Chapter 8

Eddie caught us as we were headed out. "Hey, what did you get? Did you get anything?"

I quickly gave him a status.

"Nothing new, then."

"Except that thing about Dina," Bosco answered. "She called Ted the day he died. How weird is that? Maybe we should go check her out."

I opened my mouth to protest and saw Obermeyer lurching toward us. I nudged Bosco, who patted Eddie's shoulder in a show of manly compassion.

"I think we did some really excellent grief work today, Eddie. Oh hello, Mr. Obermeyer. I was just telling Eddie what a lot of progress we made here."

Obermeyer slowed and looked bewildered as if he had forgotten who we were. "Good job," he said as he edged by. "Keep up the good work."

I exchanged glances with my brother. Warren sure was one creepy-ass old guy.

Eddie ushered us out the door and into the elevator, where a tall African-American woman was conducting a loud conversation with a short Hispanic man about how her Asian dentist had charged her $567.00 for some bridge work, dropping F-bombs and politically incorrect sentiments all the way down to the lobby.

As we exited the elevator, Bosco pulled us toward a corner.

"Listen, Eddie, maybe we should head out to Dina's house now. He may have told her who he was meeting with. We gotta know what she knows."

Eddie frowned and then nodded. He pulled out his Treo. "Here's her address—it's in Venice. Go."

"Oh come on, guys, it's five o'clock. I'm used to regular hours. I'm tired, and I'm hungry, and it's going to get dark soon."

"There's plenty of daylight."

"Eddie, why would Dina Mraz even talk to me? She sued the firm. She hates the firm. If I say I'm from Obermeyer & Schlefly, she'll just slam the door in my face."

"Don't say you're from Obermeyer & Schlefly, you idiot. Think of something. Look, we can't talk here. I shouldn't be seen talking to you." Eddie scuttled away.

Back on the 10, traffic was even worse then it had been coming in. I got off at Lincoln, navigating the truck from one gridlocked intersection to the other, until I finally got to Ashland and turned right, then left, then right again. The streets got narrower and the houses grubbier with each turn.

We were getting close to the correct address. The house, when we found it, was a dilapidated one-story clapboard. The only body of water in sight was in a plastic wading pool next door.

Three not-very-new and not-very-nice cars were crammed into the crumbling driveway, and a motorcycle presided over the dead lawn. Which meant at least four people lived in what had to be, at most, a two-bedroom. Dina would do a hell of a lot better than this, once the money from her verdict got paid.

You could only park legally on the south side, where cars were lined up nose to ass for at least three blocks. Farther than I was willing to walk. I pulled up onto the curb on the north side, right in front of Dina's house, maneuvering as far as I could onto the sidewalk. But a larger vehicle still wouldn't be able to get by.

"Stay here," I commanded Bosco as I hopped out, "and move the truck if somebody comes."

I walked up the short dirt path to the front of the house and knocked. The flimsy yellow door swung open. Startled, I took a short step backwards. The funk of marijuana and poor housekeeping wafted out of the dim interior. Nobody appeared.

I hesitated and looked at Bosco sitting in the truck. He made an impatient "get on with it" gesture. I turned back and gently knocked again, trying to keep the door semi-closed. No one answered.

"Hello?" I warbled, sticking my head in. Coming from the depths, I heard loud, obscure grunge. Maybe she couldn't hear me over the music. I gave one last glance over my shoulder at Bosco who was sliding into the driver's seat. A yellow VW van was crawling down the street, a bronzed, well-muscled arm hanging out the window. I sighed, hoping Bosco could manage to move the truck around the corner and get back without hitting anything.

I stepped into a combined living and dining room area. Beer cans, pizza boxes, two mattresses, and several once-colorful but now faded pillows littered the floor. I could see the kitchen through an archway. A food-encrusted stove top and an overflowing trashcan did not invite me to explore in that direction.

I stepped toward the only other door, knocking over a red plastic bong I had missed in the gloom. I tapped on the door in what I hoped was a non-threatening way.

"Ms. Mraz? Uh…Dina? You there?" The music abruptly stopped.

"Dina?" I called again and strained to hear a rustle, a cough, a fart, a bed squeak. Anything. But there was nothing.

Slowly, I turned the knob. After one last whispered "Dina?" I opened the door.

The room was pitch black, except for the winking blue lights of the sound system. I started to walk in and stumbled over something soft. My heart stopped in the same instant I realized that I had just kicked one of those damn floor pillows. I pawed the walls for a switch, found it and clicked on the overhead. The room was a grimy sap green, and just a little more than closet sized. Probably had been a closet at one time.

Three Polaroid photographs of hippie surfer dudes and their hippie surfer chicks were thumb-tacked up on the right-hand wall. A large daisy had been clumsily painted around another doorframe on the left. There was a narrow mattress on the floor, buried in loads of malodorous laundry.

"Oh, I'm so sorry," I gasped as I caught sight of the woman curled up on a corner of the mattress, half hidden by the pile of tie-dyed tee shirts and underwear.

I could see that she had on a bikini top and skimpy cut-off jeans. Her hair, spread out like a fan, was so dry from over-bleaching and over-perming that I was tempted to issue a brush fire warning. She had a tattoo of a skull and a thunderbolt on her meaty back.

I cleared my throat nervously. "Sorry, really, didn't mean to barge in on you..." My voice trailed away. This babe was passed out. Six empty beer cans, a bottle of vodka and a half smoked joint explained why.

I started toward her, and stopped. Fuck it. Even if she did wake up, she would be too gone to make any sense.

I sidled around and opened the daisy door, which led directly into a slightly larger bedroom with a window. Beyond that, there was a bathroom that I wouldn't enter wearing a HazMat suit. That was the entire house. No one else was home.

I tiptoed back around Sleeping Beauty, made my way to the kitchen, and tore the cover off an old pizza box on which I wrote: "Dina: Need to talk to you about Ted." I wrote my phone number, and I was just going to sign my name, when I had a better thought.

Dina would be more likely to return a call from

Bosco. He was a guy, and she might even remember him. So I signed "Bosco D." and propped the note up against the filthy toaster.

I picked my way through all the crap, got out of the house and stood on the sidewalk waiting for Bosco to return. It took a good six minutes. I relayed my findings and told him to expect a call.

"It's such a bummer. We come all this way, and she's so passed out she can't even talk. She must have started partying at, like, noon."

Bosco studied himself in the rear view mirror. "Dina Mraz is a stoner bitch. It's not our fault. It means we have to come back some other day. Eddie still has to pay us for the time."

True, I thought, we'll just talk to Dina when we come back.

Chapter 9

The second day at Obermeyer & Schlefly was very much like the first, except it was Casual Friday. Not pretty. In fact, the only thing uglier than a hot-pink polo shirt on a short, fat Korean lady is plaid pants on a skinny, old white man. We were treated to both.

Debi Kim, Corazon Villareal's secretary, breathlessly recounted finding the body, leaving out the part where she threw up.

Warren Obermeyer avoided the subject of Ted altogether, rambling on about Nebraska football and the sound system in his new Mercedes Benz. We didn't learn anything new.

Things picked up after lunch when Belinda came into the room, leading with her hips. Mournful gray eyes, yellow-blonde hair, a low-cut black sweater. Her open-toed, faux-patent-leather sling-backs screamed Payless Shoe Source.

I was prepared to pretend that we didn't know of her true relationship with Ted, but this proved unnecessary. Belinda, drama queen, broke the news to us almost the instant she sat down, tears welling up.

Bosco moved immediately from across the table to the chair at her side. I was not deceived into believing this was strictly in the line of duty. Cleavage called.

"We've been together for four years," she admitted. "I never asked him to leave his wife, I wouldn't break up a home, especially not when there are kids." Bosco was quick to congratulate her on her respect for family values.

"I mean, I've almost been married myself. Twice before, actually. One of the guys was a doctor, too. It's never worked out for me, though. I am not really looking for anything permanent any more. Ted and I just always had a really good time together, and you know how it is."

She was looking at Bosco, not me, when she said this.

"We didn't hurt anyone. I know people say I was sleeping with the boss, but I've been at this place for nine years. I was here way before Ted got here, and no one ever criticized my work."

This was exactly what we had been told by the secretaries.

"Belinda, do you want to talk about the last time you saw him?" Bosco prompted.

Belinda's tears spilled over.

"It's so horrible. After all those years of being my best friend, after all the fun times, and him always supporting me and me always supporting him, the last thing I said to him was 'You are the biggest turd I have ever met.'" She choked on a sob. "Isn't that just, like, tragic?"

Pure Shakespeare, I thought to myself.

Belinda sniffled. "I was just so mad. He wouldn't tell me what was going on. He said 'It's none of your business' and 'Just go do what I need you to do in Laguna, I can't explain.' He meant he couldn't explain to *me*. It just really offended my dignity as a person. I'm not just some doll, you know. I am a person."

Belinda thumped her chest for emphasis. Her declaration of personhood would have resonated more effectively with me if she were thumping flesh rather than silicone, but Bosco's eyes glazed over. I guess she knew her audience.

"You don't know why he cancelled on you?" I asked dismally.

"No. He just said he couldn't go, and Karen was supposed to go in his place. I think he would have preferred to send one of the men, but they couldn't stay in the same room as me, and he had only booked one room. I mean not that he didn't trust Karen–he depended totally on her–but she isn't really, you know...I mean, like, for client entertainment, and getting cozy with the underwriters from the various insurance companies."

"It must really eat you up, huh, that you were there having a great time, eating and drinking and socializing, when all that time Ted had already died?" I asked.

I was just trying to get her to say something specific about Friday night, so we could get independent verification from someone other than Karen that she was really there. But I guess my question sounded kind of harsh. Belinda started to bawl in earnest.

Bosco kicked me under the table, then quickly added, "You shouldn't feel bad, not in any way. You couldn't possibly have known. Hey, grief and guilt and anger, you know, these emotions get very mixed up in our minds. We have to work our way through this." He looked into her eyes. "That's why we're here."

Belinda melted. She aimed her false eyelashes at Bosco, and murmured, "That's so true, I have all these different emotions. I'm sad and then I really feel mad at him for dying, for leaving me."

Bosco drew her out while I struggled to keep my very light lunch down.

"I slept really badly that night, being in a hotel, with the pillow and the mattress all different, and Karen in the other bed. She doesn't snore, but you can hear her breathe, she breathes kind of loud. You know, I live alone," Belinda glanced sideways at Bosco again, "and I'm not used to sharing a room. And when I did fall asleep, I had really weird dreams. Like I would be at home in bed, not my home now, the one when I was little girl, and then, like, someone was trying to break in, to hurt me, or even kill me, and I was really scared, but I couldn't move. Then I'd wake up, and fall back to sleep, like over and over again."

She went on like this for the rest of her time slot, establishing a pretty thorough alibi for Karen.

Still, did she have to go into such detail? Nothing, and I mean nothing, is more boring than other people telling you their dreams. I was so ready to be done with her. Bosco was, predictably, not ready at all and mentioned something about a follow-up session after work as she exited the room.

Next in was a man of about thirty, Brooks Brothers and bland, but something was sort of overeager and goofy about him. The almost-really-good-looking guy from the funeral. He shook hands like a car salesman, looked me right in the eye and gave a great a big smile.

Turn it down a watt, buddy, I thought, you're supposed to be here for grief counseling, for God's sake. The fact that we were much phonier than he was didn't lessen my instant resentment, though, perhaps, on reflection, it should have. What can I say? I didn't like the guy then, and I never came to like him any better.

"Keith Gursky. Glad you folks are here. It's really great of Obermeyer & Schlefly to think of this. Just goes to show what class people they are."

Nice smarm. Maybe he thought we were reporting back. Which of course we were, but only to Eddie—not to anyone who would do Keith Gursky any good.

We discussed Keith's grief for a few minutes before he admitted that he didn't really know Ted that well. He only joined the company recently and had really signed up for counseling for "Karen and Belinda's sake," since they were the closest to Ted.

I read that as meaning for Belinda's sake, which was confirmed as we spent the next five minutes hearing about how brave Belinda was being, and how loyal she had been to Ted, even though he didn't treat her the way a guy should treat "a woman of her caliber," and how did we think she was doing? Was she okay?

"Well, I have to tell you, with all our patients…er…clients, I mean, the people we counsel," Bosco cleared his throat and tried again. "The thing is, we have very high standards of confidentiality in our...um...profession."

Keith raised his hand. Were those nails manicured? I think they were.

"I understand," he said. "I was just asking as a friend." He straightened up and looked like he was about to leave, so I jumped in.

"How long exactly have you been here?" I asked.

"Five months," he replied, a little taken aback, but I figured I wouldn't give him a chance to think.

"Where did you work before?"

He hesitated. "ViKon," he finally admitted. ViKon Melbye was one of the really big outfits, the conglomerate that was created when Viking Ins. merged with Connecticut Group and then, more recently, with Melbye and Melbye.

"What brought you to Obermeyer?" I asked, meaning, why would an ambitious guy leave a big, growing outfit to come to a much smaller group that was obviously having some problems?

"Obermeyer & Schlefly presented me with an outstanding opportunity to work with some of the most innovative brokers in the business today. In a smaller firm I could be much more flexible to meet my clients' needs, and be able to take charge of my own career."

That was pretty easy to translate. He'd been let go from ViKon because he only had a few, small accounts. He probably took a cut in pay and then had to move from Connecticut to Los Angeles.

"Has it worked out the way you had hoped?"

"Yes," he said, the lie so palpable I was almost embarrassed for him.

"So, how does your family feel about the move?" I pressed to find out if Keith was married, wondering if there might be a triangle between Keith, Belinda and Ted that could be a motive.

Keith looked even more uncomfortable as he mumbled,

"I'm separated—well, getting divorced, really. The wife didn't really care for the idea of moving out here. I mean, her family is all back there."

"Was it a friendly split?" I persisted.

Keith wriggled and gave a short laugh. "Yeah, sure, for a divorce–you know how these things go. Some bitterness, I guess. Bound to be. Actually, not too friendly, I guess."

What a useless, pathetic waste of protein, I thought to myself. But at least the day ended early. No cubicle dweller would sign up for anything after 3:00 PM on a Friday afternoon, no matter how casually dressed.

*   *   *

Eddie stuck his head in as we were preparing to leave.

"You get a name of a handwriting expert yet?"

"Yeah. Can't see him until Monday, though," I lied. Actually, I had completely forgotten my promise to Eddie to find an expert.

"But you got somebody?"

I nodded. Eddie's eyes narrowed. "Really? So, what's his name?" I opened my mouth and nothing came out.

"We located two possibles." Bosco saved me. "Delia Hight and Derrick Applebaum, but it doesn't look like Hight's going to be available. She's the top of her profession, you know, waiting list a yard long. We'll probably go with Applebaum, but I'd like to check out a few more leads."

Eddie looked at us. He had been pretty sure I was BS-ing him, but not so sure about Bosco.

"Just get it done," he growled and slammed the door to the conference room.

I turned to the telephone on the credenza and begged Mandy to give me an outside line (after reassuring her it wasn't a long distance call). What a bunch of cheapskates.

"Who're you calling?" Bosco asked.

"My buddy, Jack, at Colchester." Yes, it was Friday, but I knew he would still be there. Jack was old school—Middle

America. Wide waist and narrow views. He told me once that, although he liked me "just fine," and had "nothin' against the blacks in general," he wouldn't want me dating his son. One look at the photo of the pimply- faced pudge-wad displayed on Jack's desk and I was able to assure him the feeling was mutual.

Thing is, though, Jack was one person who had genuine faith in my abilities. He always gave me credit for cracking that fraud ring.

"Jack Summer, what can I do you for?" Jack always answered the telephone the same way.

"Hey, Jack, it's me, Fifi."

"Hey, Fifi, good to hear from you. How's it going?"

"Good, I'll have those reports to you in today's mail."

"That's fine, Fifi, I should have something more for you next week."

"Great, but that's not why I'm calling. I need a good handwriting analyst."

"A handwriting analyst? That means you must have another client! That's super, Fifi. Congratulations. Let me see what I can turn up, hold the line."

An instrumental version of *Yesterday* filled my ear. When Jack came back on, he had a name for me. "John Yoo. He's on Wilshire, and he's very good. I used him in a case a few years ago. It was a pretty interesting case..."

I spent twelve and a half minutes trying to get out of hearing about Jack's interesting case, and about the other interesting case that the first case reminded him of.

Finally, I managed to get Yoo's address and phone number. Thank God the next day was Saturday. For some misguided reason, I thought Saturday would be more enjoyable than Friday had been.

Chapter 10

But it wasn't. I was awakened at 5:50 AM by Bosco's dad in New York.

"Do you know what time it is here?" I wailed.

"Well, goddammit, I know it's almost nine o'clock here!" he barked back.

Sadly, Mr. Dorff had finally realized where his credit card was, and he didn't sound happy.

After getting Bosco up to be yelled at, I couldn't get back to sleep. I went down to the kitchen and waited for the paper.

When the battered delivery car turned around in front of my house without stopping to toss out the morning edition, I finally had to admit that my delivery had been cancelled for non-payment. I crept out in the grey light and swiped my neighbor's paper.

I'm not sure why I bothered. Nothing ever changes. A politician had been caught taking a bribe. The cops were, once again, cracking down on pornography. Somebody killed somebody else. Some rare and beautiful species was now extinct.

I put the paper down and went into the dining room to the card table-desk and sat down to pay bills, anticipating the check we would get from Obermeyer & Schlefly on Monday. Electricity, gas, phone, Visa bill, water, first mortgage and second mortgage ate up the entire $1,200.00 and another $320.00 on top of that. I realized with a jolt of dismay, I was still short of what I needed to pay the property taxes. I wrote out a check to cover my homeowner's insurance, which was in danger of lapsing, adding a note to cancel the theft coverage. There was nothing to steal now.

By the time I was done with the paper and the bills, I heard Bosco in the shower upstairs. I wandered into the living room. A shaft of bright morning light penetrated the darkness. I lounged on the floor where the couch used to be, turning my face to the warmth, dozing a little. A knock on the door interrupted me. I got up, walked over, and peeped through the peephole. And then I peeped again.

An African-American man of middle age, middle height, and middle color bounced anxiously in and out of my vision. The guy looked just like my cousin D'Metree.

I hadn't spoken to D'Metree since Pop's funeral, when he took sides with my brother Joey in blaming me for inheriting the house. He totally yelled at me, accusing me of taking advantage of my old man. In fact, by the time he was done, D'Metree practically accused me of killing Pop.

But I got right back in his grill. I told him it was no goddamn business of his what my father did with his earthly stuff. I also pointed out that if Pop's family hadn't virtually disowned him when he married my mother, then maybe he woulda left something to Joey Three. And then I told him that as far as I was concerned, the Cutter family was a bunch of reverse racist hypocrites who shouldn't even be at the funeral.

After that, D'Metree promised never to speak to me again.

So I didn't figure it could really be D'Metree, and I foolishly opened the door. There he was. D'Metree.

"What are you doing here?"

"Hey, little cuz, how've you been? Everything going okay? You're looking very fine. How's the new job? That working out for you? Isn't this just the nicest day? They're freezin' out in Buffalo, huh?"

"Have you lost your mind?" It was the only explanation I could come up with.

"Now, don't be that way. We're family, aren't we?"

I glared.

He stepped back.

"I sincerely doubt we are in any way related, D'Metree. You must have been adopted." That last, of course, was not said with any conviction. I already knew that I was related to losers of all colors.

D'Metree's face became serious. "Hey, listen, no fooling, now. I need a favor. I need you to store some things for me." He gestured toward his car, a newish tan Honda parked by the old camphor tree in front of the house. This particular Honda had a U-Haul trailer attached.

Before I could slam the door in his face, Bosco popped up at my shoulder, wearing a Calvin Klein bathrobe fresh from his self-indulgently long shower.

"Hi, you must be Fifi's other brother," he said.

D'Metree backed up even further. "Cousin, man, not brother."

Bosco grinned like an idiot. "Hey, I remember you. D'Metree, right? Jeez, I don't think I've seen you since I moved to New York to live with my dad. I'm Bosco, Fifi's brother on her Mom's side."

"Half brother," I corrected.

Bosco stuck out his hand with a big smile.

I gave up and invited D'Metree in.

D'Metree looked around. "Whoa, what happened to all your shit? You moving or something?"

"No, I am not moving, and it's too hard to explain." No way was I giving him something to criticize my mother about. He would have spread the story to every member of the Cutter clan from South Central to Missouri. "We can sit in the kitchen," I offered without enthusiasm. "While you tell me why you are here and what it is that you erroneously believe I will help you with."

"Man, you are in one bad mood, Fifi."

"Bad mood? You yell at me at my father's funeral, you practically accuse me of stealing this house, you don't talk to me for months, then you show up and expect favors."

"Bygones, girl, bygones."

I shook my head in disgust as we entered the kitchen. Bosco trailed along. D'Metree didn't seem put out by Bosco's butting in, perhaps judging (correctly) that Bosco would be a much easier sell for any dodgy scheme he had in mind.

Bosco and D'Metree sat down at the table. I perched up on the counter. D'Metree cleared his throat. "See, you know I'm working for Party All-night," he began.

"Cool!" Bosco exclaimed. "You make a living out of partying?"

I kicked Bosco in the arm. From where I was sitting, I was a little far away to get a real good toe in, but I made contact. "It's a chain of stores that sells party supplies, you dumbshit. Go on, D'Metree." His hesitation put me on guard. "If you stole stuff from your employer and you expect me to receive stolen goods, you are too dumb to live."

"What kind of racist shit is that?" D'Metree demanded. "You assume because I am a young black man, I have stolen goods in the trunk of my car all the time? That's what I do, just drive around with stolen goods? Like I hit the Fry's Electronics, and then I knock over the liquor store, and finish off with an early morning raid on Circuit City? Is that what you think?"

"You are not a young black man. At thirty-five years old, you are a middle-aged black man," I responded. Although I admit he almost succeeded in making me feel bad. Until I noticed Bosco had perked up at the mention of Fry's.

"Do you have a TV in there?"

D'Metree stared. I rubbed my forehead and hopped off the counter.

"Don't pay any attention to him. Just go ahead and tell me your little story."

"Well, so you know I'm the buyer there?"

I nodded.

"And there's this supplier, you see, they put out a nice product. Very cheap, very cheap goods."

"Made by little Indonesian children?" I inquired.

"People who need the work," D'Metree countered. "This supplier, him and his partner, well, they aren't too good at figuring out American holidays. I mean, when stuff happens and all. So they offered us these Halloween-themed items. Either Party Palace or Party All-night would have been interested, and they will be interested again next year. Right now, though, I'm pretty sure that if I brought this to the attention of the boss, he would say no way, we got to get by Thanksgiving, and we are in the middle of major Christmas mania, and then we got Valentine's Day, Easter, Fourth of July. I mean, we are a long, long way from next Halloween. You following me?"

"No, I'm not following you. I'm way ahead of you. You got these very cheap goods at an even cheaper off-season price. You bought them yourself, rather than bringing the deal to your employer, and next—shall we say August—you will put them back on the market? You expect me to store them for you here, for free, I assume? And then you will have some convenient shill offer them to Party Palace and Party All-night at what? Double what you paid for them? Triple?"

D'Metree smiled modestly.

"Hey, cuz, this is a big step for the race," I said. "You didn't steal the merchandise, you stole the opportunity. It's like a white-collar crime."

Sarcasm was wasted. "It's not a crime. The most they could do is fire me. And they won't fire me because even at twice what I paid, it's a bargain. And if I did offer it to them now, they wouldn't take it because it's just a storage issue for them. Hey, if they don't want it then, they don't have to buy it."

He spread his hands in a trust-me gesture. "Look, whatever they pay me, they'll mark it up 100% again, and everybody profits. Everybody's happy. It's just that I can't store them at my home, I have people from work over to my house all the time." D'Metree looked around. "You owe the Cutter side of the family a little something, Fifi. You got this house. And you got plenty of room here," he pointed out. Or, from my perspective, rubbed in.

I gritted my teeth and told D'Metree he could store the boxes of exciting Halloween novelty items in the spare bedroom, declining a request to assist in the unloading.

"What exactly is in these boxes, anyway?" I asked.

"Door mats," he replied. "They got, like, pictures of skeletons and witches. When you step on them, they scream."

"Very amusing. I'll see you out."

*   *   *

I put a call into Yoo, expecting to leave a message, since it was Saturday, but he answered the phone. Turns out he was another home-office worker. I explained what I was after.

"I don't think I'm interested. I'm really busy right now," Yoo informed me.

I begged.

"Well, look, if you can wait a while, I guess I can squeeze you in. But it might be several days, so don't say I didn't warn you."

"I'll bring the stuff right over, if that's okay. And I won't say you didn't warn me," I promised. I hung up and yelled for Bosco to get dressed and come on.

*   *   *

The office/condo of John Yoo, handwriting analyst, was small but furnished nicely in a bland, modernist style. A lack of ornamentation suggested to me that Yoo, a tired-looking, grey-haired man, might be a bachelor.

Yoo's manner was abrupt but professional. He led us from the cramped entry hall into the main room where I unfurled the banner onto a table, sprinkling glitter around. Bosco wandered over to inspect the state-of-the-art entertainment center on the far wall. "Shit! Fifi!" he exclaimed, "This is a Kaiyoshi, exactly what I was talking about! Hey, look at this screen! Look, look, he's got a DVD player. Hey, TiVo! He's got TiVo!"

Yoo looked annoyed and growled at me not to let Bosco touch anything. He leaned across the table and inspected the signatures scrawled every which way over the paper.

"I can compare two samples for $400.00. Cash up front. If you pay by check, I start work when the check clears. Those are my standard terms."

I sat down and wrote him a check, knowing that Eddie was going to have to cover it soon, or I was going to be in serious overdraft trouble. Yoo also told me, with unseemly glee, that if we wanted all of the samples checked, it would be considerably more.

"I can't really afford more right now. Just start with the Rob Schlefly and Warren Obermeyer signatures. If those two are genuine, that should be enough."

I handed Yoo the envelope with the samples Eddie had scrounged up, and he shook them out. For Obermeyer, we had several typed letters with his signature appended. For Schlefly, we had an old Christmas card, apparently addressed to a client, and a greeting card to his wife, inscribed, "To my sweetie of sweeties. We'll always have Paris. Love from Bobby." I couldn't even imagine how Eddie had managed to filch these items.

"This isn't enough," Yoo advised me. "I need five to ten samples apiece in order to be able to testify to a reasonable degree of certainty that these samples match those signatures."

"Not going to happen," I said. "I can't get any more samples right now."

"I won't testify in court on this skimpy evidence." Yoo was adamant.

"We'll worry about the testifying part later. Just do the best you can for now."

Chapter 11

The following morning, after reading my neighbor's Sunday paper, which I carefully put back together and returned before he was even awake—hey, I'm not a monster—Bosco suggested we pay a visit to Angela Heffernan.

"I don't want to. It's Sunday. I don't like working on Sunday. I don't like working on Saturday. I don't like working."

But Bosco called anyway, and advised me that Aunt Angela would be delighted to see us.

We drove out the 10 freeeway. Ted and Angela lived in the non-hilly part of Beverly Hills. You could call it Beverly Flats.

A small lot, but a nice-sized Mediterranean. A variety of palms and birds of paradise filled the front yard. We strolled up the tile walkway to the highly polished door, which had a small beveled glass window in the center.

Aunt Angela's housekeeper answered our knock and led us through the entryway to the right, into a large living room with a cathedral ceiling. The furniture, French Regency reproduction in soft grey and yellow, smothered in a profusion of brocade accent pillows and big silk tassels.

The housekeeper offered iced tea, which Bosco accepted, and then left us alone to wait. It was then I started to notice that the pillows weren't all shiny and new, the legs of the chairs were scuffed, and a cat had definitely been having its way with the back of the sofa pushed up against the far wall.

Angela came tentatively into the room. She was, I had to admit, still trophy material, not that much past thirty. Her streaked blonde hair was casually fluffed. Her nails were French tipped. Her collagened lips were just perfect.

On the other hand, she wasn't nearly as trim as she had been when the huge wedding photograph over the fake fireplace had been taken.

"Aunt Angela," Bosco extended both hands and kissed her on the cheek. "It's great to see you. This is my half-sister, Fifi."

Angela looked at me. "Oh yes, Bobby told me you guys had gone into business together. Grief counseling."

"Yes, yes that's right. Fifi's in LA I'm in New York. That way, we keep both coasts covered, you know."

We all sat down, Bosco and I on the cat-damaged sofa and Angela on a side chair, her back to the large front window.

"In fact," Bosco smiled, "that's partly why we wanted to see you. To make sure you're doing okay."

Angela gave that expression, like she was trying to look sad, except the toxin which she had injected into her face every six weeks at $350 a pop was preventing her muscles from responding.

"You heard that Obermeyer & Schlefly has retained us to counsel the firm—and certainly the family of the firm—through this troubling time."

Angela smiled. "I know. Bobby told me." That was the second time she had referred to "Bobby." Who the hell was Bobby?

Seeing my confusion, Angela said, "Robert Schlefly. Most people call him Rob, but I call him Bobby."

Bosco started in on his grief-counseling shtick. Angela responded immediately to his sympathy.

"It really does suck," she sighed. "I mean, I just don't

know what to do. I'm gonna sell this place," she gestured airily. "Maybe move to the Palisades. I would really like to be closer to my gym."

Has to get back in shape for the next manhunt, I thought. As she fluffed her hair with her left hand, Angela's wedding ring sparkled—a lozenge-shaped diamond on a band of gold so wide it almost reached her knuckle.

Bosco tried every empty phrase he could think of to get her to talk about her grief, but in the end we had to conclude that this was one more person who didn't actually feel grief.

She was upset, but mostly about having to sell Ted's Porsche and not being able to find the pink slip and about how inadequate his life insurance was, and how ironic she found that to be, since she had married an insurance broker. The firm, she noted bitterly, had more insurance on Ted than his own family did.

I was about to continue this line of questioning when Bosco leaned in front of me, pushing me up against the back of the couch with his elbow. "Aunt Angela," he said, "I know you and Uncle Ted were going through a temporary separation. I want you to know that you are not to feel guilty about that. Uncle Ted doesn't get a free pass just because he's dead. Your feelings of abandonment are just as valid as they were before Ted passed on. You were the one wronged here. You can't keep it all bottled up."

OK. This, I admit, was brilliant. Bosco's implication that the split-up had been Uncle Ted's idea opened the floodgates.

"I was wronged," Angela declared. "Just so you understand, though, I threw him out. I mean, it was getting very embarrassing for me. I totally get that men are not always going to be faithful. I'm not the jealous type. You know, people make mistakes and if they are truly repentant, they should be forgiven." Her eyes strayed to a hunky diamond bracelet on her right wrist, a symbol of true repentance.

"But being so balls-out about it. That's different. I mean, everyone knew. The firm was our social set. Everybody in that office was my friend."

I doubted that. A woman this self-centered probably had fewer friends than I did.

"And I think he was spending money on her." Angela spat this out with a depth of feeling we had not seen before. "He said the firm was going to pay for that little love tryst in Laguna. Yeah, right. I know how that goes. You have a little dinner, you do a little shopping on the main drag, she sees something pretty, he's thinking about that night, and," she snapped her fingers, "there goes five hundred bucks."

She did, indeed, appear to know exactly how that goes.

"And here we are, with Chloe still in college, and my Paige just starting at Concord Academy. God, educating kids these days! It's like a sucking chest wound!" Angela was looking a little frantic. "I mean, I had to throw him out," she stared at us and declared. "I have my pride."

That, I thought, was highly debatable, but I kept my mouth shut.

"It's just that when I did throw him out, things seemed to get worse." Angela hung her head.

Well, yeah, since being thrown out of his home meant that Ted had to rent a furnished apartment and pay a double set of bills. Angela could sense what I was thinking, and she hastened to explain.

"When I told him to pack his bags and get out, I didn't believe he'd really go," Angela's tone went from frustration to pleading. "Or at least not for so long. I thought a few days and he'd come to his senses. You know, he'd say he was sorry, and buy me a present, and maybe we'd go on a nice trip. I've always wanted to go to Paris."

Poor little Angela. If you weren't listening closely, you might feel sorry for her. I glanced over at Bosco, signaling, "Let's get on with it." Using his debriefing ploy, Bosco gently directed Angela to the night that Ted had met his fate.

"Oh, that was classic Ted," she fumed. "It was my big night, and he made sure he wasn't going to be there. You may have heard that I was Chair of the Diabetes Foundation Autumn Fundraiser. Adult onset," she qualified. "Juvenile diabetes was already taken. The theme was 'A Night in Tuscany' at La Fortunata. It was," she declared indignantly, "the culmination of months of hard work."

By "hard work" she had to mean two or three lunches with elderly ladies who had lots more money than she did and liked to let her know it.

As she told it, Ted had originally agreed to escort his wife to the dinner but had later cancelled on her, saying that he had to appear at the broker's convention in Laguna. Angela then found out he planned to go with Belinda. "I had to hostess the whole thing, all alone. How do you think that looked? And then it turns out he never even went to Laguna!"

No, I thought. *The creep had the nerve to die instead.*

She confirmed that the Schleflys were at the dinner, and the Obermeyers. Corazon Villareal had been there, too, but only for the appetizers. She couldn't stay for dinner for some reason.

A lot of highly respectable people were there, but nailing down reliable witnesses wasn't that easy. It turned out that only the main course was sit-down.

"We had a dessert and espresso bar set up," Angela explained. "Otherwise, you're stuck too long at one table with one set of people. You can't get the necessary mingling in. Mingling is so important at these things."

Mingling may be important, I reflected, but when some people mingle, other people can slip out, avoid mingling, and start murdering.

A few minutes later, Angela showed us to the door. To my astonishment, she gave us both little sideways hugs, being careful not to smudge her makeup.

"Thanks, guys," she chirped, "I really do feel better!"

*   *   *

Talking it over in the truck, Bosco and I agreed that Angela's revelations were suggestive, but of too many things. Angela might well have had a motive, if it was true that Ted was really going to dump her. But was she financially better off with Ted alive and obligated to pay child support for little Paige, who was only four? Or with him dead and the insurance she said was inadequate?

Chapter 12

Monday morning at the grief counseling factory was a drag. We had to endure two and a half hours of really dull people not being helpful and saying essentially the same thing: "I didn't know Mr. Heffernan very well, but it was such a shock." "He seemed like a good guy, I remember once he asked about my kids." "God. Nothing prepares you for something like this, does it?"

At the 10:40 break, I told Bosco he needed to carry on by himself for a while. I'd had enough. I went in search of coffee—even office coffee was sounding good to me by that time.

I found the lunchroom, through two doors and past a storage room and several banks of file cabinets. No windows, discolored melamine cabinets, and a dusty, plastic hanging plant suspended from the ceiling in one corner. The aroma of long-simmering coffee permeated the room, with a top note of microwave popcorn.

I gingerly took a disposable plastic cup from the stack, threw it away and took the next one. Germs lurk everywhere. I eyed the coffee pot and opted for tea. At least each bag was individually sealed.

As I stood there drinking the lukewarm beverage, a well-built Hispanic woman of about forty walked in. Her hair swept away from her face with a tapering wave. An expensive do. Her two-piece suit was a scarlet dupioni silk.

She wore plain black suede pumps, the only possible shoe for that outfit. No wedding band, but a large onyx scarab looked very comfortable on the ring finger of her right hand.

She gave me what I took to be an automatic smile, went over to the half-size refrigerator and took out a bottle of sparkling water. She wiped the top with a paper towel, a sensible precaution in my view, and turned to leave. I seized the chance.

"Are you Corazon Villareal?" I asked.

She turned and fixed me with obsidian eyes, eyes that didn't match the smile that was still fixed to her lips. Her broad face was handsome but too heavy for the Spanish beauty look. "Yes, I am. Are you the psychiatrist?"

I was about to indignantly deny being a member of any healing profession, when I realized that this is exactly what I was supposed to be.

"Grief counselor."

"I'm glad I ran into you. I signed up for the time slot at three but I have to cancel my session. A meeting got scheduled with one of Ted's clients; they want me to take over the account. Sorry."

Yikes, Eddie's client-grabbing scheme was in deep trouble. He was not only going to have to beat out Karen, but it looked like Corazon was worming her way in, too.

"Life must go on," I replied, sounding inane even to my own ears. "I...er...was just taking a little break. It gets rather...intense."

She twitched a much more genuine smile—as though she knew exactly what I had really wanted to say. "Yes, I imagine it does. How much worse would it be if there really was any grief?"

I disposed of the tea bag and jumped at the opening. "Are you saying Ted Heffernan wasn't very well liked?"

She shrugged and walked out of the kitchen, replying enigmatically, "In some quarters, I suppose he was very well liked."

I stared at her receding back. It's a disadvantage when

you don't have them confined in that small room, bound to a chair for half an hour. I began to appreciate the merits of Bosco's plan, though still very mindful of how painful it was all going to be when we were discovered.

I returned to the conference room and found the defeated brunette from the funeral, excessively nervous, uncomfortably perched in the chair. She was twisting her hands, as if strangling an imaginary chicken.

"I'm not sure I should really be here," she blurted out, "I'm not really an employee."

It was on the tip of my tongue to tell her that it was okay, we weren't really grief counselors, but Bosco, channeling my impulse, got in first.

"Hey, it's all right, Mrs. Schlefly. May I call you Dolly? Please, just sit back; we are here for anyone who needs us. This is my partner, Fifi Cutter. Fifi, Dolly; Dolly, Fifi."

At first, I wondered why Schlefly's wife would be so grief-stricken that she needed to come in and talk to us. But after a few minutes, I realized that this woman was a neurotic train wreck who would never miss an opportunity to whine.

We heard all about her low self-esteem, her lack of purpose in life, her difficulty communicating with her husband, and on and on, until she finally circled around to her grief about poor old Ted, a dear friend she didn't see all that much of, but who she was really going to miss.

I tried to herd her in the right direction when I realized that Dolly might be able to shed light on the big question: Could Robert Schlefly or Warren Obermeyer have snuck out of the dinner without being noticed? Dolly was happy to share the details of the night in Tuscany.

"It was quite elegant, candles and a beautiful arrangement of golden chrysanthemums at each table, about three hundred people, I believe, at a thousand dollars a couple for the tickets, not to mention the separate donations— that's something. I will say this about Angela, she has a nose for money," Dolly said, as if conceding a point graciously.

"Although she doesn't have—how can I say this?—natural hostess sense. Hard to blame her. You know, she grew up in a single-parent home in Petaluma, so I'm sure she didn't have a lot of experience with entertaining on a grand scale. Certain things just can't be learned later in life." Dolly's little smile was tolerantly forgiving. "For example, Angela put Robert and me at the same table with the Obermeyers. Not that I minded, dear Warren and Babs. Although, we do see such a lot of them. I mean, really, as the two senior members of the firm, we should have been at separate tables, to spread the firm's good will, don't you think?"

I had no opinion concerning the etiquette of the arrangement, but this was a great piece of news for Eddie. Rob and Warren as each other's alibi was no alibi at all.

"Was anyone else at the table?" I asked.

"Oh well, of course, we weren't isolated, for god's sake, not even Angela has manners that bad," Dolly replied, with a little laugh that was meant to take the sting out of her words, but didn't. "We were also seated with Clarissa Wheaton, you know, the actress. Omigod, I could believe the stories about her, too. You know what I mean. She had these real glassy eyes and was talking so fast. Draw your own conclusion. We were so pleased that the mayor's chief of staff was at our table, a nice man, very handsome. You know Robert plays squash with the mayor. Oh yes, known each other for years. Robert and—oh, now his name escapes me—anyway, they had lots to talk about."

She paused to catch her breath, and I did the same. The cokehead actress might not be much of an alibi, but the mayor's chief of staff, whatever his name was, was a different story. I was just about to regretfully conclude that Rob and Warren's alibi was going to stand up when Dolly started her prattling again.

"This poor man did not, however, seem to me to be getting along with his wife. I mean, she wouldn't look directly at him, and hardly said a word to any of us. She was sulking about something. Not the ideal political wife. I hope he dumps her before his career goes much further. You know, a divorce is nothing to a politician nowadays, but a problem wife, it's so hard to overcome. And he did seem very distracted."

So the mayor's chief of staff might not be such a good alibi-confirmer, after all. "Were a lot of people from the firm there?"

"Oh yes, well, the Obermeyers, of course, and Corazon Villareal, who didn't even sit down, just put in an appearance. I can't say I really like that woman. She seems hard. A number of the other brokers were there. Not Karen, of course, she had to take Ted's place at the convention. Ugly woman, isn't she? I remember that Keith Gursky fellow, he tries a bit too hard, if I can say that. This is all privileged, right? Like my therapist? Well, he kept coming up to Robert and trying to talk to him, but, really, Robert was there for client development. He had to talk to a number of different people. I mean that was the point of the donation, wasn't it?"

I agreed with her that curing diabetes was probably not a sufficiently good reason to attend a high-priced charity dinner.

Dolly was at least able to confirm that Angela had not only been there but had been seated at the head table. "The center of attention in that gold dress. I thought it was a bit over the top, and more than a bit revealing for a woman of Angela's age."

After Dolly, the afternoon ground on to little good effect. Do I even have to describe how I felt at the end of that day? It all worked out, though. I saw Mandy coming down the hall with the envelope in her hand just a split second before Bosco did and managed to rush out in front of him and collect the $1,200 check from Obermeyer & Schlefly. Sweet.

Chapter 13

"What do we do next?" I asked as we began the long crawl home.

"We can check with the valet guys at the restaurant. See if they remember anyone leaving and coming back that night."

"Maybe they took a taxi."

"Then we can trace the taxi cab."

"Bosco, the chances of convincing some driver from Guadalajara, operating a unlicensed cab and overstaying his green card, to ever talk to us, even if we could find him, which we can't, is zero."

"We have to be able to prove it somehow."

"Prove what? We still don't even know that it's murder. From what Angela told us, it could just as easily be suicide. Money troubles, mood swings, marital troubles. Plus, you know, Bosco, Robert Schlefly must have told Angela how much the insurance was. That's a little suggestive." I looked over at Bosco, who nodded. "You thinking what I'm thinking? I'm thinking Angela is the only one who calls Robert Schlefly 'Bobby.'"

"That's right. And that card we gave to Yoo was signed 'Bobby.' It said, 'We'll always have Paris.' When we talked to Angela, she mentioned she wanted to see Paris. Plus, that isn't the kind of thing you say to your wife."

"No, it isn't," I agreed, "Maybe the key-man insurance was just chocolate icing on the adultery cake for Rob Schlefly."

*   *   *

I picked up the mail on the way in. One letter, cream envelope, stiff paper. Looked like an invitation, but I was pretty spooked from the last time I got a hand-addressed letter. Except when I looked at it, it was addressed to Bosco. I handed it to him without a glance. After all, I didn't care if he got a threatening note.

The telephone message light was on. I let it play:

"Bosco, this is your mother. I understand that there is to be a memorial for my dear friend Ted Heffernan at St. Michael's. I further understand that you have been invited and asked to speak, but apparently due to some silly oversight, your stepfather and I have not been included. Please arrange an invitation for us. We feel it is important for us to attend, and we are more than willing to make a small contribution."

I was stunned. Mother talking to Bosco. Mother talking to Bosco and asking Bosco for a favor. Mother talking to Bosco and asking Bosco for a favor when that favor would actually cost her money? It was too weird.

Bosco ripped open the envelope as we listened to the message again.

Sure enough, there was a lovely engraved invitation to a memorial for Theodore Patrick Heffernan at St. Michael's the following Sunday, suggested contribution to the Theodore P. Heffernan Memorial Scholarship fund a mere fifty dollars a head.

Also included, on gold embossed, tissue-thin stationery, was a handwritten request from a "Father Paul" asking Bosco, as Ted's "ward," to say a few words.

"We gotta go, Fifi. I mean, if Mom wants us to. Looks like she finally wants to bury the hatchet."

I looked at my brother in dismay. Could he really be so naive? The king of conning others? "You've got to be kidding me. I've never known Mother to forgive anyone. For anything. Ever. I'm sorry, man, but it's just that I know her a lot better than you do..."

"That's bullshit, Fifi. I knew her before you were even born. You don't know her at all. You always think she's so mean. She isn't mean. She's strong and tough. That's because she's had to be. But she's got a really good heart."

"Sure, Bosco, Mother's got a good heart, a great heart. In fact, she's got the best heart money can buy."

Bosco actually snarled at me. I backed up and raised my hands. "Hey, I didn't say you couldn't go with Mother. I'm just saying I'm not going to go."

Bosco eyed me speculatively. In a different tone he said, "But we have to go. We never got to interview Schlefly or Villareal in our grief counseling sessions. And we talked to Obermeyer, but we didn't get anything out of him. We've got to give him another shot. We can bill for this. It's perfect. It's part of the job."

Bosco was right, which didn't make me any happier. "Okay, I'll go. But only if you get Eddie to pay the one hundred dollars for us."

"Consider it done."

*   *   *

Tuesday afternoon I cleaned the gutters, which gave me a view of the very sad state of my roof. Then I did laundry and re-caulked the shower/tub in the bathroom. None of which Bosco helped with.

By 4:15 I was tired and achy. The good tired and achy. I headed for my favorite spot on the floor in the living room. Bosco was on the phone.

"Aw Jeez, Eddie, I don't think it would be too cool to give less than a hundred dollars. I know, I know. It's a suggested contribution.But I think that's a euphemism...Well, you want us to go, don't you? Anyway, I bet it's tax deductible, so it's really only fifty dollars...Why wouldn't it be tax deductible?"

I rolled my eyes. Bosco winked. "Great. Then we'll go. What? No, she's right here." I shook my head vigorously, but Bosco paid no attention. "Hold on." He held the phone out.

I snatched it from him. "Hi, Eddie, Fifi here."

"Did you talk to Dina Mraz?"

"Uh, not exactly, see…"

"Oh shit!"

"Hey, chill out. I'll go back to see her tomorrow. No big deal."

Eddie started to laugh. It wasn't a merry sound.

"You're aren't going to see her tomorrow. Not unless you got a Ouija board."

"What do you mean?"

"I mean Dina bought the farm," Eddie barked. "Bit the big weenie. Or, if you're Baptist, went home to Papa."

"Are you trying to tell me she died?"

"You got it. OD'd on heroin, that's what Mandy told me this morning. Some guy she was living with found her Friday night."

"Oh my God," I moaned. I was there, actually there… I recalled the music cutting off as I tapped on the bedroom door. I realized now that no one had switched it off, it was just the CD ending. Which means that she hadn't been dead very long. Crap! I had been alone in a room with a dead person. A dead person. An eternally and forever dead person. Don't think about it, don't think about it, don't think about it, I chanted to myself.

I decided right then not to mention to Eddie that I had been there. He'd never know. No one would ever know. Except…Oh fuck, I left a note!

Maybe no one would notice it. The place was a landfill. Wait, wait, I tried to collect my thoughts. I didn't sign the note. I signed Bosco's name to the note. I started to calm down.

"Eddie," I made myself ask, "You don't think it has anything like…she wasn't killed, was she? I mean, because you know, the phone call, and it's a pretty big coincidence…"

"Naaaaah, you're crazy," said Eddie. His contempt was

comforting. "She went way downhill during these years, waiting for the verdict to pay off, not working, nothing to do all day, partying all night. I heard she had a bunch of druggie roommates."

"So, you really don't think it had anything to do with...?"

"Of course not, why would it? She and Ted hadn't been together for years."

"But maybe it is connected, in a different way." My brain had clicked back on after the initial shock. "Now Obermeyer & Schlefly don't have to pay the judgment. That's motive."

"I wish. But it ain't so. Schlefly already asked our lawyer. First thing he thought of. The money will go to Dina's heir. She didn't leave a will, so it'll all go to her mother in Tennessee. Probably spend it all on a nice, long trip to Dollywood in an RV."

The tight band of iron around my chest loosened a little. It was only a coincidence that Dina just happened to die when I just happened to be there. Sure, that was it.

*   *   *

On Wednesday I got up early, after a restless night, which was not all due to the fact I was sleeping on a pool raft, either. I got some reports written and waited for Bosco to get up, which he didn't, or at least not before noon.

When he finally made his appearance, we sat down in the kitchen and had a cup of peppermint tea, the last item left from the gift basket that Colchester Casualty had given to its employees for Christmas the year before. Instead of a bonus.

"I don't know what to do next, Bosco. The personal angle seems fantastic. A lot of guys screw around on their wives and don't get killed by mysterious, untraceable poisons. And if Angela had something on the side with Schlefly, that makes it somewhat less likely that she killed Ted out of jealousy.

Anyway, these people all know good divorce lawyers."

Back to Eddie's idea that Ted was somehow running a scam. This would be a great motive for Obermeyer & Schlefly, especially if Ted was looking to make a move to another firm, as Karen had seemed to suggest in our counseling session.

How mad would they be at Ted for leaving his partners with a big judgment and no future income stream to make up for it?

The stuff from Ted's office was still piled on the floor. We went over the information we had about SXYFX. Bosco seemed to think that if there was something hinky going on, it would have to involve Ms. Ng.

"You should check these companies out. You said Ms. Ng adjusts all the claims for SXYFX and Dobbins/McCray. Two of Ted's biggest accounts, right?"

"Dobbins/McCray is the biggest account, it's a huge publishing empire, but SXYFX isn't so big," I corrected him. "They make a ton of money, but I don't think they buy all that much insurance. At least not workers' comp. They don't seem to have a lot of employees. Seem to mostly hire independent contractors. Otherwise known as people you don't have to pay workers' compensation benefits to."

"If there is funny business going on, I wouldn't approach Ms. Ng directly. And you aren't going to find out anything from Dobbins/McCray," Bosco said. "You might have more luck finding something out at a small company like SXYFX."

"Finding out what? I don't even know what you're talking about!"

"Neither do I," Bosco admitted in a rare moment of candor. "But it's a place to start. And don't forget…"

"Yeah, I know." I finished the sentence for him. "It's billable."

I consulted the client information card and called Stanley Gastukian, the designated contact person. I explained that I was calling "on behalf" of Obermeyer & Schlefly in the wake of the death of Mr. Heffernan and would like to meet with him to go over the insurance coverages that were in place.

"You can come over this afternoon," Mr. Gastukian said, in a strongly accented voice. "But I usually deal with Ms. Odom."

"Ms. Odom has so much on her plate right now. We thought it best for all of us to pitch in and help."

"Three o'clock then. Don't be late; I have a busy afternoon."

I changed into a light green crepe A-line, with a round white collar and white cuffs. It was simply cut with a wide matching belt. A classic. I squashed my hair into a bun, which really made my nose look huge. Bosco said I looked "nice."

I glanced at the notes Bosco had made and stuffed them into the briefcase I had bought when I graduated from college and believed that all adults needed a briefcase.

Then Bosco sat me down at the kitchen table and tried to coach me on my lying. First, he said the key was confidence in yourself. Then he said that the important thing was to really believe in what you were saying.

I asked him how could I have confidence in myself if I was stupid enough to believe something I knew wasn't true?

Bosco told me to picture Mr. Gastukian in his underwear and gave up.

Chapter 14

The drive to Van Nuys took a mind-boggling fifty-two minutes. An overturned big rig in Burbank and a work crew on the shoulder all the way through Studio City.

I took a deep breath and tried to focus on the money. I needed the money to pay the taxes. I needed to pay the taxes to save the house. I needed to save the house because...why? Because Pop wanted me to have a good place to live, a good job, a good life.

I finally transitioned to the 170 freeway, swinging into the crappiest part of the Valley, and exited at Roscoe Blvd. The humble address on Damon Road belied the huge money I knew SXYFX was pulling in. I was not, at that moment, exactly sure of how those millions were pulled in, but I was about to find out.

I parked in a tawdry mini-mall about a block away, taking a space around the side of the Coin King Laundromat on the end, pulling in face-to-face with a concrete wall. As I opened the driver's side door, the smell of Thai take-out nearly knocked me down.

And yet, in just a few minutes, I would recall the smell of Thai take-out with nostalgia.

I walked down the long block of one-story shop fronts. I glanced up as I passed a particularly dingy pet shop. Not really a full-service pet shop. More of a piranha-and-skink pet shop, but if you wanted a piranha or a skink, "Al's

Exotic Animals" was certainly the place you would go.

The one story building which housed SXYFX was as non-descript as buildings get: light pink brick, no windows, no signage. Just the address in silver and black stick-me numbers over a very heavy metal door, in front of which a tattered smelly bundle squatted right where I wanted to be.

"Mind moving?" I asked.

No response. I fished in my light green clutch for a quarter. The figure regarded me. I could not, at first, discern gender, but I was going to vote "Woman." At any rate, she—I'll say she—scooted over when the quarter was displayed.

"You've got no boobies," she said, as I tossed the coin in her direction.

"What?" I answered stupidly.

"You got no boobies," she repeated, confirming that, other anatomical deficiencies aside, there was nothing the matter with my hearing.

"I don't know what you're talking about."

"I SAID, YOU GOT NO BOOBIES," the harridan screamed.

"Well, you've got no teeth, no shoes, and no home, so I'm doing better than you!" I snapped back at her.

I tried the door. Locked.

I spied a white button and pushed it.

"You can't be in those pictures if you got no boobies," she explained.

I tossed her another quarter but accidentally on purpose missed. She gimped off after it, lessening the toxic air quality slightly.

I started as the door clicked open. I was not as Zen-like as I had hoped. I went in.

The small room was windowless. The only possible natural light would have come from the back door, which had a safety glass inset. But a sheet of white tissue paper was taped over it, eerily reminiscent of Ted's door-sized birthday card. I shivered.

The walls were cubbyholed from floor-to-ceiling, each niche stuffed with tapes, CDs, DVDs and papers.

A middle-aged man, tall, pockmarked and pudgy, blinked at me from behind a small wood veneer desk, mottled with cigarette burns and filthy with ash and old butts. Smoking, it appeared, was not only permitted but actively encouraged in this office.

"I'll be with you in a minute." The accented voice told me this was Stan Gastukian, or a close relative. He held a slim cell phone up to his ear. He turned slightly away, but he needn't have bothered, since he was speaking some language that they didn't teach at Eastbridge Academy for Girls.

My eyes fell upon the titles of the product stacked up carelessly in the cubbyholes—demo tapes, some hand-lettered plastic boxes, some professionally packaged, but all very bad. I mean very bad. SXYFX was not "Zizafix" I realized, but "SexEffects." Which also explained the crone's delightful commentary on my cup size.

I shouldn't have been surprised. The porn industry was huge in the Valley, bringing VD, AIDS, and the abuse of prescription pain medication to the doorstep of Middle America. If I had ever thought about it, I would have fig-ured that even the porn industry needed insurance. I'm sure their vehicles crashed into telephone poles at about the same rate as those of other businesses. Maybe even more so, considering that the drivers might be distracted.

In fact, this just proved that the mainstreaming of porno-graphy into American culture was pretty complete. Regular Guy and the Little Woman didn't seem to mind that most of these films were shot right next door to their three bedroom split-level tract home. Why should Obermeyer & Schlefly?

I waited patiently until Stan punched the phone off and turned toward me again.

"I am so sorry to disturb you, Mr. Gastukian. Certain matters have arisen in connection the death of Mr. Heffernan, your insurance broker. We are following up on the accounts handled at Obermeyer & Schlefly. I believe Mr. Heffernan handled your insurance needs for some time." I paused.

The pudgy man, who did not deny being Mr. Gastukian, knocked the ashes off the end of his cigarette onto the floor.

"Twelve years," he confirmed. "Hell of a thing. Ted was a great guy."

I bobbed my head to acknowledge that he had expressed the appropriate level of regret at the passing of a long-term business acquaintance who was in no way a personal friend. We chatted a few more minutes. He invited me to call him Stan. I invited him to call me Catherine.

"Could we just go over your coverage needs?" I sat down on a strictly functional metal-and-vinyl chair. It looked pretty grimy.

Ordinarily, of course, I would have wiped it off and not worried about appearing rude, but I was nervous, being here alone with a scary pornographer, and lying like a legless dog. So I sat down and tried not to think about what the backside of my A-line would look like when I stood up.

I pulled the SXYFX file out of my briefcase. It took just a few minutes to match policy numbers and dates. None of the coverages were up for renewal for several months, and there was clearly no urgency to the situation. Which made it even more awkward for me to explain what I was doing there.

"And Ms. Ng is handling your claims? No complaints there?"

"Strange thing that," Stan shook his head. "She died too, just a few days after Ted did."

I blinked. "Died?"

"Yeah, she was hit by a bus on Wilshire Blvd. Terrible shame, survive fucking Vietnam, and get hit by a bus. She was old, though, you know, and didn't walk so well, had that brace thing on her leg." Stan looked at me, and puckered his brow. "Didn't you know that? I woulda thought the company woulda told you guys? Karen knew, she told me she sent a wreath."

"Oh, um, she probably just forgot to mention it." The chill in my heart was replaced with heat that spread up my neck onto my face to the roots of my hair. To cover my confusion, I glanced at Bosco's notes on the payment schedules.

"Premium finance payments all caught up to date?" I asked brightly.

"What the hell are you talking about?" growled Stan. I hastily looked at the notes again. Bosco had written "SXYFX general liability and commercial auto, premium finance with Phoenix Premium Finance, $164,010.26." I was reading it right, and yet, quite evidently I had said something extremely wrong.

"We didn't finance any premium." Stan glared at me. "You mean take a loan and pay outrageous interest to one of those premium finance outfits? You gotta be joking. We paid those premiums 100% up front. We got a discount for pre-payment. We always do that. We have the cash, why wouldn't we do that?"

Stan pointed at me. "This is a cash rich business, girlie. Especially with the blockbuster year we had last year. We signed Suzie Double-Q to an exclusive contract, five years, the rest of her professional life, and she is the hottest thing in the Valley right now. She's starring in twenty-seven movies this year, plus merchandising contracts. We've never had anything move off the shelves so fast as Suzie Double-Q."

Stan puffed on his cigarette, whipped a creased and stained photo off a stack on his desk and slammed it down in front of me. I glanced at it. It was captioned "Introducing Suzie Double-Q" and gave new meaning to the term "head shot." I looked away.

Stan continued to stare at me, his lips tight. Suddenly, he didn't seem pudgy. He just seemed big.

"I...uh...I...uh...not sure...some mistake..." I stuttered and looked down at the material on my lap. So was Stan lying or did Bosco just screw up? Well, that was easy, I couldn't think of any reason for Stan to lie to Catherine, the insurance broker.

"Oh, yes, yes, I see, looking at the wrong form here. Silly." I shook my head in stern reproach at myself and forced a smile.

Stan did not smile back. "Do you have a card?" He asked the ordinary question in a quiet voice, which unaccountably flooded me with fear.

Damning Eddie and Bosco both to the toastiest reaches of hell for getting me into this ridiculous situation, I flicked open the briefcase flap and blinked, I hoped, in a natural manner. "Whoops, so sorry, I seem to be out. You're the fourth meeting I've had today. You know, you just get so busy." Stop babbling, I ordered myself.

Stan was silent for a good minute. Then he excused himself and exited a side door, telling me to stay right there. I bolted instantly for the front door and pulled at the knob, but it was locked.

I looked up. Fuck! My craven escape attempt had been caught on videotape. I scooted back to the chair and sweated out several long minutes before Stan came back.

I wondered if he was calling Obermeyer & Schlefly. Was there any chance that Mandy the transvestite receptionist would put him through to Eddie? If Mandy put him through to Eddie, would Eddie be quick enough to know what to say to get me out of this predicament?

My chances weren't good. Stan would probably ask for, and get, Karen, who would instantly raise a very red flag. I tried to maintain calm. What could he really do to me? I asked myself. White slavery? Wouldn't work, I'm not that white.

No one outside could see into the building at all, and only Bosco knew where I had gone, and he certainly wouldn't worry his pretty little head about me in anything like enough time.

This is why I don't lie, I reminded myself. I'm not good at it.

Stan returned, expressionless and pushed a button behind his desk. The front door clicked open. Relief flooded in with the dazzling sunshine.

"It appears we have concluded our business," he said coldly. "Goodbye, Catherine."

I fumbled the papers into the briefcase, thought about saying something to keep up appearances, balked, and darted out.

The metal door clanged behind me and I screeched to a halt. I realized that I was not as alone as I would like to be.

*　　*　　*

Standing in front of me, and looking considerably taller than my memory of her, was the homeless crone. Around her stood three companions who, despite a marked similarity to the crone in personal style, were indisputably male.

Eight pale eyes stared at me as if I was a computer screen. Maybe only seven eyes, one of them seemed to be focused on a spot over my head, a little to the left.

"Get away," I said, trying to sound stern. No effect. I took a step forward and ran into a wall of stench. It was horrible, like being thrown into a deep pit of restaurant garbage, hospital waste and day care sewage.

I quickly stepped back. Could you die from body odor, I wondered? Wouldn't that be the absolute worst way to go?

"I'm afraid I don't have any folding money, gentlemen. I gave it all to your lady friend there."

Five eyes shifted toward the crone.

"She didn't give me nothin'," the crone shrieked.

"I wouldn't call twenty dollars nothing," I protested.

"Twenty dollars?" repeated the oldest guy, nattily attired in a stained, grey blanket and battered bowler.

Even through the layers of grime, I could see the process of thought beginning to crank up on the faces of the male contingent. Granted, it wasn't deep philosophical thought that would lead one day to the meaning of life or proof of God's existence. It was something more like: "She got twenty dollars. I want twenty dollars."

Still, it was thought, and it was working to my advantage. There was a shuffling of feet. The solid unit of four weakened.

"She put it with her stuff in her shopping cart," I gestured toward pile of rags and cans and unspeakable things. The one who was wearing shoes started toward the cart. I strode through the opening, giving Grey Blanket a vicious elbow-shove that sent him into the crone.

I proceeded directly into the street, slowing if not actually stopping traffic. I didn't know what it would take to get those nimrod drivers to stop and ask if they could help.

Not that I wanted any help, I wanted to get out of there. I walked in the middle of the street all the way to the mini-mall where my car was parked, accompanied by the frenzied wailings of an old woman who only had a shopping cart full of trash in all this world, and was about to lose it.

As I approached the truck, I rolled up my sleeves, loosened my collar and twisted off the elastic that held my hair in place. I couldn't wait to get home.

I slid onto the driver's seat and locked the door, for once not all that bothered by whatever it was that jabbed through the material in the seat and stuck me in the left buttock. I steadied my shaking hands, placing the purse and the brief-case in the passenger seat well.

And then, just as I was putting the key into the ignition, the back window behind my head exploded.

Chapter 15

I glimpsed the brief reflection of a baseball bat in the rear view mirror. Glass shards shot into my right cheek and the back of my neck as I half turned. I saw a dark shape bounce out of the back of the truck.

Thank God I had loosened my hair. Its indestructible mass had caught most of the tiny glass darts. Not safety glass, my insurance adjustor instincts automatically noted.

I gasped and turned the key, revved the engine and slammed into reverse. I turned and sped off, hardly able to breathe. I did not, for the slightest beat of a heart, think about going after the dark shape.

I was still gasping, so hard my throat was sore, when I got home. I had made the return trip in an amazing twenty minutes flat, virtually balancing out the horrendous fifty-two minute trip there, traffic time-wise.

"Bosco! Bosco!" I croaked as I let myself in. I ran from the living room to the kitchen, then upstairs. He was nowhere to be found. How he had managed to be somewhere else without a car? I slowly retraced my steps throughout the house. No Bosco.

I headed for the bathroom and examined the damage to my face in the mirror. There wasn't as much blood as I would have thought, but it took a long time for what there was to stop beading up. I luxuriated in a hot shower, with citrus-scented moisturizing gel. It stung but helped me forget the bad smells. So many bad smells. The A-line would have to be immediately taken to the dry cleaner. I didn't even want it in the house.

I re-examined my face when I got out and decided a little Neosporin was all that was needed. Except for two fairly deep cuts on the back of my neck, which I covered with a patchwork of small and medium band aids, the bloody pin pricks were pretty small. Not stitch worthy, even if I'd had health insurance. And I didn't.

Believing I had jinxed the day by going for the wrong look, I opted for zebra-striped stretch pants, fuchsia tube top, red high-heeled open-toed mules and fruit cluster earrings. I felt a little better.

Except Bosco still hadn't returned. I went to the kitchen and checked his notes against the computer printouts. The records of Obermeyer & Schlefly reflected that SXYFX had indeed financed the premium. Someone had made a mistake, but it wasn't Bosco.

Or maybe it wasn't a mistake at all. Maybe I was on to something.

I cleaned the glass out of the cab of the truck and wondered if I was going to be able to fix the window. My expert eye put the replacement cost at $175.00, minimum, and then only if I could get a used part—unlikely, given the relative rarity of twenty-year-old flatbeds in LA. Shit!

I tried to conjure up an image of the figure with the baseball bat, but I hadn't had time to register anything at all, not height, weight, not even a general build.

Could it have been a random act of violence? Or was my assailant the person that Stan had been calling when he left me alone to sweat? Had the homeless crew been instructed to slow me down while Mr. Baseball Bat got in position to follow me from SXYFX?

He couldn't have known that the truck was my truck until I go into it. Right? Except I had given Eddie the make, model and license plate number of the truck so we could park in the Obermeyer & Schlefly reserved parking. Could someone else at the company have gotten the information from the parking records?

I returned my thoughts to the Obermeyer & Schlefly documents. I wasn't really clear on premium financing. I decided to go visit the one friend I had boasted to Bosco about: Victoria Jane Smith. We had gone to Eastbridge together, and when she graduated from law school two years ago, my Pop had given her a job at his firm.

I hadn't called or IMed her in a long time, and I couldn't text her since I didn't even have a cell phone any more. I had pretty much just totally blown her off. I'm so not a good friend. I sat down at my card table and clicked open to e-mail.

"U there? Can I come C U today? How R U?"

Thirty-two minutes later I got back:

"Who are U?"

"It's Feef. S'up?"

"Feef who?"

Aw shit. She was pissed. I would have to call her. I dialed the number I knew so well and asked to be put through to Victoria Smith.

Her very British voice came through loud and clear and not warm. "Fifi Cutter. I thought for sure you'd been incarcerated incommunicado in Gitmo for the duration."

"Sorry about that, VJ. I know it's been a while. It's just that after my Pop died, I've been all sad. It took me a really long time to get over it, you know. Well, I guess you don't exactly know. How could you? Your father is still alive. How are your folks doing by the way? They good?"

"They are very well, thank you." A slight softening. "What have you been up to?"

I laid it on. "You wouldn't believe the year I've had. After Pop died, I got laid off from my job. My car was repossessed. And today, I got mugged. Seriously. Some guy took a swing at me with a baseball bat. It's been awful."

"Oh well, of course. I'm so sorry to hear that things haven't been going well." Pause. "You want to come over to talk? I could spare a few minutes. If you bring me a sandwich. I haven't had time for lunch."

"Sure.

"A pastrami on rye, with mustard, pickles, no lettuce. Double onion. And chips. And an oatmeal cookie."

"And a bottle of Chateau Lafitte to go with it?"

"A small price to pay for your shameful neglect," VJ responded. I smiled. We were good. I hopped in the truck, stopped off at the Eagle Rock Deli, and took the 134 to the 2 to the 110. Downtown in twelve minutes.

My father's old law firm was housed on the sixth floor of a mid-grade high-rise. I hadn't been there since he died. I noticed the new name plate, changing the name from Cutter, Strachan and Silverstein to Strachan and Silverstein.

I suppose the people who worked there had gotten used to Pop's absence by then, and it wasn't strange for them, walking into that space and not seeing him. For me, it was strange.

When I was a kid, I used to come here with him sometimes, playing in the lobby while he worked. He always said I'd make a good lawyer. There was no way I was spending three years of law school with a bunch of stick-up-the-ass over-achievers, but it was nice of him to say. Anyway, it was through Pop's contacts that I got into claims work. Pop had taken a lot of money from insurance companies over the years and, yet, they loved him. That was Pop.

There was a new receptionist who didn't know me. She asked for my name, and it didn't even register with her when I said "Cutter."

The lobby was kind of run down, but I knew this didn't mean lack of success. It was just that plaintiffs' attorneys don't usually care much about interior decoration. They are, as my Pop used to say, champions of the people. Champions of the people get their office furniture slightly used. Champions of the people put cheaply-framed posters on their walls. Champions of the people mend the carpet with duct tape.

VJ came out to greet me, commented tersely and

unfavorably on my zebra-striped Capris, and led me back to her office, dodging Bekins boxes piled high in the corridors, bursting with documents that somebody would have to go through some day, just not today.

VJ was tall, well-muscled and very dark. Her eyes were huge. She was wearing a severely cut navy-blue suit with a plain white blouse and navy flats. No trim, no jewelry, no makeup.

Victoria Jane Smith had stood out from the crowd from the time she entered Eastbridge Academy for Girls, in our freshman year of high school. She was from London, and she had that accent. We made friends because, in a weird way, she was like me. Black but not black.

"Career stuff going okay?" I asked.

"Yes, very well, thank you, I have had a few modest successes."

I handed her the sandwich bag as we wound back to her office. "I'm sure you're great in court. You've got that big head. My Pop always said a good trial lawyer's got to have a big head."

"Yes, well, so kind of you to mention it. Right now, though, I'm still a grunt. Welcome to the barracks."

VJ's office was small but neat, a great contrast to the rest of the offices. Reference books lined up on the low bookshelf, a file open before her on the otherwise bare desk, her diplomas framed in back behind her. One photo of her family, mother, father, sister, brother. No knickknacks.

I'm with her on that one. In some ways having to share space with balloon bouquets ("To the Best Boss Ever"), pictures of kittens dangling from branches ("Hang In There"), and Hallmark figurines ("Bless this Mess") could be the worst part of real jobs.

Victoria's expression relaxed a tiny fraction as she sat, a slight release around the eyes and the corners of the mouth. Pretty much the closest thing you could expect to a smile from VJ.

"Hey, Veej, howya been?"

"Excellent, Feef, good to see you, then. What's up?"

Another great VJ feature. No small talk.

"Got a question. What do you know about insurance law?"

VJ's mouth tensed a millimeter. "That it is incredibly tedious," she replied.

"But you know something about it, right?"

"Your father was good enough to apprentice me on two rather high-stakes insurance bad-faith cases when I started with the firm. Insurance bad-faith can be lucrative, you know. Juries do tend to vent a great deal of rage against insurance companies. We settled the one before trial for $1.3 million and got a verdict of over ten million in the other, but it's on appeal, and I am not entirely sanguine." She shrugged her shoulders the tiniest fraction. "It will probably be overturned."

I nodded, the ups and downs of a plaintiffs' practice was the story of my childhood.

"What precisely was your question, then?" VJ prompted.

I gave her a snapshot, without mentioning Bosco. I didn't want him hitting on my only real friend. "I guess, what I need to know, is what does it mean to finance the premium, and why is it so bad?"

"Well, it isn't necessarily so bad, although premium-finance companies can charge very high interest. To finance the premium simply means that you are borrowing the money to pay for the insurance policy. You pay the premium to the insurance carrier, and you pay the lender back over time. If you don't pay, the lender can cancel the policy."

"Can the insurance broker finance the premium without the insured knowing about it?" I asked.

"Well, they certainly shouldn't. Whether they can—I suppose so. They might be able to sign as the agent of the insured. But why would the broker do that?"

VJ looked at me quizzically. Now that I was there, I really wanted to tell her the whole story and get her advice. She was always so sane. I opened my mouth, but the phone rang before I could begin. I could tell from VJ's end of the conversation that some paper-driven emergency had arisen, needing immediate attention. She mimed apology and I backed out of her office, mouthing "Thank you," and "We'll get together soon."

I debated with myself on the way home. It was possible that SXYFX had nothing to do with the murder. Ted, after all, had represented them for years and nothing had happened to him. But there was the fact that I had been assaulted right outside their offices.

On the other hand, you could say I got what I asked for. I had gone to the SXYFX office under false pretenses, and I had been found out. It wasn't much of an assault, anyway. Just property damage and, unbeknownst to Mr. Baseball Bat, not even my property.

I wished I could talk it over with Bosco. I wished I knew where Bosco was.

Chapter 16

I found out when I got home and was unable to park in my own driveway because a silver S-series Beamer was ensconced in the middle of it.

Bosco and Eddie were in the kitchen, hunched around the Formica table.

"How could you not leave me a note?" I yelled.

"I don't have to leave you a note, you're not my mother," Bosco yelled back.

"No, apparently I'm just your concierge, you inconsiderate slob."

"Hey, Fifi," Eddie butted in. "Just calm down, I was taking Bosco for a ride in my new pre-owned vehicle. Did you see it? It's great, I'm telling you. Fully loaded, got heated seats, and a six-CD changer..."

"Your new car? What are you doing buying a new car when you owe me five hundred dollars for the handwriting analyst?"

"Hey, I'll pay, I'll pay. First thing tomorrow. Anyway, you don't look like you've been working real hard on the case, Fifi," Eddie eyed my outfit.

I shook the fruit cluster earrings at him. "That's where you're wrong, Eddie. I have been working on your case. In fact, I have been assaulted in the line of duty. And, since you're such a cheapskate, you will be pleased to know that, due to my great contacts, I was able to get you some free legal advice."

I explained. Bosco thought the whack with the baseball bat was pretty cool. Eddie didn't give a shit about the fact I was nearly killed, but got all excited by the free legal advice.

"Your friend is right about premium financing," he said. "The broker can sign the finance agreement on behalf of the insured."

"What if Ted needed a lot of money right away, for a short period of time, and took the whole SXYFX premium, expecting to be able to pay the premium installments over time? He could have short-term use of like a hundred thousand dollars. It seems like he needed money. You say things were not looking great at Obermeyer & Schlefly for the year-end bonus, his wife can't find the pink slip on his Porsche, which probably means he took out a loan on it. His furniture at home all needs replacing."

"He's also going through this separation thing," Bosco added. "Collecting ex-wives has got to be the most expensive hobby a man could have."

"You got that right," I said. "The only problem is, it seems like SXYFX would find out pretty quickly when the monthly payment notices started coming in."

Eddie chewed his lower lip. "It wouldn't be that unusual for the installment notices go to the broker, rather than the insured. If Ted made the monthly payments, SXYFX might never have known."

"So if he did it with SXYFX, maybe he did it with other clients too."

"Schlefly woulda killed him for that." Eddie grinned.

"And what about Ms. Ng, the claims adjustor?" I demanded. "You could have told me she died. Don't you think that's pretty important information?"

"Ms. Ng?" said Eddie in surprise. "That old bat? So she died. She got run over by a bus. What do you care?"

"I don't know. SXYFX and Dobbins/McCray both had her

as a claims adjustor, so I thought maybe there was some kind of phony claims scheme, and maybe she was in on it."

Eddie grimaced. "Ms. Ng wasn't the sharpest tool in the shed, but she was honest. She worked on both accounts because Ted liked to place insurance with that company. They took him out to dinner a lot. So what?'

"So I don't believe in coincidences."

"If you think SXYFX put a hit out on Ted, you're barking up the wrong tree. They aren't the Mafia."

"Yeah, well, what about the little matter of the baseball bat to my back window? That was pretty clearly connected to SXYFX, wasn't it? And while we're on the subject, Eddie, I've been wondering how they knew which car was mine. You need to tell me who could have gotten that information."

"Anybody who asked Mandy. But we don't need to guess. It was Schlefly or Obermeyer. I'm telling you. I have proof, and if you would shut up for a moment, I'll show you."

Eddie reached into his jacket and pulled out a Xerox copy of a computer printout. He spread it out on the kitchen table, a complex grid of numbers that at first glance looked like Sudoku on steroids.

Then Eddie pointed out that 1026 1100 was October 26 at 11:00 AM, and the columns began to make some sense. The time and date columns were in sequential order. The last column on the right-hand side of the page was a very long series of seemingly random numbers. These numbers, Eddie explained, corresponded to parking cards issued to the monthly parkers. This was a record of who came in and out of the parking garage.

"See here," Eddie tapped the top of the page with his finger. "This is the Friday of the murder. It shows that not that many people came in between 8:00 PM and midnight, when the building shuts down. Only a few. And only one," Eddie jabbed the page, "whose number corresponds to a parking card issued by Obermeyer & Schlefly. In fact," he paused for dramatic effect, "this number is the second card we issued: Robert Schlefly."

"Are you sure?" I asked.

"Yes, I'm sure. Mandy told me. Mandy has to keep a list of whose parking card is whose. If you lose your card, it's ten dollars to replace it. This number is Schlefly's, and that means that Schlefly was in the office that night."

"Let me see that," I pushed Bosco out of the way. Eddie had penciled little initials next to the Obermeyer & Schlefly numbers. There was Obermeyer leaving at 2:02; Karen at 4:16; Belinda at 4:43; Villareal at 5:10; Schlefly at 6:00 on the dot; and Gursky at 6:57. And there was Schlefly coming back in at 7:53. And leaving again at 8:27.

"But," protested Bosco, "he was at the dinner. Everyone says so."

Eddie shook the parking card register in Bosco's face. "Apparently he was not at the dinner. At least not for the whole time. Schlefly was there at the beginning, sure. But who was he sitting with, huh? His own wife, and the Obermeyers, plus a couple in crisis, and a cokehead actress. Who would notice if he was gone for an hour or so? His wife probably, but she wouldn't say, would she? And Obermeyer would notice, but he wouldn't say, either, not if he was in on it. Right?"

"Yeah, I can see how that could work. Rob and Warren find out about the unauthorized use of client funds. They get really steamed. They let Ted know that they know and they want to talk to him about it in private. They want to make sure no one from the firm is around, so they deliberately set it up for the night of the dinner, when most of the brokers will be at La Fortunata, and they have an alibi. But that's assuming they didn't get mad and kill him accidentally. That's like first degree murder. Premeditated."

"Exactly," said Eddie.

I looked over at Bosco. If Eddie was right, the job might be over. If not right now, then soon. I should have been very relieved. Except I realized that I wasn't going to make nearly enough this month to afford my property taxes. I wondered how long it would be before they took away my house and swallowed the lump in my throat.

Bosco was made of sterner stuff. "You're really on to something, Eddie. Not quite enough to go to the police though, huh? I mean, we need some conclusive proof. We have got to make this stick. So, what's our next move?"

Eddie eyed him warily. "You don't think this is enough to go to the police?"

"Are you kidding?" Bosco was scornful. "The cops don't even have an open file. And even if we could convince them that it was murder, it would take a hell of a lot more to get the cops to actually arrest somebody like Schlefly. He knows the mayor, Eddie, think about that."

"Everybody knows the mayor," Eddie argued. "That's how he got to be mayor."

"Not everybody plays squash with the mayor, Eddie."

"Once. Once Rob Schlefly played squash with the mayor. And he wasn't even the mayor then, he was just the City Attorney."

Eddie frowned.

"What's bothering me is, what could Schlefly have possibly said to Ted to get him to cancel his plans to go with Belinda for the weekend, and just sit there in his office?"

"I don't know. Something," Eddie said weakly.

"And no way this implicates Obermeyer, either."

"Maybe Schlefly will rat out Obermeyer," Eddie said, in that wistfully hopeful tone of voice my second grade teacher had used to say, "Maybe someday there will be world peace."

"Eddie, Eddie," said Bosco shaking his head "That kind of crap only works on poor people. Rich people have lawyers. Nobody's ratting anybody out. You can bet on that."

Eddie thought for a few minutes and then did, indeed, bet on that.

"Okay, you go get more proof, but you gotta get it soon."

I stared at Eddie, wondering how much he had bribed the parking garage attendant for the card readout. I hoped it was enough to keep anyone else from also bribing the garage attendant, but I realized it probably wasn't. I still had no idea what Eddie's real interest in all this was, but if he was right, it might be a good idea for him to watch his step.

*　　*　　*

Before he took off, Eddie made me come out and admire his new car. We wasted at least six minutes while he told us how he had gotten a really great deal on it.

"So, what did you get for your old one?" I asked. Just professional curiosity.

"I gave it to my son," Eddie replied. "Eddie Jr. just got his license."

Eddie Jr. The kid at the funeral.

Eddie took out his wallet and showed us a picture of Eddie Jr., and I snatched the wallet away.

"What are you doing?" Eddie yelled and started pulling on my arm to get the wallet back. I turned around, hunched over, and pulled out five hundred dollars in new twenties. Bingo, he had just visited the ATM.

I pocketed the cash and tossed the wallet back.

"I want a receipt!" he sputtered.

"I'll send you a receipt. I'll send you an invoice too because this doesn't square us. We've been working long hours, and you're behind."

After Eddie had driven off, Bosco and I had a lengthy and unpleasant discussion of why bills have to be paid before luxuries are purchased and why we must categorize television sets as luxuries. I finally just told him, "As long as you're living under my roof, young man, you'll do as I say."

At 7:00 I got hungry and made a sprout salad with rice vinegar. Bosco, still pouting, picked up the phone and ordered

Thai food. That shows you how inconsiderate he is. I mean, really, Thai food. After I almost got my head knocked off right in front of a Thai take-out.

*   *   *

The following Monday, Eddie called. "Hey, listen, I had a thought."

"You had a thought? Did the new car smell go your head?"

"What I'm thinking is, there's only one way we can know for sure if Ted financed the premium for some emergency shortfall, like you said. You gotta ask Karen."

I laughed. "No, you're going to have to ask Karen, Eddie, cause I really can't think of any convincing cover story to explain why the grief counselor is asking about the details of her client's financial affairs."

"Maybe it's time to drop the grief-counseling thing."

"What? After we went through all that trouble to set it up? What if Obermeyer & Schlefly find out. They'll want their money back."

"At least just let Karen in on it. Karen's a good person," Eddie reasoned, "and she won't blab, she's very discreet."

I translated "she won't blab" to "she doesn't have any friends left to tell, now that Ted is gone" easily enough, but couldn't quite figure out what he meant by "she's a good person." A really good person, when learning how we defrauded Obermeyer & Schlefly out of $1,200, might go right to the cops.

"What do you mean by she's a good person?" I asked Eddie.

"Well, she's always really nice, and I've never seen her get mad. She spends her free time taking care of babies with AIDS down at Temple Hospital."

"This information does not reassure me, Eddie. I am not comfortable confessing to what might be a crime and is certainly a sin to the new Mother Theresa."

"I didn't say she was Mother Theresa...," Eddie began.

"Besides," I interrupted, "It would be very natural for you, as a member of the firm, to think of a reason to pose these kinds of questions."

"I disagree. Karen might think it unethical to share private information about her clients with me, since I am not, personally, their broker."

That was as easy as Pig Latin to translate into "Karen doesn't trust me around Ted's clients." Which only verified my pre-existing opinion that Karen Odom was pretty smart.

"Fine. I'll do it. You got my invoice?"

"Check's in the mail."

"It better be."

I called Karen up at the office, and asked her to join me for drinks or dinner and said there was something I had to tell her. I learned that she didn't drink, and while she certainly ate—the evidence of that was undeniable—she wasn't going to eat with me.

"I go to the hospital from 6:00 to 8:00 PM every Monday. You can come see me at the office. "

For obvious reasons I didn't want to have this conversation at the office.

"Can't you miss just one night?" I pleaded.

"No." Karen replied frostily. "It's too late to get a substitute, and they need to be held every night."

I took a deep breath. "Let me meet you there and help you. I can do it. I can hold babies."

"Are you sure?"

"Sure, I'm sure. How hard could it be?"

"You can't drop them," Karen warned.

"I'm not going drop a baby," I promised.

Karen finally relented. As I hung up, I vowed this was going to cost Eddie big, and Bosco was coming with me.

I spent the day going though the Mraz deposition transcripts that Eddie had given me the night we searched

Ted's office. Seemed like just about everybody had been deposed.

I started with Dina. She had sounded like a phony, parroting phases her attorney had fed her: "Mr. Heffernan would stare at my chest area and make me feel very self-conscious;" and "After I complained the first time, I was much too afraid of Mr. Schlefly to complain again because he told me the whole company depended on Mr. Heffernan's bringing in so much business;" and the coup de grâce, "I'm just so upset, I don't know if I can ever go back to work in an office again."

Obermeyer had been caught between trying to make it sound like he did a lot more work than he actually did and not wanting to admit he knew anything at all about what went on in the office.

Schlefly had sounded pompous. He was clever though, for the most part seeing through the questions and providing the smooth, agenda-forwarding answers. When attacked for not having any women partners, he ambiguously responded that: "Two women were under consideration at that very moment." Apparently, partnership decisions were made by the partners in October, but announcements were made in December, just in time for the Christmas party. I looked at the date of the deposition. Two years ago. No women partners yet.

Schlefly, of course, had insisted he had no idea that Ted was using the office as his personal dating service. But then he was also forced to admit (after much "objection as to relevance" and "can you re-phrase the question" and "I'm afraid I don't understand what you're getting at") that he, himself, had met the present Mrs. Schlefly at the office, and that it was possible their relationship had begun before the divorce to his prior wife was completely final.

Ted had sounded defensive and, even in cold print, his protestations that he had never so much as looked sideways at "Ms. Mraz" were not very believable. When confronted with receipts for dinners and motels, he said that he had been accompanied by his wife on those occasions.

Not so surprisingly, Angela had backed him up, but reading the transcript, you could actually hear her grinding her teeth.

Karen had stoutly denied knowledge of any impropriety and suggested that all Ms. Mraz had to do was come to her, and she would have ensured that the "unfortunate miscommunication" between Ms. Mraz and Mr. Heffernan was resolved. Still, having known Ted so long, she had to admit to a long line of wives and girlfriends.

Belinda had refused to admit anything was going on between her and Ted, and had plenty of venomous things to say about Dina Mraz, who was lazy, rude, unprofessional and (according to Belinda) bragged about how many men she had slept with. But not Ted. Apparently, Dina had slept with everyone except Ted.

Because I am a complete idiot I didn't realize, until later, that I actually learned something useful.

Chapter 17

We arrived at the hospital just after six. The hospice where the AIDS babies were housed was in a separate wing, the Hannah Feinberg Memorial Nursery.

A teenage volunteer sat at the front desk, padding her resume to get into college. She interrupted her text messaging long enough to direct us down the hall.

The room was long and narrow, with a big picture window into the corridor. The walls were papered in a pink and yellow check. A large white bookshelf filled with stuffed bears and Raggedy Anns stood at one end.

Karen sat in a sturdy rocker, her back to the door. She was curved protectively around a particularly teeny bundle, rocking back and forth, cooing and cuddling.

Four industrial cribs occupied the center of the room. Each had a cardboard name tag dangling on a white string from the ceiling: Timothy, Danielle, Fernando, and Elise.

Timothy looked older than the others. He was sitting up and staring at Karen, blue-grey eyes, wispy blonde hair, blowing bubbles. He looked plump and alert. Danielle, too, looked like any old baby, peaceably asleep on her back with her fists in the air. Fernando didn't look as good, thin and tense, his face knotted up in anger or pain. Presumably Elise was the baby being rocked.

I motioned Bosco back away from the open door and down the hall.

Bosco looked puzzled.

"I just feel like we're spying," I whispered.

"We are spying," Bosco reminded me.

"Yeah, but..." I stopped. For a moment my cynicism failed me.

"Come on," Bosco urged. "Pull yourself together. The babies aren't going to know what you're doing. They'll be happy for the distraction. They like to hear people talk. That's how they learn."

I sincerely doubted the babies were going to benefit from hearing us talk about premium financing and insurance policies. But I realized that guilt was an unproductive emotion. Especially for something that was clearly not my fault, and—whatever else I had done in my life—the fate of these babies was not my fault.

This time we cleared our collective throat as we approached the open door, and Karen turned around.

"Oh, there you are," she said. "You sit there and you sit there," she indicated two molded plastic chairs. We sat and she placed Elise in my arms, Fernando in Bosco's and picked up the more active Timothy herself. There was a moment of awkward silence as I adjusted to the unaccustomed weight.

"How long have you been doing this?" I asked. The baby was looking at me. It was hard not to look back.

"Six years," she replied.

"Every Monday night for six years?" I exclaimed.

Karen began bouncing Timothy gently on her knee. "Pretty much. I don't really take a lot of vacations."

"So you've seen a lot of babies...?" Bosco began, asking the question I really, really didn't want an answer to.

Karen nodded and replied, as if chanting, "Anthony, Amber, Polly, Miguel, Christopher I and Christopher II." She nodded toward the right-hand wall. I glanced over; there were photographs of babies attached to brightly colored construction paper, decorated with bows, each with a name. Under the names were two dates, dates that were too close to each other by about seventy years.

"It's gotta be tough on you," Bosco said, sympathy dripping from his voice. Had he forgotten we didn't have to be grief counselors any more?

"Tough? Not at all," Karen said. "You don't understand. These babies are angels, wonderful gifts. They bring me nothing but happiness." She surprised Timothy with an over-emphatic bounce. "They don't ask for anything but love."

I could have debated that point. It seemed to me that maybe, had they been given any say in the matter, the babies would have asked for a lot more than love, like the prospect of a normal life span. I felt a little nauseous.

"What did you want to tell me?" Karen asked.

Bosco put on his sincere face, not as effective as it could have been, since Fernando had chosen that moment to spit up. Karen leaned over and calmly wiped the knee of Bosco's tailored grays with a cloth diaper.

"Karen," Bosco began, recovering some degree of composure, "I have to tell you, first, that I am not really a grief counselor. Neither is she." He gestured in my direction.

Karen shook her head. "I wondered. I really should have paid attention to my instincts. I mean, give me a break, the thought that you would ever qualify as a grief counselor, Bosco. You'd have to at least finish college for that, wouldn't you? I presume this was another one of your stupid schemes to con a little money out of honest people?"

Bosco plunged on. "No, no, no, you have it all wrong. See, what I meant was, grief counseling isn't our primary occupation."

Karen's eyes narrowed.

"The truth is, we were hired by an individual at Obermeyer & Schlefly to look into the death of Ted Heffernan. Not just the grief aspect, you see, look into the death in a more general kind of way."

"An individual?" asked Karen in a soft voice that scared me. "You aren't acting on behalf of the firm?"

"Well," Bosco hedged, "we are acting in the interests of the firm, certainly. But not exactly retained by..."

"Oh for God's sake. Eddie hired you," Karen interrupted, "He's the only one who could be behind this farce." She shook her head as if to chase away a swarm of gnats. "You want to tell me why?"

Bosco glanced at me. I gave him eyebrows up. We had permission to spill.

"Eddie thinks that Uncle Ted's death was not natural."

As Bosco proceeded with the explanation, Karen's face closed down. Was she furious or hurt or just processing the information? I couldn't tell.

When Bosco finally ran out of ways to try to justify what we had done, she took a moment, then said, "This is insane. Eddie thinks–let me get this straight–that Ted was deliberately killed and he wants you...," she paused, as if trying not to say something rude, "you two, to find out who and why and how? Is that it?"

"Yes, that is it. Fifi here is an investigator."

"Licensed?" Karen demanded.

"Look, I don't want to make this sound more dramatic than it is," I said, sidestepping the awkward question.

"It's a little hard not to make this sound dramatic," Karen pointed out—with some justification. She fanned herself with one hand, that gigantic diamond ring winking in the fluorescent lights.

"I know, but really, at the present we are just informally asking a few questions. We're trying to make sure somebody doesn't get away with murder, the murder of Ted. Trust me, if there is anything, anything at all to go on, we'll take it to the authorities." I tried to stress the "informally" part. It's no crime to ask questions.

Karen shook her head. "Even for Eddie, this is a new low. I could probably get him fired for this."

"But he did it for Ted. I think you should consider that."

Karen scoffed. "I doubt he's doing this for Ted. Eddie is not an altruistic kind of guy."

She had me there.

A pretty young nurse came in, smiled and wrote something on a chart. I thought Bosco was going to follow her out when she left. Hell, with Karen sitting there glaring at us, *I* was ready to follow her out.

"We don't deny anything you say, Karen." Bosco had decided to ease the tension by falling on his sword. "You're perfectly right. If there had been another way, we certainly would have pursued that. You have to understand, though, the police would never open the case with no evidence."

"You have evidence?" Karen asked.

"Not really," Bosco admitted. "I mean, we have..."

This time, I interrupted him. "We don't have jack shit," I said. I didn't think we should necessarily tell Karen about the parking printout or Ted's calendar or even the stolen sign-in book, not at this stage. I didn't exactly suspect her. On the other hand, you never know.

Karen considered for a long time, then shook her head with a rueful little smile. "Eddie is unbelievable. You know he's the biggest plotter and schemer in the office, but it doesn't really do him any good. People aren't stupid. At least, they aren't as stupid as Eddie thinks they are. If he would spend half of his energy just servicing his accounts and paying attention to his work, he would be a lot better off."

I shrugged. I wasn't going to waste any sympathy on Eddie, especially not in present company.

"But nothing excuses what you did," Karen continued. "You bear a lot of the responsibility. Grief counseling? God, whose sick idea was that?"

I was about to enlighten her, but Bosco got in first. "Karen, I know it sounds bad, but we really did help a lot of people. Angela, for instance."

Karen looked skeptical.

Bosco raised his hand in acknowledgment. "I know,

I know. But the sad truth is, Karen, there wasn't really a lot of grief. Chloe. You, maybe. And Belinda, in her way."

A shadow of sadness darkened Karen's face. She stared at the top of Timothy's head and hugged him a little more closely. A smile drifted across her face. Hugging that boy really did seem to do her good.

We kept silent. Danielle woke up and began fussing. Karen broke from her reverie, placed Timothy back in this crib and picked up the girl. Without looking at us, she said, "Tell me what you want from me."

Bosco skipped over a whole lot of background and simply said, "We need to know whether SXYFX financed their premiums for their policies."

"What does that have to do with anything?" Karen demanded, her face registering genuine surprise, but whether it was surprise at the suggestion that SXYFX financed the premium, or because we knew about it, I couldn't tell.

"I don't know," Bosco admitted, "But it's weird because they say they didn't, but Eddie says that the firm's records show they did. Fifi here went to see Stan Gastukian and asked him."

"Eddie has no business looking at the records of Ted's clients and you have no right to talk to Ted's clients. I'm the one working on those accounts now." She pointed to me.

"'Nuff said. Sorry. It won't happen again, Karen."

She glared for a few more seconds, and then said, "It's got to be a bookkeeping mistake. I have never known SXYFX to finance their premium. I personally handled this account for Ted. They have never been short of cash. In fact, I understand they are rolling in cash. SXYFX has had a particularly good year."

I snorted. "Suzy Double-Q. Nice."

"It's protected by the First Amendment," she snapped back.

"Oh please, I really don't think the founding fathers meant to protect the right of pervert losers to watch girl-on-girl orgies."

"Well, it's legal."

"It's still wrong."

"Most of the people in the industry are just trying to earn a living. Although," Karen looked at me, "you should keep in mind that the nature of the industry attracts a certain type of person. There are undoubtedly some people who have money tied up in the company" (by "tied up in" I assumed she meant "laundered by") "who are not people you would want to cross."

"You mean that there might be a criminal element? But that's what we're saying. Maybe that's what's behind Ted's death!"

"I didn't say criminal."

"Alright, then, you win. Pornographers are the salt of the earth, the most misunderstood minority since the Flat Earth Society. Fine. Can we ask you some questions anyway?"

"Go right ahead."

"You told us you were down in Laguna that Friday night?"

She nodded. "Ted had been scheduled to make some introductory remarks and be a sort of master of ceremonies at the opening reception that night, so I had to fill in for him."

"And Belinda was with you the whole time?"

"Oh yes. She made the circuit. She flirted with all the right people, and when she finally had too much to drink, I took her back to the room and made her go to bed."

"What time was this?"

"Around ten, I guess. I went back for a late coffee with some acquaintances of mine from the old days, and turned in around eleven-ish. It wasn't really that late."

"And Belinda was still in the room?" I asked, thinking it was just possible she had been faking drunk and had jumped into car and sped back up to LA.

"Yeah, she was throwing up in the toilet." Karen dashed my idea. "She has a very bad drinking problem, you know. I gave her water and about a half an hour later she could hold down some aspirin and Pepto Bismol." She really must be a saint, I thought. She couldn't like Belinda.

"So how was she the next morning?"

Karen gave me her 'you've-got-to-be-kidding-me' look. "The next morning? The next afternoon is more like it. We left around one. Got to Century City a little late. Leah was a bit peeved."

Bosco pointedly stared at the Mickey Mouse clock on the wall. It was 6:36, and it had become painfully evident that one of the babies needed changing. Time to go.

Chapter 18

At Eddie's insistence, we met at Aldo's again the next day.

"You guys need to be working on breaking Schlef's alibi," Eddie said around a mouthful of meatloaf and gravy. "Schlef's parking card, that proves it. You just need to get confirmation, then we'll have him."

"Really?" I asked skeptically. "You mean if we get proof that Robert Schlefly slipped away from the Diabetes Dinner, that's all it will take? And how does this fit in with the theft of the sign-in book? That's been bothering me. I just don't see the point of clocking in with your own parking card, using your real name when signing in, and then stealing the sign-in book. And if he didn't use his real name, why bother to steal the book?"

"I don't know," Eddie said, "But why should anyone bother to steal the book?"

"I don't know either, but it has to be explained somehow. And anyway," I continued, "Just because it's Schlefly's card, doesn't mean he was using it. Anybody could lift a parking card."

"Schlefly keeps his card in the glove compartment of his car, which has a very sophisticated alarm system. I think it's time to go talk to the valet guys at the restaurant. They might remember Schlefly leaving."

"Impossible," I interjected, "All middle-aged white guys look alike."

"Maybe so," Eddie growled, "But there is at least a chance that one of those boys would remember the car. Schlefly drives a pearl grey Lexus." Eddie stared meaningfully at me. "A pearl grey Lexus that he doesn't let anyone else drive."

"What about his wife? I bet he lets her drive it."

Bosco tried to smooth things over. "We're happy to go to La Fortunata and ask questions. It's just that we can't ignore the other possibilities."

We went over each of the people known to be close enough to Ted to want him dead. I suggested Karen, based on the general principle of the least likely, but she and Belinda alibied each other.

Besides they wouldn't lie for each other. Karen was kind enough to let Belinda sleep off a hangover, but that is a far cry from risking an accessory rap. And it was equally hard to see Belinda lying for Karen. Karen had a lot of excellent virtues: intelligence, efficiency, compassion. But these were not the type of virtues to earn her any loyalty from Belinda, who probably didn't have a lot of close female friends.

Angela was clearly out of it—the hostess at a big event like that slip out? Impossible.

We still needed to check on Corazon. She was there, but what time exactly did she leave, and where did she go?

"And what would Corazon's motive be?" Bosco asked.

"Right, exactly," Eddie answered. "Forget about her. She doesn't have a motive."

"Oh yes she does," I slammed my palm on the table. "The insurance money."

"What do you mean?" Eddie said. "That's only a motive for the partners."

"Yeah, but I read those deposition transcripts. Obermeyer & Schlefly are under a lot of pressure to make a woman partner. And who else but Corazon?"

I pointed out that so far Corazon had no alibi. Everyone agreed she had left the dinner early.

But Eddie didn't want it to be Corazon. He wanted it to

be Rob Schlefly. And maybe it was Rob Schlefly. How the hell would I know?

The key card thing at least made Rob the front-runner. Maybe he hadn't meant to kill Ted. If Rob had gone to the office that night, the most likely scenario is that he went to confront Ted and then got into an argument, and Ted suffered a heart attack. Rob got scared, left, and then arranged for Eddie to find the body.

But why go to such lengths to distance himself from a natural death? So he didn't call an ambulance. It's not a crime. Right? Isn't that what I had told myself a thousand times since I hadn't tried to wake up Dina Mraz?

"Okay, Eddie," Bosco interjected, "so we're going with the theory that Schlefly killed Uncle Ted for the insurance money to pay off the Dina Mraz judgment? "

Eddie hopped up and down in his seat. "I think that's gotta be it. I mean, you read the deposition transcripts, Fifi. I heard from Mandy, who had a clear and unobstructed view of the conference room the whole time, that Schlefly had to be taken out of the room and calmed downed by our attorneys more than once. His depo lasted three days. Mandy said he was so livid he could hardly see straight."

"I noticed quite a few potty breaks in reading through it. I just figured, you know, it was because Schlefly was getting up there in years."

Jessie brought us our orders. This time I went for Chinese chicken salad, hold the chicken. Bosco went with honey glaze chicken, hold the honey glaze. Eddie got a Rueben, don't hold anything, and added extra fries.

He wolfed it all down and tried to excuse himself to go to the bathroom when the check came, but he made the strategic error of being on the inside of the booth, and Bosco wouldn't let him out until he came up with a credit card. It still wasn't what he owed us, but it was something.

Chapter 19

The memorial service was at St. Michael's High School for Boys, in LaCanada, a nice suburb north of LA, 3,000 square foot houses with barely adequate yards, creeping up into the San Gabriel mountains. The chapel building was neo-Spanish revival and situated front and center, with the rest of the buildings more neo than Spanish.

We got to the chapel a little late—not my fault. The priest spoke long and earnestly on the topics of the day. "How Much Can You Afford to Give?" was the main theme, the secondary message being "Ted Heffernan Gave Us Some Money and Was a Really Good Guy in Other Ways, Too." I'm paraphrasing here.

Chloe Heffernan, wearing her teeny black mini-skirt, got up and said a brief thank you to everyone for coming. Her voice was so soft I could hardly hear her.

Bosco gave a good eleven minutes of humorous anecdotes about his Old Uncle Ted, none of which were true. But his delivery was excellent.

The priest intoned a lengthy prayer. I dozed off, coming back to consciousness when Corazon Villareal got up to give the eulogy. She was impeccably dressed in a Dana Buchman slate-blue two-piece, silver buttons, and Stuart Weitzman pumps.

She said Ted was charming, dynamic, family oriented—which, I guess if having lots of families is "family-oriented" this was true—and "unexpectedly compassionate," a great back-handed compliment.

Most interesting, for my purposes, she said something about being at a christening the night Ted died, some kind of analogy about one candle goes out, another one gets lit. It was the christening part that I paid attention to.

When it was over, forty-two minutes that seemed a lot longer, we crossed the quad to the "All Purpose" hall, a charmless, cinderblock rectangle with fluorescent lighting and too few windows. A long buffet table was set up on one side and a cash bar on the other. A few undersized bouquets of lilies and pinks were scattered around.

Group pictures, cheaply framed in black, hung crookedly on all walls, sports teams and graduating classes from 1941 to the present. Black and white gave way to color, short buzz cuts and cowlicks were superseded by over-the-collar shags and modest mullets, then back to buzz cuts. Most years featured two to three African-American kids, even in the early days. Well, not the very early days.

I felt two lasers drilling into the back of my head. I turned uneasily, and there was Mother, all the way across the room, pinning me down with that look. She hated that I wore a pantsuit instead of a dress. And she thought I should have put on makeup. And she was silently criticizing my hair.

I could tell.

I slumped away, and she turned back to her conversation with a big-eared guy, giving him her full attention.

"Who's the big-eared guy?" I asked Bosco, who was greeting the incoming in his role as ceremonial host. Bosco shrugged. He'd been away so long he had forgotten the importance of keeping track of that woman's machinations. May not have had anything to do with us, but you never knew. It looked to me like meeting the big-eared guy was her reason for wanting to be invited.

I spotted Corazon at the buffet table, got an idea for an opening from Bosco's oratorical mendacity, told him I'd be back, and sidled on over.

"Hi, how are you?" I gushed at Corazon. "You may remember me. I'm Fifi Cutter. We met in the kitchen at the office. My brother and I are the grief counselors?" I stuck my hand out, causing Corazon to put down her drink and shift her plate of vegetables and her Prada purse to the other hand. She gave me her wide, warm client-friendly smile, and I smiled back.

"I so appreciated your talk at the service, Ms. Villareal. May I call you Corazon? Please call me Fifi. It is difficult, isn't it, finding the right tone at these things?" *As if I spoke at "these things" once a week.* "I was particularly struck by the symbolism of your being at a christening on that Friday, the very evening that Ted died." I cocked my head, and tried to look waggish. "That was really true, I suppose? I mean not just poetic license?"

Corazon looked mildly surprised. "Oh yes, it was true. My niece Glorietta's baby."

It took a while—spontaneity was not her forte—but I kept asking questions, and finally Corazon finished her glass of Sauvignon Blanc and opened up.

"It was so nice. My whole family was there. At Holy Family in Rancho Cucamonga. The reception went on until very late, after midnight," She paused. "It's a very big family. I have five brothers and a sister, and all their kids, my mom and dad, even my *abuela* , she's ninety-three, and two aunts. I was godmother to the baby."

I tried to look encouraging.

"My parents have thirteen grandchildren," she concluded.

I was momentarily distracted, trying to imagine what a big family would be like, a big family of whole siblings, not halfers, siblings who actually liked each other, that is. I told myself that just because people had genes in common and forced themselves to be together at family gatherings, it didn't mean they liked each other.

Maybe Corazon's brothers hated their more-successful sister who, in turn, hated her brothers for contributing to the all-important grandchild statistic when she never would. Maybe mama and papa were, after four decades of marriage, only restrained from a tragic murder/suicide by arthritis and cataracts.

"So the baby isn't a Villareal?" I asked, coming back to the task at hand.

"No, Glorietta married a gringo," Corazon sighed. "The baby's name is Miguel Villareal Cummings." Corazon put down her glass, seemed to realize we had just been introduced and assumed her insurance-broker persona. "So you're in the grief counseling business? Do you carry professional liability insurance? There are some excellent packages available."

Any more questions of a personal nature and Corazon would get suspicious. I repeated my appreciation of her comments, and made my exit as gracefully as I could.

I couldn't say Corazon was my favorite person. She seemed mercenary and cold. Still, nobody makes up a baby christening with dozens of people as witnesses. Even if they were family. After all, how reliable was family? On second thought, I'd better check out that alibi.

But if it held, then out with Corazon, out with Karen, out with Belinda, out with Angela. No alibi yet for Keith Gursky, the consummate brown-noser with the manicured nails.

The alibis for Schlefly and Obermeyer were still problematic, despite that parking card business. Someone would have noticed if either of them had tried to slip out of the dinner. Or, put it this way, the risk that someone might notice would be too great to take.

Maybe, I mused, it had been murder—but not even connected with someone at O & S. Some loon just happened to get hold of a card key, went up to clean out the office, found Ted hard at work, tried to knock him out and hit him, by serendipity, right on that delicate place on the skull, leaving a slight indentation where a careless coroner could miss it. Maybe this wasn't a body-in-the-library murder after all.

Maybe it was just a small-column-in-the-City-Life-section kind of murder.

Nah. I didn't believe that. The threatening letter and my cracked windshield told me otherwise.

I started circulating. I saw Dolly Schlefly, standing alone, clutching a pinkish drink, but one look at that once beautiful, now petulant face, and I chickened out. How could you open a conversation with a head that sported such a totally intimidating pile of over-processed hair? I would leave her further interrogation to Bosco.

It was time to take a break from duty and find out who the hell the guy with the big ears was.

I knew the Mutual Mother would not welcome an interruption. She was already having to contend with Belinda, who had burst into her conversation about three minutes earlier. On the other hand, I was pretty sure she wouldn't be overtly rude to me in front of strangers. I steeled my nerves and walked up, head held high.

"Hi Mom." I didn't quite have the nerve for a peck on the cheek, and her vicious glance confirmed the wisdom of my judgment.

Nonetheless, she pretended to be moderately pleased to introduce me, although Mr. Big Ears was frankly paying more attention to Belinda at that moment, his eyes glued to a generous display of bosom.

"Herbert Dobbins, my daughter. This is Mr. Dobbins." I noticed she didn't bother to provide Mr. Dobbins with my name. "Mr. Dobbins went to school here with Ted, and we've known each other for years."

Since I had never heard of him, and my mother had to scheme to run into him, I took this to mean that they had met once years ago and had not seen each other since.

"Herbert is the Dobbins in Dobbins/McCray," Mother proudly explained, as if she were personally taking credit for this fact.

"How nice," I murmured.

Belinda, sensing exclusion, leaned forward and shook my

hand. "We've met before. You do the grief counseling with Bosco." I could feel my mother's hackles rise but knew she would not make a scene in front of Herbert. For some reason, she was exerting herself to impress this stiff.

"So this is your daughter," said Belinda, addressing herself to Mother. "My, my, Mrs. Tuttle, you hardly look old enough to have a daughter in her late 20s," Belinda smirked. I mentally snorted. Belinda was a baby in the big leagues.

"Yes," Mother replied, "my daughter keeps me up on all the youthful fashions. But I'll have to rely on you, dear, to tell me what the over-30 single girls are wearing." Mother arched an eyebrow at Belinda's Victoria's Secret stretch top.

Belinda colored and glanced uncomfortably at Herbert, who was oblivious. His entire universe had funneled down to "I can almost see Belinda's boobs," and he was completely bewildered when Belinda discovered an urgent need for more refreshment and ducked away.

This was a golden opportunity to get information about Herbert out of Belinda. "I'll join you." I hurried after her, leaving her no choice but to actually head back to the buffet table.

Belinda, I realized after two more minutes in her company, was feeling a little out of place as 'the other woman' and was assuaging her social discomfort by getting plastered. I enthusiastically encouraged her, and went on to extract the information that Dobbins was a long-time client of Ted's, the old-school connection being stronger than water. Dobbins/McCray, I recalled, was the outfit that also had Ms. Ng as a claims adjustor.

I would have found out more, but Belinda attracted men like flies to road kill. Old Warren Obermeyer, his wife not in evidence, oiled over with a smile. He was smooth at the small talk, although he directed very little of it my way.

Warren was not an attractive man, and I don't believe he ever had been. He was soft in the belly and had no eyelashes. His skin was grey, except for the end of his nose, where it tended to purple. Altogether, he looked like a baby eagle. Bad breath, too, which was hard to miss, since he monopolized the conversation.

After twelve minutes of some boring work thing that had happened fifteen years ago where he saved the account by sheer brilliance, I finally got a word in, trying to steer the conversation towards the Diabetes Dinner and the night Ted died.

"I understand you're quite a supporter of charity, Mr. Obermeyer."

This was a mistake. Warren instantly became wary, thinking I was going to hit him up for something. Then again, he knew he shouldn't come out against charity. Belinda, much to my shock, saved the situation. Of course, she didn't know she was helping me out, she was merely trying to kiss some butt. Nonetheless, I was grateful.

"Oh yes," she gushed, her fourth gin fizz emphasizing her words. "Warren is one of the most generous guys ever. He is so good to us, he always does something really super nice for Christmas, and you know, he contributes quite a lot to diabetes research. I mean, he's like a patron or something."

"Really," I sliced in before she could segue away from the topic. "Diabetes research. That is something that I am very interested in. You know, as a person of color. A disproportionate number of African-Americans suffer from diabetes. But of course you know that."

Warren blinked at me with his pale eyes. He didn't know squat about diabetes and less about people of color. "We recently had our annual fundraiser, we raised over $400,000." Money was something he did know about.

"That is so wonderful!" I was gushing as bad as Belinda. Well, maybe not quite.

"Yes. Actually, Angela Heffernan was the chairman of that event." He looked slightly embarrassed. "It turns out, you know, really tragically—I mean none us of could have foreseen—but it seems as though that was the day, well, the night that Ted...er...passed on. We didn't know it until Sunday, of course."

I made encouraging noises, pretended an intense interest in the catering details of the dinner, and finally got around to quizzing him about dessert.

"Did you get to sample the profiteroles? I've heard the profiteroles at La Fortunata are just divine."

Warren agreed that all of the desserts "looked real yummy," but he couldn't tell me what any of them were because he never ate sweets and had only had a cup of after-dinner coffee.

I glanced delicately at the half-eaten Napoleon sitting on the pink paper plate he clutched in his left hand, and he smiled weakly.

Chapter 20

I edged around, trying to find an opening to talk to Schlefly, but it almost seemed as if he were avoiding me. Which he couldn't have been. I'm sure I wasn't important enough for him to bother trying to avoid me.

After I made several circuits of the room, I caught Eddie watching me from the northwest corner. He gave an offensive little "c'mere" with his head. I strolled over and gave him a progress report before Bosco joined us, his plate piled high with miniature ham sandwiches and sausage rolls.

"I want to talk to Chloe Heffernan," Bosco said. "Come with me."

As we edged away from Eddie, I asked Bosco what was the good of talking to Chloe, and he said maybe Chloe hated Angela and knew about her affair with Rob Schlefly and wouldn't mind talking about it. I reminded him that Angela was alibied for the night in question, but then Bosco went on a "hired killer" rant, and how it happens way more often than anybody knows. I told him to shut up. He told me to shut up.

Chloe was pretty adorable, in a Bratz kind of way. She and Bosco half-hugged and air-kissed. I was properly introduced.

"I've heard so much about you from Bosco," Chloe said. "You must have had a lot of fun when you were kids."

I looked at her, uncomprehending.

"I would have done anything for my own horse at that age," Chloe laughed. "It must have been so cool living on a ranch, and going riding together every day. I mean, most brothers and sisters fight a lot. You guys were really lucky."

I caught on and covered, smiling brightly as she raved on about Bosco's imaginary childhood—on a ranch, with horses, an Olympic-sized swimming pool and an Irish setter named Cody.

"Yeah, well, Cody got run over by a car a long time ago," I finally said, hoping to move onto something more pertinent to our investigation and my financial well-being. Chloe looked suitably sad, and we agreed that big dogs were great and small dogs were so annoying, the way they yipped all the time.

Bosco glided into grief counselor mode. "It must be so hard for you, losing your Dad like that. I don't know how much you saw of him recently..."

Chloe took the bait. "Yeah, not that much. I didn't really get along with Angela."

"Stepmothers," Bosco shook his head knowingly, which irritated me, because, from everything I had ever heard, Bosco's stepmother was way nicer than his real mother.

"God knows I've had enough of them." Chloe drooped momentarily and shot a look at Angela, across the width of the room, who was not acting the part of the bereaved widow at all. In fact, she had her head thrown back and was laughing merrily at something Keith Gursky had said.

I personally did not believe Keith Gursky could ever come up with something witty enough to make anyone laugh that hard, so I assumed Angela was flirting, although why she would bother to flirt with Gursky was a mystery. Then I noticed Schlefly watching the performance, doing a slow burn. He hadn't been trying to avoid me, I realized, he had been following Angela.

"My dear stepmother wants me to go to my father's apartment to clean it out," Chloe grumbled. "She said it would be too painful for her. Well, I mean, how does she think it's going to make me feel? Karen volunteered to do it, but it seems wrong."

With barely suppressed excitement, Bosco jumped in. "Hey, Chloe, what if I help you, huh?"

"You would do that for me?" she cooed.

"Yeah, I'll be happy to help. Hey, what are friends for? Why don't we do it this evening? We'll stop by a grocery store, get some cardboard boxes, what do you think?"

"Okay, that would be great," Chloe beamed.

I was as happy as a homecoming queen on Prozac. Not only getting rid of Bosco for a few hours, but having him doing something that might be useful. Bosco ruined it.

"Fifi can help, too," he said. "She's got this great truck. It would really come in handy."

Chloe and I both acted delighted at Bosco's suggestion. I excused myself and told them I would meet them at the door in ten minutes.

I found Eddie, who was being successfully avoided by many people. It appeared that the members of the crowd had spent enough time remembering Ted and were now glancing at their watches.

Eddie was not happy that he had shelled out $100 for the clue of the half-eaten Napoleon, but he cheered up when I explained we were going to clean out Ted's apartment, which was a snooper's free pass.

*   *   *

Ted's bachelor pad was off Pico, not a bad neighborhood, but not great, either, and the freeway access was a little questionable at rush hour.

It was a depressing living space. The unit came furnished, which meant plaid acrylic fabrics and graceless oak veneer. It was just three rooms, a bedroom with a small adjoining bathroom and a kitchen/living room/dining room combination. At least the job wouldn't take long.

Especially since Ted was not a "saver," and he hadn't lived there more than a month or so. I quickly perceived that this was mostly going to be about sorting out old clothes. Bosco immediately suggested that maybe we could take some of the furniture off Chloe's hands, like the TV and maybe the bed. Good thinking, but Chloe explained that since the apartment came furnished, it had to be turned back furnished.

Not wanting to paw through a dead man's blazers, khakis and topsiders, I headed for the cubbyholes built into the wall in the kitchen.

I found the rental agreement, the water and gas bill, a cellular phone owner's manual, which was about the size of the Oxford Unabridged Dictionary. Nothing of interest—or so I thought.

I walked back into the bedroom just as Chloe was asking Bosco if he would like her dad's briefcase.

"You need a job to need a briefcase," I said.

Bosco ignored me and replied with exaggerated politeness, "No, thank you, Chloe. I already have one."

They stuffed the clothes into clean lawn and leaf bags for deposit at the nearest Goodwill. We were done by 6:23.

Chloe had the good manners to treat us to dinner, but the bad taste to take us to Taco Bell.

We had to park in the back, the food was gross, we sat near a crying child, and Chloe kept tearing up. As soon as we had completed the experience with a trip to the rest room, we headed out to the truck.

"Oh no!" Chloe cried.

Bosco and I looked, frozen in our tracks. The neat little lawn and leaf bag bundles had been ripped open, and clothes were strewn all over the truck bed and onto the parking lot pavement.

It took us ten minutes to convince Chloe to please stop crying, because, after all, we were donating the clothes to poor people, and only poor people would have stolen them, so really we had just cut out the middle man.

It took us another thirteen minutes to re-pack. I couldn't

even see that anything had been taken. Except the new brief-case.

*   *   *

Chloe continued to sniffle all the way to Angela's house, where I would have been happy to let her off at the curb, but Bosco walked her to the door.

Like things weren't crappy enough, it was nearly 10:00 PM when Bosco and I finally pulled into the driveway at home, and I saw the sight that no homeowner wants to see: the side door into the kitchen was ajar, a glass pane shattered.

Chapter 21

I hustled from the truck up the side stairs and stepped inside, crumbs of glass crackling underfoot. I flipped the switch.

The light was harsh, but relief crept over me as I surveyed and confirmed that no one was there. No many-tentacled alien. No knife-wielding psychotic serial killer. No strung-out gang banger.

Bad smell, though. Body odor. Super bad body odor. I waved my arms around and grimaced.

"Smelly burglar," Bosco diagnosed, bellowing me in.

"Should we call the cops?" I asked. Bosco considered and then admitted that it couldn't hurt, so I fumbled for the number, which I did not have handily affixed to a refrigerator magnet.

The dispatcher advised us that they were having a very busy night, but if we wanted to cause everyone a lot of bother, someone would be out the next day, except we shouldn't touch anything in the kitchen until they arrived, and she couldn't say when tomorrow they would come, so we would have to stay home all day waiting. I thought that would be a good job for Bosco, but he disagreed.

I sarcastically thanked the voice and she went on to presumably more immediate emergencies.

The message light had been blinking, teasing me all during the call. As soon as I hung up, and half afraid of what we would hear, I punched the button. It was no gloating threat, however, just Yoo, the handwriting analyst.

"I'll send you a written report," he said, "but I wanted to let you know my conclusions. The two signatures both matched perfectly. There is little doubt that the two signatures on the banner are the two signatures identified as Obermeyer & Schlefly. Let me know if you want to come pick up your material, or I can mail it."

Bosco and I looked at each other. So, no tricks with the banner, and Ted had really died on Friday. It was disappointing in one way, but nice to have it settled.

"You should let Eddie know," said Bosco.

"It can wait until morning. Right now, I have to do something about the door. I can't leave it like this."

I didn't have any spare plywood hanging around. Or nails. Or a hammer, so I taped a cookie sheet over the broken pane and smeared the outside door knob with canola oil. It was all about slowing them down.

It was when I was putting on the oil that it occurred to me I might have made a mistake in having Yoo check those two particular signatures. If Obermeyer & Schlefly had torn down the original banner, killed Ted later, and put a fake banner in its place, then the only two signatures that *would* match would be theirs.

Kicking myself, I finished cleaning up the kitchen, closing the open windows and putting away the oil. I automatically picked up a stray dish towel on the counter and saw the decapitated rat.

The head was about three inches from where it should have been attached to the body. I stifled a scream and took a closer look. Its little hands and feet had also been cut off, arranged at the stumpy end of each of the arms and legs. Or are they all legs on a rat?

"Bosco!" I yelled, for once very happy Bosco was there.

"Shut up and go to bed. It's late," he yelled back.

"Get down here now!" I bellowed.

He did. I don't know which was worse. The sight of his face when he saw the rat, or the rat itself.

Still, I made him clean it up. I just couldn't. Not without puking. I have a weak stomach; it's a medical condition.

Even after the horrible little corpse had been bundled out to the bin on the curb, awaiting trash pickup the next day, neither of us was very anxious to turn off the lights and go back to our separate rooms.

I made coffee and we sat down at the card table in the dining room. Bosco suggested we call the police again, but since the broken door hadn't impressed them, I said no.

"But this looks like some kind of threat, Fifi. A warning."

"Yeah, but what exactly are we being warned about?"

"You," corrected Bosco. "Not we. Maybe you shouldn't have gotten involved."

"You...you...creep...Son of a...You're the one who... I wouldn't even be in this..." I was so furious I swallowed spit down my windpipe and choked. Bosco thumped me on the back until I was able to talk again. And when I did, he wished he hadn't.

I eventually calmed down and returned to the matter of the rat. "Whoever did it, it was a really smelly guy, though. The rat didn't smell. It was...fresh." I choked again, thinking about it.

"Well, maybe you're not worth the high-end killer. You know, the immaculately dressed Russian guy with the Matrix coat and the infrared laser scope," Bosco said. "Maybe you only rank the deranged homeless guy with the rusty razor."

"Omigod! Remember those homeless guys I ran into outside of SXYFX? An outfit like SXYFX is just the type that would hire a bunch of homeless guys as muscle. If it weren't for the rat, it'd be funny."

"But homeless people don't have cars. How did they get here from the Valley?"

"They shuffle-walked, Bosco. What do you think? Someone brought them."

Bosco shrugged. It wasn't exactly like Atlas shrugging.

"But why is SXYFX mad at me?" I continued. "I mean, even if they knew I was investigating Ted's death, which I can't see how they could, what's it to them?"

"Well, unless they killed him," Bosco said gently.

"Because he screwed up and financed their insurance premium? Get out. Your broker screws up, you yell at him, then you get another broker." I gestured toward the counter where the rat had lately been. "What's the point of this? If I don't know what I'm not supposed to do, why warn me not to do it?"

We puzzled some more as the sky grew lighter. When it was pinkish grey, I went to bed. Bosco said he still wasn't sleepy and had "some things to do." I didn't have any energy left to wonder what he had to do at dawn.

In fact, it wasn't until well after noon that I finally called Eddie. He was impressed with the rat. He said he didn't think Obermeyer & Schlefly had that much imagination.

"I don't think this is Obermeyer & Schlefly, Eddie. I think this is straight from SXYFX to me."

"Nooo, that's ridiculous."

"Why? Why is it ridiculous?"

Eddie didn't have any answer for that, not any coherent answer. He pretty much just kept saying he knew it was Schlef and Warren.

"Well, so far we haven't broken their Diabetes Dinner alibi. The Schlefly and Obermeyer signatures matched. Still we should probably get two more of those signatures on the birthday banner checked, okay?" I had decided against mentioning my colossal goof.

"Yeah, you do that. Get two more signatures checked. There's something there, I know it."

I called Yoo, the handwriting analyst, and left a message, telling him to check two more samples. I picked Karen and

Leah as the least likely to be in cahoots with one another, or with Obermeyer and Schlefly.

We retired early that evening, having reached our conversational apex when Bosco asked me for the salt.

I lay down on my raft and stared out the window, too wound up to sleep. My neck hurt. I gingerly touched the bandage. What if it got infected?

I concentrated on lying still until I couldn't stand it any more. I flailed my arms and jerked my legs and spun from the right side fetal position to the left side fetal position, little thinking that things were about to get worse.

Chapter 22

I must have dozed some, but it didn't seem like it. I only knew that a piercing scream catapulted me upright and on my feet. Screams and shrieks continued to peel out, over and over. The house was surrounded.

I flung open the door to my room and ran blindly into the jamb as I tried to swing around the corner. I saw stars as the pain stabbed right from my nose to my brain.

I headed for Bosco's room on instinct. The horrible screams and wails continued, eerily uniform in tone and duration, like a well-directed chorus of the insane. Finally, the wails stopped and I screamed, a human, jerky breathless scream, not even very loud.

Bosco opened his door and bolted out just as I reached the threshold. With a vicious smack, we bashed heads. It wasn't funny at all. It hurt like hell and I fell to the floor.

Bosco, the genius who had planted D'Metree's Halloween mats in strategic places around the perimeter of the house as an early warning system, was quicker to figure out what was going on. He was dazed but triumphant.

"It worked," he crowed. And practically skipped down the stairs, his hand clapped to his forehead, where a reddish bruise was beginning to ripen.

I picked myself up and followed more slowly. Much more slowly.

The front door was open. Bosco stood on the walk looking

up and down the street, then suddenly bolted, his sheepskin slippers slapping on the macadam surface of the street. I stared after him.

Our surly neighbors, moods not improved by the hour or the circumstances, started drifting out of their houses toward us, tentatively at first and then a lot more aggressively.

Some stringy-necked woman named Sandy or Patty or something approached first, her short hair mussed, her hands clutching at her surprisingly sumptuous bathrobe. It was probably her ex-husband's. She didn't quite know whether outrage or sympathy was appropriate, but she clearly wanted it to be outrage and demanded without preamble to know what all that noise was.

I told her I had no idea—I knew it couldn't be satisfactorily explained—but surmised that someone had tried to break in but had been scared off. People milled around.

"Was that you screaming?" demanded a tall bespectacled man who I believed to be the occupant of a modest '60s ranch two doors down.

"Well, I'm not sure what you expect me to do...," I began.

"You woke up the whole family," a disgruntled Hispanic woman interrupted, still this side of open hostility, but not by much. I guessed that her "whole family" included the residents of the faux-stone facade on the corner.

"Did they get anything?"

"Where did they go?"

"Did you see anybody?"

Finally I said I didn't know who screamed, and that they probably took everything, but thank God they didn't hurt me, because, after all I was a woman living alone (oh if only). The '60s ranch man looked a bit abashed.

Just then a beefy guy in pajama bottoms and a tee shirt (I was pretty sure he was the occupant of the do-it-yourself eyesore) approached the side of the house. He had a determined take-charge manner as he stepped, with a heavy tread, on a carefully concealed Halloween mat. The shriek lifted him into the air about a foot and he came down on his butt.

His almost-as-beefy wife rushed to help and planted her size 10s squarely on another mat. She, likewise, leaped up and landed.

People circled, staring at the downed pair, speechless. Now, that was funny.

The beefy couple sheepishly got to their feet, exaggerating their injuries to cover up embarrassment, snappishly insisting that they hadn't screamed, someone else had screamed and they were startled and that's why...

Bosco came up the street holding a struggling rag-bag. I recognized the homeless crone from the Valley. I hurried to him, avoiding the awkward questions of the neighbors.

"There were three or four of them," Bosco huffed, "the others got away."

"Let me go," the crone growled, lunging to bite Bosco's hand.

Though I like to shove as much blame onto Bosco as possible, I just couldn't fault him in this instance. He did the prudent thing, given the extreme likelihood of contracting a hideous saliva-borne disease. He let her go.

The skeletal woman scampered down the street like a wounded donkey, disappearing around a bend in the winding road and leaving that very bad distinctive odor in her wake. No one followed her. Least of all me.

This caused another fifteen minutes of conversation and speculation, focusing on the oddity of female burglars, and whether she worked alone, and didn't she look like a transient? Eventually the conversation started to turn to "who's Bosco?"

I explained that Bosco was just visiting, and he was my brother, and therefore didn't violate the single family occupancy law. One or two of the neighbors cautiously mentioned that they couldn't see the resemblance. Beefy woman wanted to make sure I knew that third-party rentals were illegal in this neighborhood. I pointed out that breaking and entering was even more illegal.

"Could we please get back to the fact that I was a victim here?" I pleaded.

"We should call the cops," someone finally said, I think it was the '60s ranch guy. I didn't disagree. I just hoped maybe someone with greater credibility than me would volunteer to actually make the call. Nobody did.

String-neck edged away, beginning the exodus. Beefy man and woman followed her.

In no time at all it was just me and Bosco and Mr. Officious '60s Ranch, who said he was head of the Community Watch program. I convinced him he should call the cops on his cell phone. While he was doing that, Bosco and I surreptitiously collected the mats and took them back to the house. A few of them, I noticed, were no longer in mint condition.

Bosco fell asleep on the floor of the living room and I was dozing when a patrol car pulled up about an hour later. I guess the Community Watch guy had some juice.

Officer Pacheco, well muscled, mustachioed, and altogether okay to look at, came to the door. I invited him in.

"Whoa," he exclaimed, looking around. "You really got cleaned out. Jesus, how could they have moved all your stuff out without waking you up?" He added suspiciously, "It must have taken hours."

"No, no," I shook my head, "I don't own anything. Or at least, not very much."

Just then Bosco woke up. "Pretty much just the TV," he said. "They got the TV."

"So just the TV then?" said Officer Pacheco, writing his report on a clipboard.

"Yeah," I said, too tired to argue.

"Well..." He looked around again. "It couldn't have been anyone who had staked the place out beforehand. It must have been quite a disappointment to go to the trouble to break into this great big place and get nothing but a TV. I guess you didn't see anybody lurking around here lately?"

I explained about the break-in the night before and let Bosco explain about the bag lady.

Officer Pacheco was not optimistic. "Not likely we'll ever catch her," he admitted. "She sounds mentally ill. That rat thing is really off the wall. But she couldn't have been working alone, not hauling around a TV set."

"Big screen," Bosco affirmed, gesturing widely.

"Yeah, unless you find it thrown into the canyon tomorrow, I guess we can write it off. But I'll file the report. You know, for your insurance company."

Bosco smiled a seraphic smile. I waited until Officer Pacheco had departed before breaking the news that his plan, brilliant as it was, wasn't going to work since I had just declined theft coverage in an effort to save a little money on my insurance premium.

Then I had to listen to Bosco wailing—a sound not unlike the ones from the Halloween mats.

Chapter 23

Monday morning I called Holy Family in Rancho Cucamonga. I asked for the parish secretary and got an older-sounding woman.

"Hello, can I help you?"

"I hope so. My name is Catherine...uh...St. Catherine..."

Damn, I should have thought of a fake name before calling.

"Catherine St. Catherine? My, what an interesting name."

"Yes, my folks were big on St. Catherine." I shook my head. "I'd like to contribute an article to the parish newsletter about the Miguel Villareal Cummings christening and I wondered if..."

"Parish newsletter? We haven't published a parish newsletter in years. Everybody's on e-mail now."

"Well, yes, that's the idea. To start an e-mail newsletter."

"That's a fantastic idea!"

"Yeah, thanks. Anyway, maybe you can tell me who the godparents were?"

"Sure I can. The baby's aunt Corazon was the godmother, and his uncle Tomas was the godfather. I wondered if Tomas would feel up to it, after all the troubles he had, but he seemed fine. I mean, it was a nice gesture, naming the baby Miguel, but it had to be painful."

I paused. Obviously she thought I knew the family. "It sounds like you were there?"

"Of course I was there. I've known Albert and Carmen for thirty three years. I go to all their grandchildren's christenings. I wouldn't miss it."

I couldn't believe my luck. "It went on a long time I heard."

"It did indeed. It was a lovely affair. Nobody got out of there before midnight."

"Not even Corazon?"

Now it was her turn to pause. "Corazon was there to the end. May I ask what your interest in Cora is? Who exactly did you say you were?"

I hung up. The phone trilled. Oh, god, she had star sixty-nined me! That *never* works. With trepidation, I punched the "talk" button.

"Hello?" I tried to speak really softly, with an unidentifiable accent.

"Hey, speak up. I can hardly hear you. You sound funny. You okay?"

"Yes, Eddie, I was just eating some jelly beans."

"Jelly beans? At nine thirty in the morning. Not healthy. Listen, the rumor is they're paying off on the key-man policy Thursday. Five million bucks. It covers the rent increase. It pays off the Mraz judgment. The partners will get bonuses. Everybody is walking around so happy, but trying not to show it. Obermeyer looks ten years younger."

"So, what, he could pass for 90?"

"And Schlefly. He looks like his face is gonna crack if he don't smile soon."

Another interesting development which didn't prove anything, and nobody was hiding it, so it wasn't like great detective work.

"I have no idea what I'm supposed to do about it," I complained.

I was about to find out. Eddie's voice twisted up into a squeak of excitement. "Here's the deal. We need to know when that policy was taken out. And why they're paying up without any questions. I found out who the adjustor is. The one who is writing the check."

He paused, presumably for dramatic effect. "Leonard Washington." The dramatic content of Eddie's announcement was a little thin. I didn't recognize the name.

"Washington," he repeated. "Washington. Come on. Think!" he urged. Nothing. He sighed. "You've got to know the guy. He's got to be black, right? There are no white people named Washington."

"Well, there was at least one," I pointed out. It took him a minute.

"Not now, though. Right? Now, there are no white Washingtons."

I was forced to admit the odds were against a white Washington. Still, the relevance of the race of the minion who was going to sign the check escaped me, and I said as much.

"I need you to talk to him. You don't know him but you know someone who knows him, right? How many black claims adjustors are there in LA, anyway?"

"I am afraid I don't have that particular statistic at my fingertips," I replied. What a bonehead.

"C'mon, c'mon. Get busy. Get on the phone, Cutter. Call all of your friends."

I didn't want to explain about not having a lot of friends, especially to Eddie, of all people. He probably still had hopes of one day having a friend himself.

"This Washington guy, he's giving up too easy," Eddie went on. "He's paying out within thirty days from death. What is that? That's not even trying."

"He probably doesn't have any reason not to pay the claim, Eddie."

"There's always a reason not to pay a five million dollar claim, Cutter. There must have been an investigation. What did that investigation show? Why was it ended? It's just strange as all get out. It makes me suspicious."

"You should just ask Obermeyer or Schlefly about it. Isn't that information you would be naturally interested in as someone who might make partner one day?"

"I can't ask them. In case you have forgotten, they are number one and two on my suspect list. They wouldn't tell me the truth. And if they did tell me the truth, I wouldn't know it was the truth, and I wouldn't believe them regardless, so it wouldn't do any good."

"You're telling me that you can't get this information from some clerk at the firm? How much of a secret could it be? Buy a crucial secretary some lunch, Eddie. Casually bring up the insurance policy. Get the scoop."

Eddie's voice trilled high enough to disorient dolphins. "I've tried that already. I have been trying to get the inside story on this insurance payout for weeks. I have bought lunch for Kathy, fetched coffee for Debbie, and if I spend any more time and money on Adele, people are going to think we are having an affair. They don't know. Obermeyer dealt with this personally. And, by the way, do you have any idea how suspicious that is? Any idea at all? Well, I'm telling you, it is very suspicious, because Obermeyer hasn't done anything personally for a decade. We've got to get on this."

I didn't understand Eddie's agitation. If the firm was saved, he should be happy. But mine was not to wonder. Mine was to make phone calls, and bill hours, and go to all kinds of trouble so my stupid half brother could one day watch reruns of *Seinfeld*.

"Sure, big guy, calm down. I'll make a few calls. Get on my homies, you know."

As per usual, all that beautiful sarcasm went to waste. Eddie merely grunted his assent.

"And what if I do get in to see him?" I asked. "What am I supposed to do, flutter my eyelashes and vamp him into telling me that he really is in cahoots with Schlefly and getting a kickback for not contesting the payment?"

"Nah, that wouldn't work," Eddie replied. "But you'll think of something. Call me this afternoon. I'm out till three."

I tried to think of a black person in the industry that I could call who didn't actually hate me. In the end, I called Jack. Of course, he wasn't black. Quite the contrary. But he knew a lot of people. And he didn't hate me.

In fact, Jack sounded glad to hear from me. It took me a moment to adjust. He thanked me for the property damage reports, and I thanked him for getting me Yoo's name.

"Jack, what I need this time is a little weirder. I need an introduction to a claims handler in life, Omega Life, out in Thousand Oaks, name of Leonard Washington. Know him?"

"Sorry, Fifi, I don't know the guy. I've never done any life."

I knew how he felt.

"I do know a few life guys, though," Jack continued. "Anita Lilianthal switched to life a few years ago. She's at Southern Sun, though, and I forget where she was before that, but not at Omega. Then there's Barry Stern, he started out at DCL, but then they went under, you know. Don't really know where he is now, maybe I can take a glance at my Rolodex. Still use the old Rolodex. Got stuff in here back twenty years. Oh yeah, Joe O'Hare, remember him?"

Jack continued to torture me for several minutes, which I billed to Eddie as double time because it seemed twice as long as it was. In the end, though, Jack spoke to Anita, who spoke to someone else, who now worked with Leonard, and I had my appointment for Wednesday at 11:15.

Eddie was smug about the success of the "black grapevine," and I didn't bother to correct him. He was less than thrilled when I told him the appointment was for Wednesday, as that was cutting it a little close, but I hung up on the ungrateful creep and charged him another fifteen minutes for his bad temper. What exactly I was supposed to say to Leonard when I met him, and what exactly I was supposed to find out from him, and why he wouldn't just kick me out of the office once I got there, was left up in the air.

Chapter 24

On Tuesday afternoon, after much internal debate, I slipped sheepishly down to Dorinda's Beauty Boutique to shell out some bucks for cornrows. It was ninety-five dollars, but I had to do it to let Leonard know I was black in case he missed it. Dorinda's is in a strip mall, in a run-down section of Pasadena, where all the apartment buildings looked like prisons—which was prophetic, since that's where one third of the young men who lived there were headed.

Dorinda, herself, was an elaborately coiffed woman in her fifties. On that particular day, her bronze-tipped tresses were positively baroque. I got my wash and was seated in the chair farthest from the plate glass window, a purple plastic sheet draped from chin to knees. Huge photographs of impossibly handsome African-Americans with impossible hairstyles grinned confidently down from the walls.

"Are you kidding me?" Dorinda exclaimed when I told her what I wanted. "Did ya'll hear that?" She played to the small crowd of regulars. "This girl wants her hair cornrowed. No, your hair is too frizzy to cornrow good. I have told you that before. It's not like a real black person's hair. Look, what it needs is conditioning and straightening and then more conditioning because of the straightening."

"I don't have time for that right now." I shrunk down even

lower in the chair. "And anyway, white people get cornrows too, sometimes."

"Yeah, if they look like Bo Derek. And honey, you ain't no Bo Derek." The regulars all chuckled at that.

"Cornrow's just gonna make that little bitty doorknob head setting there on top of your neck look even smaller. You need volume. Let people know you got a head up there. Cornrow is the opposite of volume. And what's that big old bruise on your forehead, girl? You been fightin'? Some big girl take you down? You know you too small to go lookin' for trouble," Dorinda put her hands on her hips and shook her head.

"Would you please just do something with my hair?"

Dorinda combed and teased and pulled and gooped and braided. I finally opened my eyes to a side part like a razors edge, bangs slicked down over my forehead (covering the bruise), straight cornrows from front to back, and a curly mop of a ponytail hairpiece stuck on the top "for volume."

The fake ponytail didn't exactly match the dust brown color of my hair, but Dorinda's regulars gathered around and cooed over the end result. For a brief moment I felt pretty.

*　*　*

Wednesday came and I was ready. I chose a strong yellow suit with a fitted skirt and jacket. The color sort of suggested dashiki. I shoved my feet into black patent leather spikes and got in the truck.

Thousand Oaks is a long way out the 101 freeway, west, through Glendale, Burbank, Encino, Tarzana, the great sprawling grid of mid-century urban development flashing by on either side. Lots of anonymous buildings, chain retailers, tract homes, and car dealerships. Traffic on the other side, going eastbound, was jammed. The drivers of the huge, passenger-less SUVs that crowded all four lanes, looked irritated. Bet they were wondering why traffic was so bad.

The Omega building was visible from the freeway, awkwardly placed upon a slight rise. It looked as if it might lose its balance and fall onto the freeway. It would be no loss if it did, a single-story people container, stretched out to smother as much green earth as possible. Or, as the Codden & DeBragg Development Co. sign proclaimed, "47,000 sq. ft. of prime office space!"

I parked in the lot and wandered around the perimeter trying to find the front entrance. I finally realized that what appeared to be one building for some reason had two addresses 18020 (East) and 18030 (West). It took me a few minutes longer to figure out that I wanted 18020 (East), whereupon I discovered I had gone exactly the wrong way from the parking lot.

I was already pissed off when I entered and found myself standing before a white door marked Omega Group of Insurance Companies. I entered into a sparsely furnished waiting room.

The receptionist could be seen in silhouette behind a frosted glass panel, more like a doctor's office. It even smelled kind of like a doctor's office, and I was certainly kept waiting long enough to make me think I was in a doctor's office.

I finally rapped on the glass. After several minutes an African-American woman of middle age slid back the panel.

"Yes," she said, obviously not impressed with my corn rows. Her own hair had been ruthlessly waved à la Ann Landers.

"I have an appointment with Leonard Washington."

If anything, she became even less friendly. "Have a seat," she commanded.

There were only two chairs, both low, square, and soft, a nasty light teal color that clashed with my yellow suit. The fabric was both slick and itchy.

The door eventually opened and a young, plump Asian

woman led me back to the inner office, the typical, cheesy rabbit warren of cubicles with built-in desks and stenographers' chairs. The teal was carried out through here, but to make it even more repulsive, it was combined with mauve.

Leonard, however, ranked. He had an office, all the way at the back, with a floor-to-ceiling window. The view from Leonard's window was the grill of an old Toyota Tercel.

The view of Leonard stopped me cold. White. The Last White Washington. Son of a bitch. Ninety-five dollars and two hours of discomfort for absolutely nothing.

The guy wasn't much taller than me and so frail in build I wondered if he was meeting his daily nutritional requirements. Gold-framed glasses made him look like he was a kid playing grown up.

I handed him my card. He shook my hand. Of the two visitors chairs, one was occupied by a stack of files, so I took the other. Len—I had begun to think of him as Len—retreated behind his little desk. He sat down and peered at me between two more file stacks. I wondered if his feet touched the ground. I smiled as sincerely as I could and told him it was really good of him to see me.

"No problem, Ms. Cutter, I understand you have information about a claim? Or," he paused, "you want information about a claim?"

I told Len that I had been retained by a person with a position of financial interest with respect to Obermeyer & Schlefly and that I had heard about the impeding payout. I simply wanted to know when the policy was purchased and if there had been an investigation on the cause of death.

To establish my bona fides, I laid out what I knew about the financial problems of Obermeyer & Schlefly. Len frowned and honed in precisely where I had not wanted him to hone.

"How do you know all this?" he asked.

"I've been retained to look into the matter," I repeated.

"Well, that doesn't really answer my question."

I had to admit the truth of that observation. I dodged

a little more, but he kept asking very direct questions that were really hard to dodge.

"Who is this person who retained you?" Len demanded.

"Look, all I want to know is when his policy was purchased. Is it a secret? What's the secret? 'Cause if it's a secret, that's pretty suspicious."

Unruffled, Len leaned forward, "Well, why is it a secret who you work for? Huh?" He took off his glasses and polished them with his tie.

I hate it when men do that. It's the step before wiping your nose with your sleeve. As if he had made some great debating point, Len put his glasses back on leaned back and continued.

"The payment will be made on Thursday, and that is all I am prepared to tell anybody. Are you telling me we shouldn't pay the claim?"

"I'm saying that no one knows how Ted Heffernan died. It could have been anything. It could even have been murder, for all you know. I'm kind of curious."

"Curious?" he echoed. "You sound to me as if you suspect foul play." Len infused the last two words with as much melodrama as he could muster from in between his two file stacks. "Because if so, you shouldn't be here. You should be talking to the police."

He showed me the palms of his little bitty hands.

"That's exactly what I'm doing. Gathering information to go to the police. That's why I'm here."

"Ms. Cutter, I obtained the autopsy report, and I can tell you that there was no reason not to pay the claim and no reason for us to investigate any further. Besides," Len pointed out, "This policy would pay out even if death was caused by first degree murder. So I don't really have a dog in the fight." In case I didn't understand the cliché, he clarified. "Your concern is not my concern."

"Even if that first degree murder was committed by one of the partners in the firm, who would benefit from the death?

Isn't there some rule about not being able to benefit from your own criminal act?"

Len blinked skeptically. "Yes, there is, but Warren Obermeyer? Robert Schlefly? I don't think so, Ms. Cutter. And anyway, even if one of the partners should turn out to be a deranged homicidal maniac, the other partner would still be entitled to the benefit. Unless you think that both of the partners were in it together?"

"No, I guess not." I knew the taste of defeat. It was, after all, my usual afternoon snack.

"I carefully investigated this claim, Ms. Cutter," Len's lips had thinned, "Just as I carefully investigate all of my claims. I do not work for the police, of course. I simply ascertain whether the conditions of coverage have been satisfied. That's my job."

Spare me, I thought, how pompous could a guy get in just thirty years of living?

And still, he yakked on, ticking off the elements on his fingers. "The decedent was identified by a dozen different people. The decedent had not falsified any information on his application. We do a comprehensive medical screening, you know, and an annual physical. The decedent did not die of a known pre-existing condition. Or, at least, there was no proof of anything like that. The cause of death was undetermined. Granted, they didn't look for poison," he smiled humorlessly. "But that would only be relevant to the suicide exclusion, and the suicide exclusion would only apply the first year after the policy has been taken out. If he did commit suicide, the year had long since passed..."

The silence following this break in the ramble caused my ears to perk up. Len was looking at the open file. The minute lengthened.

"The year had long since passed?" I prompted.

"Well, that's a moot point." Now Len sounded like a guy trying to convince himself. "You aren't suggesting that he poisoned himself in some insane act of altruism toward his partners, are you?" He stared at me.

I shook my head.

"So," he concluded "It's a single limit of five-million dollars, whether he died of a stroke or a mysterious South African poison. He died. We pay."

I tried to work out what had caused the momentary hesitation. Len was correct, I wasn't suggesting suicide. In spite of Angela, and the money troubles, it just didn't seem likely.

"Do you test for drugs in your annual physical?" I asked.

"I cannot share information about particular individuals, of course," he said, still more distracted than when he had begun, "but yes, it is our standard procedure, you know, in the Beverly Hills or Brentwood geographic locations, to screen yearly for certain recreational drugs."

"What about your South Central clients?" I inquired, just yanking his chain.

"We don't have South Central clients," he snapped.

"And no drugs showed up on the autopsy report?"

"No, there were no drugs or alcohol in the decedent's system."

"Was there a specific finding about time of death?"

Len looked surprised. "I suppose so. I didn't really focus on that. Clearly the man died during the policy period." He flipped through the pages in the file folder, looking for the autopsy report. "Yes, time of death between 8:00 PM Friday night and noon Saturday."

"May I have a copy of that report?" I asked, although I wasn't sure why.

Len wasn't sure either, but I gave him a smile. To my surprise, it worked. He smiled back and buzzed his toady, who came in, retrieved the report and provided me with a copy in three minutes. I picked up my knock-off Kate Spade handbag, and Len rose from his seat. Just as I had my hand on the door handle, the reason for Len's earlier hesitation hit me. I turned.

"The policy has been in effect for over a year, right?"

He nodded.

"When were the limits increased to five million?" I asked. For a moment I thought Len wasn't going to answer. I forced myself to smile again.

"October 5. This year." He grudgingly conceded.

"You mean the limits had only been one million dollars before?"

Len nodded.

"And who at Obermeyer & Schlefly contacted you to raise the limits?"

He glanced through the file for the most recent underwriting memo. He looked at me. I sat back down, and crossed my legs, hitching the skirt up a little.

"I don't see how it matters, but it appears to have been Warren Obermeyer himself."

Len looked unhappy at having capitulated, so, to make him feel better, I hiked up my skirt a little more and said, "Oh, I'm sure you're right, it doesn't matter at all. Sorry to have bothered you."

Elated by my success, I stopped in at Teru Sushi in Studio City, sat at the bar, ordered a California roll and charged it. By the time that Visa bill came in, I might have the money to pay it.

Chapter 25

I made my way to Century City from the Valley over the Hollywood Hills, via Laurel Canyon. A twisty drive through residential housing, expensive boxes in the LA mock style: mock Tudor, mock Palladian, mock Cape Cod.

It took fifty-seven minutes. I was greeting Mandy and asking for Eddie at 3:12. He appeared in the lobby, stiff around the neck, head and shoulders, grasped my elbow and sped me back to his office. Shutting the door behind me, he whispered furiously "What are you doing here? Someone might see you!"

"I'm here to report. I went to Omega and talked to Leonard Washington. Hey, what's that?" I pointed to a small, expensive-looking electronic device which Eddie had obviously just taken out of its bubble wrap.

"It's like an iPod, but you can play it without earplugs," he said proudly. "Look, it fits here in my shirt pocket. And it's got great sound. Listen to that volume." He flicked it up, and a surprisingly loud blast of "You're Having My Baby" filled the small office. Someone pounded on the wall next door.

"How much did that cost?"

"None of your beeswax," said Eddie. "What did you find out?"

"Three things. First, he didn't have any drugs or alcohol in his system. Second, they routinely tested for recreational drugs at his physical and always came up negative."

"I never thought his money was going for drugs. What else you got?"

I smiled. "Third, Obermeyer increased the policy limit from $1 million to $5 million on October 5th of this year."

"Washington told you that?"

I nodded and explained my brilliant deduction that had forced the information out of Len. "From Len's perspective it doesn't matter, because Ted didn't commit suicide. For us, the important point is that Obermeyer raised the limit the week after the court of appeal decision came down on the Mraz case. The very week after."

Eddie nodded.

"So listen, Len mentioned other partners. What other partners are there?"

Eddie shrugged. "There aren't any other partners with Ted gone."

"But I read in the deposition transcripts that they make new partner announcements around Christmas. Maybe someone is going to be made partner this year?"

Eddie flared at me, "That's irrelevant. Forget about that. You've got to concentrate on getting your buddy Washington to delay the payment."

"I don't know how to do that," I flatly replied. "He made it clear this was not his issue. He's paying on Thursday."

Eddie slumped in his chair. "Oh God, so they killed him, they get the money, and we'll never prove it."

"I don't think that's necessarily true. If it is the old guys, like you think, they'll panic if they know we're on to them. They aren't professional hit men, after all. And it seems unlikely that they know any professional hit men. If you're right and they are the ones who hired a crew of homeless people to burgle my house, they've gotta be the rankest amateurs ever. Right?"

Eddie's eyes darted nervously at the mention of homeless people, then he listlessly agreed. He seemed extremely unhappy. "Look, you've got to get over to La Fortunata as soon as possible. You have to break their alibis."

* * *

I got home at 5:40 PM. Bosco was waiting. I told him it was time to begin the panicked stampede of old white men.

La Fortunata was downtown on Figueroa, near Third, which was good, because there was no way I was going to turn around and fight traffic to get back to the west side. Not to catch a murderer, not for money, not for any reason in the world.

On the way Bosco mentioned that Yoo had called. The other two signatures matched as well.

"I guess it was kind of dumb to have him check Obermeyer and Schlefly first," he remarked.

"Do you ever shut up?" I asked. "Anyway, the other two checked out. The banner is genuine, the autopsy report is correct, and Ted died Friday night. That's all we need to know."

"Yeah, it worked out okay, I was just saying, you know, that it was dumb. That was my only point, that you were really dumb." Bosco grinned like a fool. I mentally debated a left turn into oncoming traffic. After all, Truck L'Orange was not equipped with passenger side airbags.

La Fortunata was on the street level corner space of a new and not very interesting office building. Downtown LA is usually pretty deserted after six, but a few upscale restaurants try to make believe there is really a night life. Most of them cater to the theater crowd, which means eating early and quickly.

Inside, the restaurant mimicked an Italian trattoria. The muted yellow walls were sponged and fake-aged. All it needed was a haze of cigarette smoke and the din of misbehaving children to make the European illusion complete.

Unable to come up with a convincing story on the way over, I relied heavily on the meretricious talents of Bosco as we entered the darkened interior. "This one is yours, my brother."

Bosco smirked and gestured for me to wait in the foyer as he walked up to an adorable waif who was considering her reservation list with great concentration. I wondered how hard it could be to figure out the seating for the three parties of two and the one party of four that were the restaurant's only occupants.

I heard Bosco say "Hello, there. I'm a reporter for Hollywood Lights. You may be familiar with our publication. We're an entertainment industry weekly. We're doing a little human interest piece on Clarissa Wheaton, and I would love it if you would answer just a few questions."

I grinned. Clarissa Wheaton was the blow-loving actress who had been at the table with Obermeyer and Schlefly.

"Are you on staff at the Light?" she asked, with a certain deference. Bosco had calculated correctly. The waif was a wanna-be actress who didn't figure she could afford to piss off the industry tabloids this early in her imaginary career.

Bosco smiled. "Well, freelance for right now." Ooh, nice touch of self-deprecating candor. "If you will just spare me a moment, I'm on the trail of some really hot stuff. I need some information about The Night in Tuscany Diabetes Dinner held here, a few weeks ago." He paused. "If the story pans out, my editor is willing to pay for the information."

The waif glanced my way. "Who's she?"

"That's my photographer," Bosco leaned in and became even more confiding. "She doesn't have her equipment with her right now, of course, but if the story takes off, we'll have to come and take pictures. Would you be willing to pose for her, do you think? You know, something dramatic, maybe with the light coming in like this," Bosco swooshed his left hand, "and a soft shadow like that," he waggled his right hand close to her cheek.

"Sure," she said breathlessly. "What do you want to know?"

"You remember the dinner? You were on duty that night?"

"Yes, I was in charge of the seating. André was in charge of the kitchen, but it was all me out here. They brought in their own sommelier for the wine, so I really don't know about that."

Bosco beamed his approval. "We're in luck. It's the seating I'm interested in."

I inched forward. The waif bent down and fished something out of the back of the maitre d's lectern. She brought out a seating chart and a list of names.

She glanced my way again. I slid back. Bosco congratulated her for not throwing anything away. They spent a few more minutes comparing the seating chart with the list and deciphering the notes. The waif produced what appeared to be another copy of the list, a clean copy. She made several notations on it, talking all the while, then gave it to Bosco. He made a few notes of his own.

A telephone number changed hands. I rolled my eyes and we were out the door. Bosco again told me to wait while he went to talk to the head valet guy, a conversation that lasted several minutes.

"What's the deal?" I demanded as I started up the truck.

"The deal, as you say, is quite fascinating," said Bosco complacently. "This list," he waved it in front of my face, nearly causing an unfortunate encounter with a pizza delivery guy on a bike, "is the original guest list. On it are all the folks who paid five hundred dollars a couple for a little focaccio di papate, carciofi romani, and pheasant with sausage."

"So?" I batted the list away and flipped off the protesting biker as I turned onto the 110 freeway.

"So, for one thing, Gursky was there the whole time."

"Gursky? I never seriously considered him. No motive. Too much of a dweeb."

"Better. Obermeyer spilled some wine on his pants during the main course and excused himself halfway through the meal."

I considered. "Obermeyer, huh? I could see him as a co-conspirator, but do you think he actually did the killing himself? He's kind of old to be attacking people, don't you think?"

"Maybe. Maybe it's habit."

"What are you talking about?"

"Well, remember Karen told us about that other guy Obermeyer used to be partners with who died? Ollie somebody? And Obermeyer got all his clients? Maybe Obermeyer killed Ollie, too."

"Bosco, that's wild speculation."

"It's more than that. Obermeyer could have taken Schlefly's car. We've already agreed that just because it was Schlefly's car doesn't mean Schlefly was driving it. He could have given Obermeyer the keys."

I slid over a few lanes, not wanting to get caught in the backup from traffic exiting to the 5, but still wanting to be in position to make the left hand exit to Glassell Park.

"But why couldn't Obermeyer just use his own car?" I asked. "Or are you saying that Obermeyer wanted to pin this on Schlefly?"

"Also," said Bosco replied, cruising past the question like a politician, "Obermeyer was the one who increased the limits on the key-man policy."

I considered the implications of that observation for a few moments, then Bosco continued. "Heather definitely puts Aunt Angela out of it."

"Who's Heather?"

"What do you mean, who's Heather? The woman I just spent the last twenty minutes talking to."

"Oh, the waif. Why didn't you say so?"

"Heather says that Aunt Angela was sitting at the head table in a golden Dolce and Gabbana, with her hair extensions piled eight inches high. Heather had to consult her a few times during the course of the dinner. There is no way she snuck out during the evening. After dinner she introduced the honoree, Chief Justice Alfred Chu, and gazed appreciatively at him all through the espresso and lemon timballo. By the time the subject of insulin imbalance and the wonderfulness of everybody present had been exhausted, it was midnight."

"Office locks down at midnight," I observed. "I never believed she had the guts to do it. I guess it's good to have it confirmed by an unbiased source. Could Obermeyer have made it to Century City by eight, do you think?"

"Don't know," Bosco replied.

"Can Heather confirm Schlefly was there the whole time?"

"Well, she can confirm that he was there at the very beginning to collect his name tag and then there again to say a few words at the end. There might be an hour unaccounted for, but it would be very tight and tricky."

"It's all tricky, Bosco."

Chapter 26

The next day Jack called with one of his good news/bad news assignments. I had to drive to Riverside and then to San Dimas and then to Sunland to get witness statements concerning a five-car pileup on the 219. It was good money, but I got home late and hungry; and when I walked in, I found that Bosco had turned the central heating up high enough to broil a turkey burger.

I walked into the dining room to turn it down, and saw that the message light was on. I punched and heard "Ms. Cutler? This is Lydia Long-Waller, Eddie's wife. Please call."

I noted the "Long-Waller." Great, so she used to have her own last name.

I dialed, got a wrong number, shook myself and dialed again.

"Hello?"

"Hi, is this Lydia...uh...Long-Waller? This is Fifi Cutler."

"Hello, Ms. Cutler." I didn't correct her. "Look, I have to ask you, I can't find Eddie. Is he there?"

It was a good thing she couldn't see me blanch at the sordid implications of Eddie being at my house at 9:43 PM.

"No," I hastened to assure her. "I haven't seen him since Tuesday. What's wrong?"

"Probably nothing. It's just that Eddie called me before he left work tonight, around 7:30 or so. He said he was going to come right home, except he did mention he might drop by your house tomorrow morning on his way in. He had found something at the office he wanted to give you. Anyway, now I can't get him on his cell phone, and since he hasn't come home yet," she paused. "Well, I thought maybe he just decided to stop by tonight."

"Actually, I just got back myself. Hold on. I'll check with my brother."

I found Bosco in the kitchen with his shirt off, showing way too much white skin. I yelled at him to put on some clothes. He refused.

It took a few minutes, but I was eventually able to report to Ms. Long-Waller that Eddie had not dropped by and had not called. After hanging up, I thought I'd just give him a call myself. Maybe he had caller ID and didn't want to talk to his hyphenated wife. No luck.

We tried his cell phone too. Still no luck. Which kind of made us a little uneasy.

"We should go over there," Bosco said.

"What, drive all the way to Century City just to see if we can find Eddie at the office? If he was there, why couldn't we get him on the phone?"

"Maybe he's in trouble."

"Well, if he is in trouble, we're unlikely to be any help."

"Come on, Fifi, you gotta at least try. He's our friend," Bosco argued.

"Eddie Waller is no friend of mine."

We debated the pros and cons for a full eleven minutes. Bosco suggested that, if we went, we could try a great Nicaraguan restaurant on Olympic. Bosco, otherwise known as the Freeloading Gourmet, had read about the place in the *Times* that morning.

He cemented the argument by pointing out that I could bill Eddie for the time going to Century City and back, so the dinner would be practically free.

I parked on the street, the closest legal space I could find, and we walked six blocks to the building. If I had to pay for parking in that neighborhood, the economics of the evening would be upside down. The parking attendant at the building looked at us with some degree of hostile interest as we passed his booth, but didn't try to prevent us from descending the ramp, or parking in the visitor spaces.

We thought we would first check to see if Eddie's car was there. If it was, we would find a phone and try calling him again. If it wasn't, we'd have to think of some way to get the security guard to let us up to the fifteenth floor.

Bosco remembered the section where Obermeyer & Schlefly employees parked better than I did. It was several levels down. The escalator wasn't working, so we took the stairs, which didn't smell that great, by the way.

As the heavy door to the stairwell banged shut behind us, I started to get freaked out. It wasn't just the smell. The industrial light was very unflattering to my skin tone. Even Bosco looked bad, the shadows on his face made him look like he was wearing a Batman mask.

Our steps echoed unnervingly on the metal treads. Clang, clang, clang.

Three floors down, we both suddenly stopped.

The echo of our last steps stopped ringing, and we heard a door, several floors above us, creak open and shut with a muffled whumph. Brisk footsteps started down after us.

I looked at Bosco. Bosco looked at me. Wordlessly, we started off, not quite running, but walking like we were late to the Nordstrom's shoe sale.

Finally, we reached the seventh basement level. Dante-esque. I had a flash of fear that the door to this level would be locked and we would be trapped. Bosco gave it a shoulder. Nothing. My heart lurched as I elbowed him aside and heaved. The door reluctantly opened a few inches. Not locked.

"God, Bosco, you're such a girl." The footfalls above us continued to echo down.

We emerged into a vast expanse of concrete. An array of

wing walls and pylons blocked the view in every direction and a lot of cars were still there.

"I'm not sure exactly where Eddie's space is. You take left, I'll take right." I stepped over a heavy chain barrier.

I had made my way to the north wall, when I first heard a sound penetrating the silence of the parking garage. I couldn't quite make it out. I made my way closer to the wall, veering to the left, trying to follow the sound. It got louder and louder and finally I could hear what it was.

It was the thin mewl of *Rhinestone Cowboy,* tinkling out over the expanse of cars and space.

Chapter 27

I ran back to Bosco, who stood frozen in between two rows of cars. He had heard it too, I could tell. We followed the sound of that forlorn signal and found Eddie, in section G12, lying between his silver BMW and an Audi.

He had a hole in his head.

I mean a real one. Small, black encrusted, just above the staring left eye.

I stifled a scream. Bosco had less success with stifling.

The stairway door slammed shut behind us. A tall man— in a trench coat—walked swiftly toward us. Before I could run away and leave Bosco to his fate, I recognized Keith Gursky.

A flood of relief, highly disproportionate to the sight of his goofy face, washed over me. In the next instant, I wondered if that relief was justified. Not, I realized, by anything that we actually knew about Gursky. I mean, there he was. And there Eddie was.

Keith, however, smiled as he approached, not in a sinister fashion, just in his usual dumb shit fashion.

"Hey, working late?" he hailed us. "Me, too. I usually, do, to tell you the truth. You know, you gotta be the early bird." Even he seemed to realize the stupidity of what he was saying. "And the late bird, too. Ha ha." He headed for the Audi.

He reached the Audi.

And then he screamed. He didn't even try to stifle it. Was it an act? I couldn't say for sure. I mean, I haven't heard that many men scream. It sounded like the usual "you-flushed-the-toilet-while-I-was-in-the-shower" kind of scream.

When Keith recovered himself, the three of us spent way too long exclaiming and then trying to decide who would stay and who would go for help.

We thought about using Eddie's cell phone, which had been dropped right by his hand, along with the Beamer keys and the mini-player, which was still playing. *Rhinestone Cowboy* had given way to *Witchie Woman*.

It looked like Eddie had been just about to open his car door and was getting all of his gadgets out, ready to enjoy his trip home. But I pointed out that we wouldn't get a decent signal down here. Also, nobody wanted to get that close to Eddie, especially not me.

Of course, no one wanted to be alone, either. Not alone with the body, not alone running up seven flights in the deserted stairway to the security desk, and neither Bosco nor I wanted to be alone with Gursky.

It was like that riddle about the sack of grain and the chicken and the fox and having to cross the river in a small boat that could only hold two things at a time or whatever the hell that riddle is. It was like that.

In the end, we all three left Eddie alone and wheezed up seven flights of stairs together. The cops came. They questioned us for what seemed like hours. Hours in which I had to try not to think about death, while avoiding awkward questions. We never made it to the Nicaraguan restaurant.

*   *   *

Piecing it all together from what we heard that night and gathered from the newspaper account the next morning, Eddie had been seen leaving the office by a number of people, including the security guard, my old friend Mr. Ballon.

But nobody had heard the shot or seen anybody

who looked like a killer. There were no security cameras in the garage (which had worked to my advantage when I swiped the folding chair).

One officer was reported to have said, "The known facts appear to point to an unsuccessful, interrupted random robbery situation." Nothing, in fact, had been taken.

Or had it? Lydia told me on the phone that Eddie was going to bring me something the next morning, something he had found in the office. He would have had it with him, and he never made it into the car. It should have been next to the body. But there was nothing next to the body, except his phone, his keys and the mini-player.

All my instincts told me this was a successful, completed robbery situation, with nothing random about it.

Bosco realized that recent events had put a high-definition wide-screen further out of reach. He was subdued as he got a bottle of beer out of the refrigerator. He did not offer me one, which I wouldn't have accepted even if he had, because I don't drink beer. But still, it was my refrigerator, and my beer, since I paid for it, and I think he should have offered.

I pulled out the vacuum cleaner, determined to do something constructive.

Bosco forestalled me. "Fifi, don't you think that Eddie getting killed like that, well, don't you think that it pretty much proves that Ted was murdered too?"

"Yeah, I know, Bosco. But we checked all the alibis for Friday night, right? They're all solid, except Obermeyer, who spilled wine on his pants. I just can't believe a guy that old killed someone."

"Okay, so it's not any of the people Eddie thought it was."

"Or anyone from the office at all. Angela was clearly occupied at the dinner, Schlefly was probably at the dinner the whole time. Karen alibis Belinda. Belinda alibis Karen. Corazon is alibied by a christening," I sighed. "Heather the Hostess said Gursky was at the dinner, but maybe he's so much of a loser that he could leave and no one would notice. But why? Unless he was up for partner, which I find hard to believe, we have no motive at all for him."

"Except Belinda," Bosco pointed out. "She could be a motive."

"Yeah, for a desperate guy who has no prospects," I retorted.

"Belinda, in case you're blind, is smoking hot."

"To you and Gursky maybe. Like I said, desperate guys with no prospects."

Bosco was silent for a brief moment and then shook his head. "Maybe we're wrong about the time of the crime."

"Look, Bosco, I know Eddie had a great idea that there was something off about that whole birthday banner thing. But Yoo checked the signatures," I reminded him. "There were sixteen different people who signed it. We could check them all, I suppose, but Yoo thought that at least four of them were genuine. It was a pretty conclusive finding."

"And Eddie himself took the paper and kept it," he replied. "But it's too...I don't know...too..." Bosco took a last swig. He downed that thing pretty fast for the middle of the day, if you want my opinion.

Then it struck me. Bolt of lightening right between the eyes. Big old sledge hammer on the top of the head. Huge gulp of pure Tabasco sauce straight from the bottle.

I ran to the card table where I kept my little pile of papers pertaining to the investigation. I scrutinized the autopsy report that I had managed to get—with a smile—from Len Washington. I looked at the time of death. I looked at the name on the autopsy report. Dr. Larry Stoltz.

Len had scrawled a telephone number on the report. I called it.

"Dr. Stoltz," a low tenor with a slight Philly accent answered.

"Dr. Stoltz. This is Trisha from Len Washington's office on the Heffernan case, we spoke before."

Bosco raised his eyebrows and fake clapped.

As I had hoped, Dr. Stoltz was too self-important to admit

he didn't remember me. "What's the file number, dear?" he asked. "I can't help you without the file number. I handle a lot of cases, you know."

I gave it to him and waited. After a minute or two, he responded. "Oh yeah, yeah, yeah, the birthday boy. What can I help you with? The body's long gone, cremated."

"I know that, I was just wondering, do you have the reports regarding the birthday banner on the door?"

"Yeah, yeah, I got all that information right there," he replied, a little defensively. "Witness statements, the whole thing. Found on Sunday, couldn't have died any time after Saturday at noon."

"Thanks, that's all I needed." I hung up just as Dr. Stoltz was spluttering, "Why are you asking?"

"Bosco, we are so dumb, omigod, we are so unbelievably dumb!"

"If you can't say anything nice," Bosco said, "then don't say anything at all about me."

"Bosco, listen to me. We've been looking at it all wrong."

Chapter 28

I clutched my hair. "God, what a bunch of fucking idiots we are. Of course that one was real."

"Which one what?"

"The banner that was taken off the door on Sunday. Then Eddie gave it to me and I took to the handwriting expert. It was real. But that one wasn't the one that the girls put on the door on Saturday. It was switched *before* it was put up!"

"Not following you."

"Okay. Listen. Everybody signed the banner. Then, before Ted is killed, the killer switches the banner with a forgery. A forgery that wouldn't fool an expert, but good enough. You see? That's the banner that Belinda and Leah put up. The forgery. These women aren't going to look at the banner that closely before the murder. Picture it. They come to the office on Saturday, they have absolutely no reason to think there might be a substitution. It would never enter their heads in a million years. So how good does the forgery have to be? No, from the murderer's perspective, the only remote possibility is that someone might have the paper examined by an expert after Ted's body is found."

"Not following you," Bosco repeated. There really cannot be any genetic connection between us, can there?

"Concentrate! The killer takes the real birthday banner after everyone signs it, then creates a duplicate banner and substitutes it before the weekend. The girls come in on

Saturday, put up the duplicate. The murder doesn't happen Friday night. It happens Saturday night. Killer and Ted get there on Saturday. They tear down the forged banner to get into the office. Laughing, laughing ha ha ha. Then, somehow, we still don't know how, Ted is killed. And the killer replaces the real banner, the one with all the genuine signatures on it, over the door."

"What are you saying, the coroner was in on it? And you found that out just by talking to him now?"

"No, of course he wasn't in on it, you jackass. But he knew about the birthday banner."

"I think everybody knew about it. It was bizarre enough to get mentioned on the local news."

"Yeah, but don't you see? You can't have a true opinion about time of death if the expert is told beforehand that it had to happen between Friday night and Saturday noon. Scientists are not infallible. They can be totally subjective. Especially on stuff like time of death. Especially when the office is as overworked as the coroner's office. And no one even thought this was a criminal case at the time, so who cared? He might not have even really run any tests. He probably just filled in the time of death that he thought he already knew."

I let Bosco ponder this for a few minutes before I said, "We've been looking at this all wrong. We need to look at people who have an alibi for Friday night but no alibi for Saturday."

"Or people who don't have an alibi for either night," Bosco suggested.

"Oh, why don't you just have another beer, Bosco? Come on! What would be the point of all this bullshit if the killer didn't make absolutely sure that he had an alibi for Friday night?"

Bosco shook his head. "I don't get it. Are you suggesting Ted just stayed in his office for like two days waiting for the killer? That he didn't come out when Belinda, Leah and Karen showed up at his door on Saturday? That doesn't make any sense."

"Bosco, the only reason we thought he was in there the whole time was because of the banner."

"That, and the fact nobody heard from him at all on Saturday."

"Yeah, but that could be arranged. Somehow. Okay, I don't know how yet. But this finally explains why it was necessary to steal the sign-in book. I mean, our problem with that was, why bother? You could pretty easily sign in a phony name and disguise your handwriting. But how would you explain to Ted when he came back in on Saturday evening that *he* had to sign in with a phony name? What if the thing that Eddie had wanted to give us the night he was killed was the stolen sign-in book?"

I pulled out the suspect list. Those with a solid alibi for Friday night were Angela, Schlefly, Obermeyer, Belinda, Karen, Keith and Corazon. What we needed to know was who, among this group, didn't have an alibi for Saturday night.

"Or for last night," Bosco pointed out. "Easier to get information about last night. Closer in time."

I was practically dancing the rumba when I suddenly came to my senses. "Except why bother now? It's over, Bosco. Nobody's going to pay us, right?"

"Can't we bill Lydia?"

I shook my head. "No way. Face it Bosco, she's newly widowed and I don't think she works. She's probably frantic with worry about what's going to happen to her and the kid. I don't think I even have the guts to ask her." I slumped against the wall. "This is such a bummer. We were actually getting somewhere. And now it seems like it was all for nothing." I angrily flicked on the vacuum cleaner and started pushing it across the floor.

Bosco continued to stand there as I vacuumed around him. Suddenly, he started waving his arms and talking. I have a really good vacuum cleaner, or at least a really loud one. I couldn't hear a thing he said. Finally, he pulled the plug.

"Karen Odom."

"What about her?"

"She'll hire us."

"Really? Karen? You think?"

"It's perfect. She already knows that Eddie hired us. And she has much more reason to want Ted's murderer caught."

"It would be perfect," I agreed. "But she could still be a suspect."

"I don't think so. I called Belinda a while ago and Mandy told me Karen was in New York. Staying at the Sherry-Netherland in Manhattan. She's there to visit the headquarters of Dobbins/McCray. She couldn't have killed Eddie."

I bit my lower lip. "How do you know she's really there?"

"I'll call her there and see if she answers."

He got right through to her. From Bosco's side of the conversation, I gathered she had already heard about Eddie.

"I know it's just terrible, Karen," said Bosco. "Listen, I hope you can get a plane out for the funeral. You know, if that rainstorm gets any worse, it's going to be tough taking off. I just heard on the TV that New York is getting soaked."

I stared at Bosco. Was he having a high-definition hallucination?

He knew what I was thinking, and wiggled his eyebrows at me. "In the high 60s? And clear? Sorry, my mistake; well, I guess that means you will be able to get back here with no problem." Bosco gave me a smug smile. "Yeah, I'm sure you want to get here as soon as possible...I know, I know...Listen, Karen, there's something I want you to think over. You know how we were investigating Ted's death for Eddie? We made pretty good headway. In fact, we think that's why Eddie was killed. But I know you thought the world of Ted. We were wondering if you would consider hiring us. We're so close to a solution here."

Karen's reply took several minutes, while I squirmed.

"Okay, yeah, well, just think about it. That's all I'm asking. See you at the funeral, I guess."

"What did she say? And what was all that about a rainstorm?" I demanded.

"The rainstorm was all about confirming she is definitely in New York."

"You were just talking to her at the Sherry-Netherland in Manhattan!"

"Yeah, and how hard is it to transfer a phone call? But if she was really here in LA and I had said that about a rainstorm, she wouldn't have corrected me so quickly. She would have hesitated. Trust me, she was in New York, looking out her window at Central Park."

I had to take back all the unkind things I had been thinking about Bosco. He was pretty devious. "What did she say about hiring us?"

He patted me on the shoulder. "She's going to think about it. Don't worry, Fifi, if she doesn't hire us, I'll think of some other way for you to earn money."

Our touching sibling moment was broken by a booming knock at the door. I heard the firm voice of authority: "Ms. Cutter. Los Angeles Police. We'd like to speak with you."

Chapter 29

It took me one second to realize that some bright cop had done some digging into Eddie's recent doings. I had mere seconds to hiss instructions into Bosco's ear.

"Don't say a goddam thing, you hear me? Not one goddam thing. You just sit there and smile and say you'd like to help them, but you've already told them everything you know, and you need to speak with your goddam lawyer, do you hear me?"

Bosco gaped. I grabbed his shirt. "Especially about Dina. If they ask you about her, don't say you don't remember her, don't say you haven't seen her in years, don't say anything. We don't know how much they know."

The door knocker crashed down again. I flinched. "If you lie, you'll make it worse, Bosco, do you understand?"

Pale as the Pillsbury Doughboy, Bosco nodded, and I swung the big front door open.

Two uniforms were on the porch. "May we come in?" the fatter one asked, not yet threatening, but already beginning to take a step forward.

"No," I said tersely, putting my five-foot-two-inch frame in his way, desperately trying to keep in mind Pop's advice: "Say nothin', ask for your lawyer, and then say nothin'." It was harder to do than you might think.

"No? Noooo? And why not?" The big man cocked his head to one side.

I forced myself to say nothin'.

"Maybe you want us to take you both down to the station?"

"If that's what you feel you need to do," I carefully replied, "Then we both want lawyers." Bosco made an inarticulate noise at my side.

"Oh, come on," the other cop, the good cop, piped up. "There's no need for that. We just want to talk to you. That's all. If you got nothing to hide, you shouldn't be afraid to talk. Right? You said Eddie Waller was your friend. You want to help find out who killed your friend, don't you?"

I stared at him, willing my lips not to tremble, trying to remember if I had lied and said Eddie was my friend. I conjured up a vision of Pop, laughing, telling us all the tricks the police used, and how they nearly always worked. Nearly always.

"We'd like to help you, but we gave a complete statement, and we have nothing to add."

It took another fourteen minutes, but in the end they loaded us both up in the two-tone and hauled us over to West LA Station, where they split us up as soon as we got in the front door. I only had time for one last brief warning glare at Bosco.

I was placed in an interview room, painted pea green and no more than six feet by eight feet. A woman cop came in, took my purse and watch and gave me a receipt. She had no right to do that. I knew it, and she knew it, and she knew I knew she knew it.

I glanced up at the tiny window, high above my head. It had bars. As if anyone could reach it. As if anyone could fit through it if they did reach it. No, it was just there to give you a taste of the future.

Three orange plastic chairs were lined up against the far wall, but Officer Fat and Officer Good Cop didn't sit down. I did, though. I didn't think I could keep it up if I had to stand.

The first hour—it had to be at least an hour—was wheedling of the it'll-go-a-lot-easier-on-you-if-you-just-tell-us-what-really-happened variety, including the gut-wrencher: "Some strange shit's been happening at your house, Ms. Cutter wouldn't you say? And a lot of people you know are dead."

"Not a lot. Just two. And I didn't really know Ted Heffernan."

"But you knew Eddie Waller didn't you? You did some business with him, didn't you? We know he owed you a lot of money, Ms. Cutter. Person could get really irritated at somebody who owes them a lot of money."

The fat one dangled a piece of paper before my face. I set my jaw rigidly as I recognized it as a copy of the invoice I had given Eddie, and read my comment, scrawled in red marker: "Pay me or die."

A light sheen broke out on my forehead, and both of them smiled, but all I said was, "I want a lawyer, and I cannot afford one, so one has to be provided to me at no charge."

They ignored me. Like Pop said they would.

"Doesn't say here what work you were doing for Mr. Waller. What do you think this young lady was doing for Mr. Waller, Dan?" Fat commented.

"I don't know, Kirby, but if it was something on the up and up, I'm sure Fifi would tell us, wouldn't you, Fifi? Funny thing is, some of the folks down at Obermeyer & Schlefly seem to think you and your brother are grief counselors. See, the reason that's funny is because our information has you as a licensed insurance adjustor. That's a license issued by the State of California, isn't it? What do you think a felony arrest would do to your license?"

I finally put my face in my hands and refused to look up. Officer Good Cop left the room, as Fat Kirby circled and bellowed and got way too close to me, without quite touching me.

"Look at me," he commanded. The heat in the room had

been turned up, I noticed, literally as well as figuratively. "What are you, a coward? Ya scared?"

Being called a coward stung, but I let it go. They don't hand out Purple Hearts in police stations anyway.

After that, they left me alone for about an hour. I couldn't tell the exact time, though I kept glancing at my wrist where my watch used to be. I couldn't seem to help it. When I calculated maybe fifty-five minutes, the door opened again. I put my hands over my face again, but sneaked a peek. It was Fat with a grey-haired guy in a baggy brown suit and an intelligent, horsy face.

"Ms. Cutter, I'm Detective Sweet." He had a nice voice, deep but mellow. "That's good, Kirby, you can go. Ms. Cutter and I have something very serious to talk about here."

Detective Sweet pulled up one of the other chairs and sat directly across from me. I looked wearily over at him. I felt like I'd walked across Death Valley at noon in July. He read my mind. He asked me if I would like a bottle of water, and he held one up. It glistened.

"It's cold," he coaxed.

I almost took it.

Detective Sweet smiled. "I think I can help you out here," he said, his voice low and kind. "We pretty much have it all figured out now." He gave an apologetic little shoulder twitch. "Your brother isn't made of the same strong stuff you are, Ms. Cutter."

I felt my stomach churn. Oh Bosco, you stupid turd brain. What have you said?

Detective Sweet gave a chuckle. "He tried to bamboozle us, yes he did. He's quite the story teller, he is. But I think he finally realized he had to come clean. For his own sake."

I waited.

"He says that your job with Eddie Waller, well, how should I put it? I guess you knew it wasn't legal, didn't you? He's pretty much putting this at your door, honey." Detective Sweet paused again. "I'm really sorry. I know that must hurt."

Forced out of my silence, I croaked, "But you didn't get him his lawyer. You can't use anything he said."

"Can't use it against him, that's true, Fifi." The gentle face became pained. "But we could use it against you. From what he says, I don't think Bosco did anything really wrong. It sounds like maybe he got caught up in something you and Eddie Waller were involved in. Wrong place, wrong time. But maybe he didn't tell us true, Fifi. Maybe you can straighten it out for us?"

I studied my clenched hands and tried to concentrate. I didn't really think I had committed a felony. Maybe a misdemeanor. Obviously I didn't kill anyone, but I know how cops think. They have two people in custody, and if it isn't one, it's the other.

I chewed the inside of my cheek like a fox gnawing his foot off to get out of a trap. Officer Dan was right. If I got convicted of something, my adjustor's license could be gone. I would be unemployed. I would certainly lose the house then.

This could all be the start of my own personal Martha Stewart nightmare. Maybe I should just tell the truth.

Except they hadn't mentioned Dina Mraz. Like they hadn't put that together yet. But they would. Soon. There was that note. I signed it "Bosco." They would focus on him.

Unless I confessed. I didn't want to confess. I wanted to tell them that Bosco was the one who went inside the house. That's cowardly and disloyal, I told myself. I don't want to be cowardly and disloyal.

Then again, who knows what Bosco would say? Maybe *he* would be cowardly and disloyal? Maybe it would be smart to get my version in first.

I opened my mouth to do just that, except I didn't realize what I was going to say until I had already said it. "Detective Sweet, you can arrest me and get me a lawyer, or you can kiss my semi-black ass."

*   *   *

Bosco and I were home in less than forty-five minutes, watch, purse and dignity restored.

"They were good," Bosco acknowledged, as he yawned and headed for his room. "They turned up the heat, did you notice that? God, I drank so much water, and then I had to pee so bad, I thought we were in for a forty-day flood. Then the fat cop came in and tried to tell me you broke down and spilled your guts and blamed it all on me." Bosco laughed. "Like I would fall for that."

Chapter 30

For the next several days I buried myself, with relief, back in the unexciting fender-bender business.

On Wednesday, we got in the truck to go to Eddie's funeral, which took place at the McMurdoch Funeral Home Chapel, a one-story fake-brick structure with two columns on either side of the central front door, conveniently located between a Chevron station and a Yoshinoya Beef Bowl. So if you needed beef noodles or gas while saying goodbye, you were taken care of.

When we walked in, we saw Lydia sitting next to Eddie Jr, who stared at me. It was unnerving 'cause he looked so much like his dad. On the other side of Lydia sat a woman in a red sweater, too tight and too synthetic, and a man in a tan double-stitched shirt and brown pants, with a bit of stretch in the fabric and elastic in the waistband. She looked like she could have been going to a bar and he looked like he could have been going bowling.

But at least they were there, which is more than you could say for everybody else in the world.

"Impressive wreath," I murmured to Bosco, indicating a purple and yellow horseshoe from Obermeyer & Schlefly. "But you would think an appearance could be made by his secretary, at least. Somebody who worked with him. I know he wasn't well liked, but it isn't as if they would have to talk to him."

The man standing at the front near the casket looked at his watch. Since he wasn't a minister, I suppose you could just call him a master of ceremonies. That didn't seem quite right, either. Bosco and I went up to the front and greeted Lydia.

"So sorry," Bosco said. Lydia gave a slight head tilt that could be interpreted as either "God's will be done" or "Hey, what are ya gonna do?" She motioned toward Eddie Jr. and told him to "say hello to Mr. Dorff and Ms. Cutter," but he just kept staring at me.

An older, pinch-faced woman I took to be Lydia's mother sat next to Eddie Jr. She carried an air of grim satisfaction, like it had all come to a bad end, just as she had predicted.

I jumped when the doors banged open to admit Karen, Belinda, Leah and Keith. I wondered if anyone else would notice that all four of them were dressed for a regular day at work, which meant that attending had clearly been an afterthought. No doubt when everyone had gotten to the office and realized that no one else had planned to go, these guys volunteered. Four people with heart.

Then I saw the way Keith was looking at Belinda and revised my opinion, three people with heart, one person with an entirely different organ.

Belinda stared at us, no doubt marveling at our dedication to the task of grief counseling the flock of Obermeyer & Schlefly.

The master of ceremonies guy sorted out his notes and commenced. All about how Eddie had so much yet to give, husband and father, sands of time, comfort of family and friends, strength in adversity. Considering that he was forced to be completely non-specific as to religion or any outstanding virtues Eddie actually possessed, he didn't do too bad of a job.

After it was over, Lydia stood right at the doorway, where you couldn't slip by her, and invited us all back to the house. Of course we all went. There were too few of us not to.

Eddie and Lydia's tiny tract house looked even shabbier by day than it had the night of the office snoop. The start of this whole thing, I reflected. The beige paint was sun-faded, not quite peeling.

We were met at the door by the woman in the red sweater, a neighbor named Molly who was, clearly, Taking Charge.

The inside of the house was as bad as the outside. Not call-social-services-and-take-the-children-away bad, just Lydia's apparent awareness that she had no taste and had compensated by making everything as bland as possible. Except not white, because white would show the dirt. Which, in this household, would be quite a show.

A Honey Baked spiral-cut ham and a party platter from the local grocery store were plopped down on the dining room table. A bouquet of dark red rosebuds in a cut-crystal vase sat on the mantle, perspiring on the rosewood veneer. The vase was Waterford and rather beautiful. It probably hadn't been used since Eddie and Lydia had gotten it as a wedding present from some relative who didn't know them very well.

Bosco circled, scheming how to carry away extra ham slices without ruining his suit. I hoped he wouldn't be so distracted by free food that he would forget to talk to Karen. This was like the ideal opportunity to get her to hire us, right here at the funeral.

There was an assortment of photographs of Eddie on the table. I pretended to look at them, but really I was letting my eyes drift over them without focusing. Then I got caught by one picture which showed Eddie, smiling into the camera. He was standing in front of a Christmas tree, holding his new fishing rod. Eddie had no idea that this was his last Christmas.

I felt clammy. Okay, it would be equally awful if he *had* known it was his last Christmas. I turned back to the food.

I took a mouthful of broccoli and dip, looked up and caught Eddie Jr., sitting alone on the faded plaid couch in the living room, still staring at me. He looked like he wanted to say something. I walked over.

"Can I help you?" I asked.

He jerked his shoulders. Something was going on.

"Can I sit down?" I gestured with my plate at the space beside him.

"You're the one who was working for my dad."

"Yeah. How did you know?" I took a deep breath and started choking on a little piece of broccoli.

He waited until I had finished coughing.

"Did you know what I was doing for him?"

"Yeah," Eddie Jr.s' voice was so low I could hardly hear him.

"Really? Did he talk about it a lot, or what?"

I sat down and the boy flicked a glance my way.

"What's the deal?" I tried to look friendly, but it's hard to do with my eyebrows and I think I ended up just looking surprised. It seemed to work, though. Eddie Jr. relaxed.

"I was helping him. My dad, I mean."

"You were?" Hope rose up. "Well, that's great Eddie. I can tell your dad must have had a lot of confidence in you." I leaned in. "Listen, Eddie, did your dad tell you what he was bringing me that night?"

Hope was dashed. Eddie Jr. shook his head. "But I know that he was trying to prove that Mr. Schlefly and Mr. Obermeyer killed Mr. Heffernan."

That didn't tell me anything new. I tried hard to keep my patience.

"So what is it, Eddie? What do you want from me?"

"I want to know if they killed my dad, " he blurted out.

"Oh. Well, I don't know. I mean, I don't really know that they killed Mr. Heffernan. There were other people…"

Eddie angrily wiped his nose on the sleeve of his bright blue polyester jacket. "My dad said they did it."

Obviously, for Eddie Jr., this was good enough.

"Okay, I hear you, I hear you. But what did he actually tell you? C'mon Eddie, maybe you'll help us prove it."

Eddie Jr. considered. "He told me you went to that sex place, and how they bashed your window in." He darted a quick look from under his stringy bangs. "Were you scared?"

"No," I lied. "What else?" When he hesitated, I added. "Eddie, your dad would want you to tell me."

"He told me that the guy at the sex place did it because he was mad you lied to him."

"I don't lie," I lied again. "And if your dad knew that, why didn't he tell me?"

"Because he said if you knew the sex guy had your windshield bashed in, you would stop thinking Mr. Schlefly and Mr. Obermeyer killed Mr. Heffernan. He knew they did."

"Okay, fine. But how did he know the sex guy had my windshield bashed in?"

"The homeless people told us. They said a lot of people get beat up around there. They have a guy who just does stuff like that for them."

"Wait a minute, you said 'told us'? You mean you and your dad? You talked to homeless people?"

Eddie Jr. fidgeted. "Uh, yeah."

"You went out there?"

His lack of response was a neon sign.

"You went out there and brought them back to my house, didn't you?"

Eddie Jr.'s face went so white that the flesh-colored acne medication on his cheeks and chin stood out like spots on a piebald pony.

"You went out there, you brought them back to my house and gave them the rat, didn't you?" Bosco looked over from across the room and frowned. I forced my voice down to a loud whisper. "Why did you do that, Eddie, Jr.?"

Eddie squirmed. "To help my dad. I wanted to help my dad. He said if you thought the bad guys were trying to get you, you'd want to get them back. Except my dad was really mad when he found out what I did. He said he didn't need my help."

Eddie embarrassed both of us by breaking out a sob. A few people looked over sympathetically. It was a good thing we were at a funeral.

"How was I supposed to 'get' the bad guys, Eddie Jr.?"

"I don't know. I didn't know what you looked like. I thought you'd be bigger for one thing. With muscles. You know, like Xena. Or at least carry a gun." I gripped his upper arm, and squeezed. "Please don't tell," he whimpered. "I took the rat, from my biology class. If they knew they might not let me graduate."

"Might not let you graduate? I might not let you live, you bratty, booger-eating moron. Why in the name of God would you even think your dad would want somebody to put a dead rat in my kitchen?"

"Because he told me to write the letter."

"What letter?"

"The letter that would prove Mr. Heffernan was murdered by those old farts. The one that told you to stop investigating. That always works in books. If you warn the hero to stop, then he doesn't stop. He gets, like, more determined. Plus the letter had a really good clue in it that would put you on the right track."

I thought for a minute. "'Bottom line?' Like Mr. Schlefly always says? I assume your dad dictated the wording?"

"Yeah, he wanted to make it really scary and mean."

"And you thought you would do something even scarier?"

"I did it to help my dad," he repeated. "To get you mad."

I crossed my arms and fumed. I was mad alright. "How did you get the homeless people to come with you? How do you even have a car? You're like fourteen."

"I'm seventeen!" Eddie Jr. squeaked. "And my dad gave me his old car, you know, when he bought the Beamer."

Right, Eddie had given his old car to Eddie Jr. I knew that.

"And the second break-in attempt?"

"I didn't tell them to do that, it was just that I sort of forgot to pick them up again, you know."

"You forgot?"

Eddie Jr. squirmed. "They smelled so bad, I didn't want them in the car any more. Anyway, they're homeless. What difference does it make where they don't have a home?"

I stared at him, totally stymied. If I smacked Eddie Jr. the way he deserved to be smacked, the cops would certainly come. I couldn't afford any more contact with the cops right now, especially at the funeral of the guy they think maybe I killed.

The unappetizing little puke snurfled out "I'm really, really sorry." I swallowed bile and grudgingly accepted his apology. If there's one thing I know, it's when I'm beat.

Chapter 31

I disentangled Bosco from Belinda, much to Keith Gursky's relief, and pulled him aside. "You won't believe what I'm about to tell you," I said. "We should get out of here. Did you get a chance to talk to Karen?"

"Just briefly. She said to meet her back at her office to talk about it."

"What, now? It's nearly four o'clock. Do you actually like sitting in freeway traffic, Bosco? I mean, is it fun for you?"

"It won't be that bad, Fifi."

I argued some more. Bosco won.

In the truck on the way over, with traffic every bit as horrible as I had expected, I told Bosco that there was no way in hell Karen was going to hire us. "She's too smart."

"It has nothing to do with being smart. Ted was her mentor. And she seems like she's going to stay at Obermeyer & Schlefly so she would want this cleared up."

"I hope you're right. But what's she going to do if it does turn out to be Obermeyer or Schlefly, after all? From what Eddie Jr. said, Eddie really was convinced about it. I mean, they could have killed Eddie if he was getting close."

"Hey, as long as Karen doesn't turn out to be the killer."

"Nah, you proved her alibi for Eddie's shooting. Besides, I think she really is one of the good guys. I mean,

I know she's the approximate size of a mini-mall, but she's actually intelligent, and her kindness appears to be genuine."

"One thing still bothers me, Fifi. We have established that Schlefly wasn't at the office on Friday night. Right?"

I agreed. After all, the whole point of the birthday banner charade was for the murderer to establish an alibi for Friday night. And Schlefly did establish an alibi.

"Then how do we explain why his car was there? Remember the parking printout? It still showed his car going in and out. I mean, even if that's not when the murder happened it's still weird."

I had no answer.

We were shown to Karen's office, and it took fifty-two minutes to explain everything. Karen was mostly interested in the details of the premium-financing scheme, naturally.

"So you see, Karen, we've made some very significant progress," Bosco stated.

"Except you spent most of the time checking alibis for the wrong night."

"But it was important to do that. Now we know that the suspects are those people who have an alibi for that night."

"That's true. And you did so some good work. Except we don't know what it was Eddie was bringing you that night. The night he was killed."

"I think I do know," I announced.

"What?" Karen asked.

"The sign-in book. Remember how it was stolen? The murderer must have signed in on Saturday. Employees have to sign in on weekends. The book was evidence."

"But how did Eddie get it?" Karen asked.

"There's no way to tell now. Out of somebody's office, I guess. You know, Eddie had keys to all the offices?"

Karen slammed her hand down on the desk. "You mean he came into our offices when we were out? My office?

He had no right..." She made a visible effort to compose herself. "Okay, okay. He's dead. Gotta be nice. But what a jerk he was."

Bosco started in again on his sales pitch, to get Karen to hire us. With a sinking heart, I saw she wasn't convinced. A sort of fixedness to her smile. Finally, she confirmed my fears. "You are right. I do owe it to Ted to take this further. And you guys did so some really good work, like I said. But I think it's better to hire a pro. Really, I do. I've done a lot of research."

She would, I thought.

"And I've narrowed it down to two firms."

"Why start over? We already know the players, there's no learning curve," I pointed out.

"All great arguments. On the other hand, there's so much to be said for fresh eyes. I'll tell you what I will do though. For the work you've already done." She whipped out a checkbook, wrote a check and handed it to me. A thousand dollars. I stared.

"Wow, that's really generous of you, Karen. We appreciate it." I put it in my purse.

Bosco would have argued further but I knew it was time to move on.

*   *   *

The next day I had to take a statement from a witness to a four-car pileup in Brentwood. Guy named Earl Ettinger was looking out his third floor window, and allegedly saw it all. Bosco volunteered to come with me, hoping no doubt that we'd stop off at some charming sidewalk café for lunch. I wondered why he was still living in my house.

The little apartment complex didn't have any parking, and the streets were packed. I cruised back onto the main drag, circling in increasing frustration, trying to find a parking space.

I finally found a semi-legal spot about four blocks away,

in front of a very upscale laundry—make that an upscale French laundry, I guess, for dainty things so precious you wouldn't trust them to the maid. The parking was for thirty minutes only, and only if you had, in fact, a soiled dainty thing good enough for French cleaning.

On our way back to Ettinger's place, we walked past a restaurant featuring Tibetan-Swiss fusion cuisine; an Italian shoe store window full of strappy, glittery, impossibly steep-heeled slides at breathtaking prices (apparently catering to the billionaire stripper demographic); and an "Emporium" selling items so high-end that not the smallest clue as to what those items might be was revealed to the mere passerby.

Earl was pleasant, quite clear in his recitation, and would have been a great witness if he hadn't been home from work because he was recovering from laser eye surgery. Nonetheless, I recorded his statement right there with my portable recorder. The whole thing took less than seventeen minutes, so I was very pleased as we walked back to the truck.

I glanced at my watch to see if we were in parking ticket danger; we had six minutes. Not really enough time to stand in line and acquire the rights to a mocha latte, but I gazed longingly at the Coffee Connection as we passed. I consoled myself that it would cost me ten bucks to get out of there for both me and Bosco.

Parking ticket reminded me of parking card.

A parking card is just a parking card. If you keep saying parking card over and over, it starts to sound funny. Anyone can have a parking card. In fact, it wasn't necessarily a question of having Schlefly's whole car. Anyone can have anyone's parking card.

Dolly Schlefly. Who would have better access to her husband's parking card? But why kill *Ted* if she was jealous of Angela and Rob? I shook myself. You don't care any more.

An Islamic woman in a white scarf and Reeboks pushing a baby carriage powered past us on the left, curbside. We approached the truck.

I can't honestly say that I felt a premonition, the world was ordinary and sunny, and I wanted a latte. I grabbed Bosco by the arm and started to turn back toward the Coffee Connection. That's the moment it happened.

The blast was so loud it was like silence. I was slammed to the pavement. I saw, as if in a series of still frames, the Islamic woman smashing into a mail box, the baby carriage flying high in the air, a man in a black suit engulfed in debris, sinking to his knees, the window of the French laundry shattering and the remains of Truck L'Orange catching fire, in a desultory, anticlimactic way.

Chapter 32

I pulled myself to my feet. All I could hear was the ringing in my head. Pale terrified faces floated around me. I dashed wildly into the street, frantically trying to locate the baby carriage. The eddy of screaming people swirled around, blocking, then revealing, vignettes of fear.

I was pushed north and then east to the other side of the street, trying to stand on tiptoe and making little jumps to see over the heads of the idiots who surrounded me. Idiots who weren't helping, who were just moving, inexorably but pointlessly, like the tide.

I broke free after what seemed like an eternity but was probably only thirty seconds. I realized with a sharp gasp that I had lost track of time.

But at least I was now unencumbered by the horrible flesh of other, taller people on all sides of me. I swung around, keeping my elbows up. I spotted the carriage, some thirteen feet away. Sickeningly, it was upside down against the curb.

I rushed over, unable to breathe as I lifted up the tangled mass of scorched dark canvas, twisted pieces of thin metal poking out at random angles. For a fraction of a second, I thought I saw the tiny limp body. But it was just a momentary mirage. There was nothing. Nothing.

I whipped around in new horror, surveying the street to see where the infant had landed. I climbed onto a low wall surrounding a parking lot (why hadn't I noticed that when I was looking for a place to park?).

My lungs hurt, I still hadn't been able to breathe, I couldn't hear and I couldn't see anything but the tops of heads. Then, back across the street in the glistening debris of the shattered window, I saw a man help the mother up, clumsily try to replace her headscarf and then grasp her to him, a dark, black-bearded man. A man with a curly-haired toddler wailing on his shoulders.

Bosco rushed up. I saw his lips move, but I still couldn't hear. "It's all right," I thought he was saying. "It's all right."

I must have been staring. Bosco shouted louder. "The father had the baby. The baby wasn't in the carriage. The baby wasn't in the carriage." He pointed back across the street to the trio, now being escorted away by an assortment of good Samaritans mopping up a dramatic but not life-threatening amount of blood.

"She looks like she's going to be all right," he yelled, and I heard him.

"Shut up, you don't have to yell!"

Bosco looked like he was going to take offense and then gave me an affectionate noogie. "It's going to be okay, Fifi."

Further communication was cut off by the screeching arrival of an ambulance and two patrol cars. Instantly, loudspeakers were blaring, warning us away from the truck, away from the gas tank which could blow any moment. I could have told them there wasn't enough gas in the tank to do any more damage.

Two news vans swooped in and set up camp. Helicopters circled like vultures. An emergency first-aid station was set up in front of the Coffee Connection. A bruise had appeared on Bosco's chin (he tripped and fell trying to get out of the way of the fire hose), so I brought him over and we stood our turn in line.

Eventually, a smart-alecky kind of paramedic wiped

the wound with antiseptic, said there was no need to bandage it, and supplied the really helpful information that it would hurt for a few days. But the Coffee Connection was giving away free coffee drinks so I did eventually get my latte.

Refreshed, I strolled over to the crowd control officer. "Just so you know, that was my truck," I told him. He looked at me sharply, trying to decide if I was a nut ball.

"No, really," I took a sip of the latte. "It was my truck. License number 1NGA399."

"C'mere," he hollered over his shoulder to a young officer nervously hovering around the entrance to the branch bank on the corner, where the cops had set up temporary headquarters.

"Says she's the owner of the demolished vehicle. Take her to the detective." The young officer, Cambodian or Vietnamese, wrote my name and address in a notebook and gestured Bosco and me into the bank.

We waited a good forty minutes in the lobby, where officers and important plain-clothes lawmen swarmed. No one paid any attention to us until, of all people, Detective Sweet marched through the door. I shrank down in my chair as he conferred with the officer in charge, glaring at us out of the corner of his eye. Then he sat himself down on the loan officer's side of the desk and gestured us over.

"Let me do the talking," I said out of the corner of my mouth. As the purported victim of this crime, I realized that stonewalling was no longer a viable option. I steeled myself to tell them, within narrow parameters, what they absolutely had the right to know, to stop myself from blurting out anything that would lead to awkward questions, and to manfully resist any urge to prevaricate. A narrow tightrope over a deep, rock-strewn ravine.

Detective Sweet's eyes were like burning coals as Bosco and I perched uncomfortably in the two chairs on the customer side of the desk.

"I got the word that you were claiming ownership of the

truck that blew up here. Blowing up property in Brentwood is a very serious offense," he informed us. Needlessly. "No more bullshit."

"I'm not going to bullshit you, but it's hardly my fault my truck got vandalized," I protested, sounding more petulant than defiant.

"Vandalized? You call that vandalized? Vandalized is when somebody keys your new paint job. Vandalized is when somebody snaps the side view mirror off. When somebody blows your car up with a remote-controlled bomb, I think we're beyond vandalized."

Detective Sweet then let me know, in a few well-chosen words, that he had already come to the conclusion that the bombing was geo-politically motivated. Apparently, there was a Middle Eastern grocery store a few doors down from the laundry, and, after all, the woman most affected had been a rag head. Plus the license plate had been run and Detective Sweet learned to whom the truck really belonged. He knew that person wasn't me.

I forced myself to be calm. I thought of an ice-blue stream babbling over round rocks, down into a dark, deep pool and took a deep cleansing breath.

"Are you revising your original theory? You have now concluded that I am Muslim terrorist? On what evidence? Do I look Middle Eastern to you? Oh, no, no, don't tell me, you've concluded I am a black Muslim, right? And somehow I've gotten into some unspecified feud with my Arabic brothers, stole the truck, planted a bomb in the back seat, and detonated it next to the Middle Eastern grocery store. All to send a terrible message, the meaning of which could be known only to me and the poor bewildered owners of the grocery store, who are probably still hiding in the produce aisle, clutching kumquats, parlayzed with fear. Do I have that right?"

A look of chagrin passed over Detective Sweet's face. That was exactly what he had been thinking.

My confidence growing, I pointed out that if Detective Sweet had been even close to accurate in his deduction, I would be in Panorama City by now, on my way to parts unknown. I would hardly hang around to get my free latte. Much less would I admit to possession of the truck.

I also informed him, with some heat, that the truck was not parked in front of the Middle Eastern grocery store. It was parked in front of the French laundry.

Detective Sweet replied, in all seriousness, "It's very difficult to find parking around here."

"Look, I don't know how to make a bomb, even a small bomb. How would I know how to do that?"

"You can get instructions on how to build bombs off the Internet. This one was efficient, but not particularly elaborate," Detective Sweet countered.

"You can look on my computer! Go ahead, look!"

"You are giving us permission? To search your house, to search your computer?" Detective Sweet snapped his fingers at a uniformed officer who quickly left the room.

"No! I mean, yes, I mean," I looked helplessly at Bosco, my erstwhile confidence erased. Bosco looked back at me and said, "Tape recorder."

Detective Sweet stared at him, uncomprehendingly, but I got it.

"I'm an insurance adjustor, you already know that, right? I was just taking a statement from a witness down the street. Listen," I said, pulling out the portable tape recorder from my bag and setting it on the desk. I rewound the tape, and it started playing, first me recording the date and address of Earl Ettinger, and then the interview:

"Mr. Ettinger, were you a witness to an accident which occurred on..."

Detective Sweet listened through the mundane account of how one car stopped short to let a passenger out and the other car was going too fast and hit him from behind and the third car swerved to avoid the mess and hit the fourth car coming in the other direction. When we got to "That is the end of this interview," Detective Sweet switched off the machine.

"He's right down the street, you can check it out. Our being here today had nothing to do with the Middle Eastern grocery store."

Detective Sweet looked frustrated, like a race horse being forced to run the race backward. He dispatched another uniform to go talk to Ettinger, who was shortly going to wish he had closed his curtains and gone back to bed and had never run down to see if everybody was okay.

"And you can get in touch with Harold Krasner, and he will tell you that he lent the truck to me as a favor to my mother. Oh wait. No. You can't get in touch with Harold Krasner," I realized, "since the reason he lent the truck to my mother is that he is in…" I stopped myself before I said it, but Detective Sweet was way ahead of me.

"In Egypt," he said meaningfully.

Chapter 33

"He's there on business," I protested. "Look, I don't even know the guy. He's a friend of my mother's. She arranged for me to borrow the truck. She can tell you how to get hold of him."

"Why did you need to borrow a truck?" asked the detective.

"Because I'm poor," I snapped, before realizing that nothing, absolutely nothing, is more suspicious than a poor person on the west side. It was time to stop talking. "Oh God. Let me call my mother. Come on, you don't want to look like a major idiot on the evening news, do you?"

Detective Sweet jerked his head angrily at another uniformed officer, who handed me a phone. I punched in the number, my hand trembling a little. Of course, I didn't get my mother.

I got Delia, the housekeeper, who advised me that this was my mother's nail day, as of course I should know. It took some explaining and a lot of pleading and, finally, a command to turn on the television to verify I was telling the truth before Delia would give me the number of the nail salon.

I met with the same resistance from the salon. My mother, I was informed in singsong, broken English, was having her "long soak with moisturizer" and that this was "quiet time, relax time, not good time for telephone call from daughter."

In somewhat less singsong English, I convinced the nail diva to turn the phone over to my mother now.

With Detective Sweet's eyes fixed on me, I told my mother about the untimely demise of Truck L'Orange.

"What am I going to tell Harold?" she demanded.

"You could tell him that I'm okay."

"How am I going to explain this to Harold?" Mother demanded again.

"Yes, Bosco's fine, too." I gave a tight nod to Bosco who beamed. He is pathetic.

"Was it at least insured?"

"Not for this," I admitted between clenched teeth. "But Mother, I need you to put that aside for a moment."

"You mean you borrow a car and you don't have the courtesy to insure it?"

"I had liability coverage, mother, it was an old truck. Do you know what the premium is to add property damage coverage? More than the truck is worth. Even the insurance agent didn't have the stones to try and talk me into p.d. coverage."

I saw Detective Sweet's eyes narrow. Maybe he was starting to believe me.

"Look Mother, really, we have to discuss this at a later time. Right now, the police want to talk to you."

I held the phone out. "She wants to speak to you," I said brightly.

"This is...this is...Please madam...this is Detective Sweet...no, I need to speak to you...madam, we will need the car for evidence...no, I can't...look, I just need you to verify..."

It took fourteen highly enjoyable minutes before Detective Sweet could finally disconnect. He still wasn't completely convinced, but I was beginning to hope that we had thrown enough doubt into the mix that he wouldn't risk a premature, and ridiculously erroneous arrest in a case as high profile as a car bomb in Brentwood was likely to be.

The final straw came at 3:53, while we were waiting for the

officer who had been sent to get confirmation from Ettinger. A thin policewoman came in with a cell phone and handed it to Detective Sweet, saying "It's Joe, Vice."

Detective Sweet jovially addressed the caller as "Jojo" and then stared at me, his eyes getting bigger and bigger before he finally exploded, not as loud as the car bomb, but pretty loud. "You've got to be fucking kidding me! Your sister? Jesus H. Christ..."

Detective Sweet leaped out of his seat, whirled around and stomped over to the far side of the lobby. I could still hear him, though, since he continued to yell.

"You coulda have fucking told me that earlier, Jojo. What do you mean you didn't know? How could you not know? What do you mean, you aren't speaking to her?" A long period of silence and then Detective Sweet looked over at me over his shoulder and shook his head. He lowered his voice, and I could only catch a few words. "We all have someone...Yeah, she's a piece of work...I hear ya..." And then, "We don't have to do anything right now...Could you at least get her to tell me..."

He hung up with a heartfelt "If that ain't a pisser!" and stomped back over to the loan-officer's desk.

"I'm gonna let you go for now. But just because you got a brother on the force doesn't mean you can't be arrested. Do you hear me? We're gonna keep investigating, and if I find out you've lied to me in any teeny tiny particular, I will have your ass in a sling." He leaned over and put his face close enough to mine that I could smell his caramel frappachino. "And if you're guilty, don't think your brother can do anything for you, you got me? I told him I wouldn't lock you up now, I didn't say anything about later, understand?"

"Um, yeah, but somebody's gonna have to drive us home," I reminded him in a small voice, any trace of bravado spent.

*   *   *

The tragedy of not having a car didn't really sink in until the next day. There was no use asking the Mutual Mother for help. I was sure she felt she had done all she needed to do by calling in my brother—"Jojo" to his friends—and twisting his arm to come to the rescue. I thought about calling Lloyd, because sometimes he could be guilted. But not when it was me against Mother.

I worked on reports (a series of food-poisoning cases allegedly owing to the careless refrigeration practices of a local purveyor of pork burritos—unpleasant but no lasting effects) until Bosco made his noontime appearance. He was smirking.

"Got the car situation covered," he announced. "You just have to get us to Century City."

"Century City? Where the car dispensers are?"

"No," he said heading for the kitchen. "Where a perfectly good silver BMW is waiting for us."

Chapter 34

"A Beamer? Get out of here," I muttered. Then the description clicked. "Eddie's car? We're going to drive Eddie's car? And what's Lydia gonna say about that?"

"Lydia is very grateful that we had the thoughtfulness to volunteer to sell the car for her and drive it to the used car dealership, which happens to be owned by the family of an old friend of mine from UCLA."

"What old friend? You didn't go to UCLA."

"I did not actually attend UCLA, no," Bosco admitted. "But UCLA sounds friendlier than USC."

"You didn't go to USC, either."

"Nor do I have a friend in the used car business, sis. Are you starting to catch on?" Bosco asked with mock patience. I hate mock patience.

"The car is still at the office, and the firm wants the parking space. We have to get it out by the end of today. He kept a spare set of keys in his desk at work to give to the oil change guy who sets up in the basement." Apparently our Eddie, so lax about his personal appearance, and perhaps not the cleanest guy in the world, had proper regard for car maintenance.

Then the only problem was getting to Century City. I tried calling VJ, but she was with a client or some goddam thing. So then I called D'Metree, who was rude, but agreed to drive us to Century City, when I reminded him that I was storing his Halloween mats. No reason to tell him there might not be as many of them as when we last met.

D'Metree picked us up several hours later and opted for surface streets, which was not a choice I understood at noon. During rush hour, maybe.

He let us off in front of the 4747 building. Mandy the transvestite receptionist was, as one would expect, delighted to see us, or at least delighted to see Bosco, and handed over the spare keys to Eddie's car.

I must admit Eddie's Beamer was by far the nicest thing he owned. I slid into the driver's seat. The new car smell was gone. In fact, it smelled a little funky. But it was still excellent.

We approached the exit, one line for visitors, one line for monthly. Monthly was the indicated line, but—ironically, in the circumstances—I couldn't find the parking card.

"Where's the fucking card? We need a parking card to get out of here." I fumbled around as we crept closer to the mechanical card reader, with cars lining up behind us leaving only inches to spare, thus making getting out of line awkward. No, not awkward. Impossible.

Bosco riffled though the change island between the seats and opened up the glove compartment, but he couldn't find the card.

I finally found it, in the driver's side door pocket, after we had pulled up to the front of the line and delayed the anxious, high-stress Century City types about twenty precious seconds, which caused a cacophony of honking that would have rendered me deaf if the bomb the day before hadn't temporarily blunted my hearing.

Bosco continued to rustle through the side pocket. He was driving me crazy. I yelled at him to stop it and sit still.

"Don't you smell that?" he replied.

I sniffed as I maneuvered my way out of the intestines of Century City. Bosco was right. The nauseating pine-smell emanating from the tree hanging from the rearview mirror masked an even nastier odor, and it wasn't just generalized kid smell. I waved my hand in acknowledgment and opened my window. Bosco released the latch on his seat, and it snapped it all the way back with a jerk.

He was rewarded. Sticking out from under the seat was a squashed McDonald's milkshake cup. The stench wafted up with new force. Bosco stared down between his feet in revulsion and made a little gagging sound. In that instant I emerged from parking hell and into the glare of the sun. I pulled over to the side of the road. Asshole behind me honked again. Screw him, we had a serious situation here.

Bosco opened the door. I avoided looking at him, as we briefly sparred to see who would pick it up and toss it out. I gagged a little, too. But it was no good, he won.

I held my breath, reached over and tossed the mess out of the car on the side of the road. I really hate littering, and this was even worse than ordinary littering because a McDonald's shake isn't biodegradable, but there was no choice.

Bosco was shrieking something about how I had gotten some on his pants, which wasn't true, and really not more than one little drip, and it was definitely not deliberate. Hey, I had no more interest in riding home with eau de old milk-shake then he did.

"You've ruined my pants, my favorite pants," Bosco yelped.

"I think there's some tissue under the seat," I said

"How could you know that?"

"Everybody has tissue under the seat. Especially if they have kids," I shrugged.

"Yeah, but that's used tissue," Bosco objected. "And if you think I'm going to put old snot on top of..." He couldn't even finish.

He reached under, anyway, and joyously pulled out a wad of unused napkins. As he was wiping the imaginary speck of off his cuff, he noticed something else under the seat and pulled out several sheets of Obermeyer & Schlefly bond and a small, cheap, vinyl-covered notebook.

Chapter 35

"Goddamn," Bosco breathed. "Goddamn."

"What? What?"

"Look at this," Bosco said.

"I can't look, I'm driving, you dumb shit. Tell me."

"These are copies of minutes from the October partner meeting. They were not only going to finally make Corazon a partner, they were going to make Gursky and Karen partners. Jesus! They were going to make Eddie a partner!" Bosco remarked, looking over the loose sheets first.

"Poignant," I remarked, as I headed towards the freeway, as any normal person would do at that hour of the day. The Beamer was fun to drive, especially after the truck, but the seats were kind of hard. Germans don't want you to get too comfortable.

"Hey, Bosco, Remember when Eddie first took us to Aldo's? And he said he had lots of keys to things? He also said that Obermeyer usually locked his office, because he had the firm's confidential information in there. They vote on partners in October but they don't announce who made partner until December."

"How do you know that?"

"I read it in the deposition transcripts."

"Why didn't you say something?"

"I didn't see how it was important then."

As we drove downtown, Bosco read from the thick

sheaf of bond, providing a running commentary on the firm's finances and operations as outlined in the attachments to the minutes. There was a proposed partnership agreement under the seat as well. It didn't sound like such a sweet deal to me. Schlefly and Obermeyer would still own most of the firm.

"And the firm was in bad shape," I remarked. "Signing on for partner meant signing on for debt. From what you just read, Obermeyer and Schlefly keep most of the profit, but everyone shares the debt equally. Pretty crappy deal, although," I snickered, "it does explain why they finally made Eddie a partner.

"Not so bad after Ted died," Bosco reminded me. "And here's the kicker, at the death or incapacity of any partner, the shares would be divided up among the remaining partners in accordance with their then-existing shares."

Bosco started on the notebook. The handwriting was small and ugly, Eddie's for sure, and there were pages of arithmetic. I didn't really give a rat's ass about it, but it kept Bosco quiet for a while, so I was grateful. Boy, the Beamer drove nice.

As we squeezed past downtown on the 10 transition to the 110, Bosco muttered "Hire pinhead and his weird sister." He looked at me. I concentrated on not rear-ending the RTD bus that was about to merge into my right-front bumper. We had three minutes of real stop and go down the slot as I edged over.

"I wonder what the definition of 'incapacity' is."

"What do you mean, what does it mean?" Bosco responded.

"I mean, is it defined in the partnership agreement?"

Bosco flipped though the pages. "Yep, incapacity means loss of broker's license or inability to substantially perform services as an insurance broker for a period of six consecutive months."

"Well, do you think a prison term for murder, or even

conspiracy to commit murder, would be longer than six months?" I asked.

"Shit! Do you think Eddie was setting O&S up?"

"It's possible."

"That's diabolical, Fifi. Two old men, they might have gone to prison for years for something they didn't do."

"Maybe Eddie didn't think it would go that far. But even just waiting for trial would be longer than six months. During which time their broker's licenses would be suspended. So it wouldn't even have to be a conviction. He'd get a hefty share of the firm. Explains his sudden spending spree."

"Even so. Their lives would be ruined. Could Eddie really do that to somebody?" Bosco was stunned.

"What if he really believed they were guilty. Eddie Jr. said his dad was convinced. Manufacturing evidence against someone you really think is guilty, I mean, it's still bad. But it's not puppy-torturing evil."

"You're saying that just because someone is framing you, that doesn't mean you're not guilty?"

"Exactly." I pulled into the driveway.

Bosco frowned and shook his head.

"Of course there is another alternative. That Eddie actually killed Ted and then blamed it on the old guys."

"You're insane, Fifi. Eddie didn't have a lot of social skills, but he wasn't a killer. I can't believe he would do that," Bosco said. "There are other suspects, you know."

"That's true. You get rid of Ted, and Eddie, and then shift the blame to Robert and Warren, there's a lot of firm to split up between Gursky, Karen and Corazon. A firm that used to be worse than worthless suddenly becomes worth, say, three million, and has a future."

"The other thing is, Fifi, if Eddie killed Ted, why did he try so hard to make it look like he was killed on Friday? That doesn't make any sense if he was pinning it on Schlefly and Obermeyer."

"That's a good point," I conceded. "Besides, if Eddie killed Ted, who killed Eddie?"

Chapter 36

Several days later, Bosco confronted me in the kitchen. "Are we going over to Mom's?"

"Why would we do that?" I replied as I scraped the last bit of coffee from the can into the filter.

"Um, you know," said Bosco, "'Cause it's Thanksgiving and all."

I snorted. What fantasy land did this geek inhabit? Bosco persisted.

"Fifi, really, you and Mom have to stop this feud. It's Thanksgiving." Bosco said "T-h-a-n-k-s-g-i-v-i-n-g" really slowly, like I wouldn't otherwise get it.

"I haven't had Thanksgiving with Mother for several years, Bo, and I really doubt having you along will increase our chances of an invitation."

"But Feef," Bosco gestured toward the refrigerator. "We don't have anything to eat."

I opened the refrigerator door. Two mummified oranges, a half full bottle of Thai garlic sauce, a frozen lasagne in the freezer. And a box of baking soda.

"And," he added, "You've just run out of coffee."

I hesitated, but I was hungry, too.

"Well, okay, but I'm not gonna call her; you call her," I said.

"Great!" Bosco bounced to the phone. He had to look up the number and mis-dialed at least twice, but finally got it right, and eventually convinced Delia to put Mother on. Bosco's side of the conversation didn't seem to go well at first.

"But I thought you expected us...No, of course, we didn't make any other plans...Where else would your son and daughter spend Thanksgiving?"

I sighed, but after a long period of silence on this end, I sensed a change in the direction:

"No, it would just be the two of us...It's catered? You catered Thanksgiving dinner?"

I shot the dimwit a warning look, and he quickly added, "What a great idea. Saves so much work...Oh, you know Fifi hardly eats anything...I'll make sure she's dressed nicely. Well, no...I doubt there's time for her to buy anything new, you know the stores probably aren't open now, but, really, I'll make sure she's wearing something nice."

Until, finally: "Around three then? Oh, right. Three sharp. Got it. See you then, Mom."

At 2:20 we hopped in the Beamer, crossed over to the Valley via the Hollywood Freeway to the Ventura and were there at 3:17. Bosco was presentable in his Armani, and I looked fabulous in vintage bronze satin, short, full skirt, fitted bodice and cap sleeves, peek-a-boo sling backs and faux Jackie pearls. I had French-twisted the hair, and calmed it down with Ultra Sheen.

Mother and Lloyd's new house was a pink brick, white-shuttered ranch, with a three-car garage and a low profile, modestly concealing from the street the fact that it was nearly 4,000 square feet.

Lloyd greeted us with cordial indifference and steered us through a long central hallway—dove-grey carpet, lighter grey walls and white trim—opening into the large living room, richly furnished in pale jade greens, with apricot and silver accents. A floor-to-ceiling window looked out over a Japanese garden.

Several people who didn't look like any relatives of mine were milling around. Lloyd dutifully made introductions,

I didn't catch all the names, but I already knew Lucy and Ralph Thornton. Ralph was Lloyd's sometime partner in various real estate ventures. And I recognized Valley Councilman Chip Bowers, although his perky wife Marcy and his sullen teenage daughter, Dawn, came as an ugly surprise.

There were two other couples. I couldn't possibly be expected to tell them apart. One of the couples had a kid about nine who looked like he could give Dawn a run for the money in the pouty, whiny, bratty race.

And then there was the guy with big ears. His wife had little ears. Otherwise, they matched pretty well.

"Herbert and Carolyn Dobbins. My stepchildren, Fifi and...er...Bosco."

I smiled a really fake smile and said to Big Ears, "Yes, I believe we met at Ted's memorial service. And nice to meet you," nodding to the little woman.

Mother zoomed over and carried them away before Bosco or I could say anything offensive. What was the deal with that guy? I wondered. But not too much.

The point of the day was to make sure we got enough to eat, and it was like falling into food heaven. I nibbled on some figs with warm Gorgonzola and goat cheese with mango chutney on toast points, while Bosco shoveled down huge quantities of prosciutto and melon, sashimi, and lobster in filo wrap.

Before we could ruin our appetites, Delia called us into the big feast. We all trooped into the dining room. Muted gold wallpaper and warm brown Persian carpets darkened the room and helped disguise the fact that it was as big as a cafeteria.

I stopped dead when I entered, and Bosco ran into my back. The long table was covered in several layers of ivory lace, graced with massively baroque candlesticks and peach roses. Mother gestured us toward a small folding table, covered in what had to be a poly blend tablecloth from Linens 'N Things. It was pushed up next to the sideboard against the wall, and it was set for four. A kid's table.

Bosco and I reluctantly sat down with Dawn and the boy as everyone else took their appointed places. I prayed nobody would say grace. Councilman Bowers had to do it, though; if he didn't, somebody might leak it to the press.

When we finally got to eat, Bosco devoured everything in sight and washed it down with chocolate milk, although he looked like he could use a drink. He was doing his best to talk to the boy, whose name, I was completely uninterested to learn, was Trevor. Bosco kept yammering on about sports or something. Trevor looked more like a chess player to me.

Kid caught my attention, though, just after we had been served the remnants of a very fine chestnut and Stilton cheese casserole, by mentioning "Uncle Herbie" and gesturing over to Mr. Dobbins.

"That guy your uncle?" I asked.

"Not my real uncle," said Trevor, as though only a moron wouldn't know that.

"What's he do?" I figured I didn't need to be subtle with this booger eater.

"Money man." Trevor rubbed his thumb and index finger together.

"Really? He invests?"

"Yeah, that's why he gets invited everywhere. Everyone wants him to invest. That's why he's my Uncle Herbie." Trevor smiled. "He put together a group to invest in this high-concept teen magazine. My Dad supplies the paper." Trevor waved airily, doing a very good imitation of an asshole.

I wondered what my mother wanted Herbert Dobbins to invest in. I eyed Trevor. Couldn't hurt. So I asked.

"That guy," said Trevor, pointing at Lloyd with his fork. Lloyd, vaguely aware that he was being pointed at, looked up for a moment and smiled benignly in our general direction.

"Lloyd? How can you invest in Lloyd?'

Trevor, now convinced I was a moron, said, "I thought he was your father?"

"My stepfather," I corrected. "I hardly know him."

"Well, you should know he wants to run for state senator," said Trevor, abandoning the fork and picking up his turkey leg.

"So that's what this is all about? A campaign contribution?" I was relieved to know that Mother's interest in Dobbins was completely unrelated to my ill-fated investigation.

"Politicians need Uncle Herbie. Here in the Valley, he can make or break you," said Trevor smugly, obviously parroting things his parents said. "He's for Christians."

Great, I thought, another constitutional scholar who thinks that freedom of religion means you get to choose between being Baptist or Methodist.

Trevor continued. "And for business. He's really for business."

"Screw him," muttered Dawn, startling me by vocalizing my very thought. I began to feel a bit more warmly toward the little misfit.

After the meal, Delia served coffee and pie in the living room. Lloyd politely sat down next to me in the plush armchair catty-corner to the sofa. He smiled an embarrassed "I have no idea what I can possibly talk to you about" kind of smile. I made it easy on him.

"What's this about running for office?"

He actually blushed. "Your mother's idea. You know."

I bobbed my head to show my sympathy. "She's going to get Dobbins to come up with the cash?" I asked, keeping my voice down, although I could see Dobbin and Chip Bowers strolling through the Japanese garden. Trevor's parents were itching to chase them down, I could tell.

"Well, I don't know. He didn't commit. But your mother is very persuasive." Again Lloyd looked uncomfortable.

"He's in publishing?"

Lloyd perked up, relieved he could talk business, and bored me for at least twelve minutes with all of the various holdings of Dobbins/McCray, which ones were up, which ones were down, how much Dobbins had made off this one, what his plans were for that one.

"I hear he's involved in some high-concept teen magazine now," I added, just for something to say when Lloyd finally paused for breath.

But he shook his head. "He put together the deal, but he didn't put in any of his own money. New magazines, that's too risky a venture." Lloyd glanced up to make sure no one could hear him. "And a good thing, I hear they are having major distribution problems. Probably going to fold."

I was sorry to hear that Trevor's parents might not get paid for supplying the paper. Maybe they would lose so much money they would have to send Trevor to public school. He could take the bus and make the acquaintance of Chaco and Lil' Pete and all rest of the Ripple Street Gang.

From across the room I saw people start the process of leave-taking. Mother gave a nearly imperceptible signal, and Delia carried out the cups. Dismissed, we rose, and said our thanks. As I started back down the long grey corridor, I saw Bosco out of the corner of my eye try to give Mother a hug. I wondered if he had managed to get at the Chablis after all.

Chapter 37

Around two on Friday, Bosco asked if I could take him to the Beverly Center. I tried to dissuade him—the biggest shopping day of the year, only a masochist would go to the Beverly Center.

"I'm not going to buy anything, don't worry," Bosco said. "I'm looking for a job. They hire extra people during the Christmas season, you know. I think I'll be able to catch a ride back."

Why did I believe a lame old lie like that? Bosco? Job? And what kind of job would he interview for at the Beverly Center? Matching black socks and red ties to gray suits for the colorblind businessman, at minimum wage?

Of course, if I had been thinking, I would have realized the grotesque improbability of Bosco standing in a dressing room with a load of rayon blend over his arm, gushing out, "This ensemble is superb and looks so good on you, in fact, it almost covers up that unsightly goiter on your neck!"

I thought of all that later. At the moment, I was distracted. The sky was dark and grey. I couldn't afford to repair the roof, but if the rains started, and the roof leaked, the hardwood floors would get ruined, which I also couldn't afford to repair, and what if the water got behind the walls and it got all rotten back there, and poisonous mold spores started to seep out and cause strange flu-like symptoms? I didn't have health insurance.

By the time I got back from dropping Bosco off, it was drizzling.

*   *   *

Time changes your perspective. For example, when Bosco had not returned by 7:30, I was happy I could have the lasagna I had defrosted for dinner all to myself. It was good, too.

But when he hadn't returned by 8:30, I was a little peeved. He should tell a person when he's going to be out for so long. Hadn't I explained that the last time he went missing?

When he hadn't returned by ten, I started to get concerned.

By 10:34 I was panicked.

I catalogued all of the possible places he could be. I called Karen, no answer.

I called Aunt Angela and got Chloe. Aunt Angela was out at some premier with some guy, Chloe told me, but the guy was definitely not Bosco.

I called Mother but hung up when she answered, then called back later, got Delia and learned that Bosco was certainly not there.

I even called D'Metree, got his wife Sharlene who told me that D'Metree was in the shower, and Bosco wasn't there.

I called Eddie Jr., but he was already in bed. As Lydia irritably noted, teenage boys need their sleep. I could have reminded her how nice we had been the night she called us with Eddie Sr. missing, and had gone out looking for him and all, but considering the way that had turned out—best not.

I looked for Belinda's number, but it wasn't in my book.

I went up to Bosco's room to find it. I felt bad about going through his drawers and reading his stuff and looking in his pockets. Which is where I found a crumpled envelope addressed to Belinda Barrett at an address in Toluca Lake, from The Tree People. She had flipped it over and written today's date, and "Trinidad Café, Beverly Center 3:00." With a little smiley heart face.

241

I went a little faint for a minute. He had to remember, under all that slutty exterior, that she was a suspect, right? A murder suspect. In fact, the more I thought about it, the number one suspect. Of course.

The whole staging of the Laguna thing, to give her an alibi for Friday. She could easily have set up some phony meeting for Ted that night. Ted would believe Belinda if she told him a hot prospect was coming to meet him, but was too busy running Microsoft, or taking over Disney, to come to the office during normal business hours. Ted would buy that.

And then, what? I thought hard, imagining the scene. Belinda would just pretend to be drunk, get back to the room before Karen did, call Ted and tell him that Big Shot couldn't make it. They would have to reschedule the meeting for Saturday.

And who had a better chance to mess with the birthday banner than Belinda? She was the one who put it up. She was the one, Eddie told us, who had tried to throw it away.

Was she smart enough to figure all this out? I remembered all the secretaries we had talked to in grief counseling. They all agreed Belinda did her job well. You can't do your job well if you aren't smart. See, I thought, just because a person has great big, world-class hooters, doesn't mean she's not smart.

And the parking cards? Belinda could have stolen Schlefly's card and switched it with Ted's. The parking register showed Schlefly going out at 4:30 PM and then back at around eight and then out again. That was Ted.

Not Obermeyer. Not Schlefly. Belinda. Because she was in it with Gursky, who was going to make partner this year and get his share of the key-man insurance.

And Bosco had walked right into the spider's web. I stared at the crumpled wad in my hand. I called Information, but Belinda wasn't listed. Single woman living alone, she'd be an idiot to be listed.

Of course, *I* was listed, I reflected. Maybe I shouldn't be?

Maybe it was dangerous? Think about that some other time, I ordered myself.

I called Keith Gursky's number. He was listed but he wasn't home.

I had to sit down. After ten minutes, I called the only person whose judgment I had any respect for.

"Veej? It's Feef. I need your help. I know it's late, but I've got a bad problem," I paused. "I think my brother may have been kidnapped, and they may kill him."

I heard a Grand Canyon-sized sigh. "Okay, you're going to have to explain this a little more slowly, Feef. First of all, what brother?"

"You remember, that brother I had? Ruined graduation? The white one? Lives in New York?"

"Right. Your mum's kid. New York." VJ paused. "You know, if he's in New York, I'm afraid my usefulness is going to be rather limited. What would be wrong with calling the police? That would be my standard advice in this sort of situation."

Great big sigh right back at her.

"He's not in New York, Veej. He's here in LA. He came out to visit. Actually, he came out for a funeral, but then he stayed."

"I've got that then. But I still haven't got why you don't call the police. After all," she said with heavy emphasis, "it is the white brother who's gone missing, right?"

That was a VJ joke. British humor is very easy to miss.

"He hasn't been gone that long. They won't help. I could explain why I think he is in danger, but they wouldn't believe me, and I'm not sure, but I think I might have to admit to something illegal to get them to believe me, and under the circumstances, well, that might make things really worse. And then if it turns out he isn't kidnapped, but is just, you know..."

"What, precisely, is it that I know?"

"I think he went to the apartment of a real skank," I admitted.

"But," said VJ, "for some reason, you think that, instead of enjoying the late-night favors of this skank, he has been kidnapped and is in some considerable danger of getting whacked? Have I got that right?"

"Not just for some reason, for a bunch of really good reasons. Listen, I don't have time to explain. But the skank may be poisoning him to death right now."

"She really is a skank then, isn't she?"

"Will you help me or not?" I demanded. "Just let me know. If I have to call someone else, I will."

"Oh, stop it. Who else could you call? Of course I'll help. But I have to be in court in San Bernardino tomorrow at 8:30 to argue some rather important motions, so let's make this snappy, shall we?"

Not willing to let VJ know the depth of my relief, I was very cold when I asked her to please meet me at the parking lot of Bionic Sushi in Toluca Lake.

I dressed warmly and went out the front door, turning on the front porch light and locking it behind me. Just as I started down the walk, I heard the phone ring.

I turned and fumbled to get the door open, dropped my keys and finally burst in just as the caller was starting to leave a message. "This is Detective Sweet. I'd like to speak to Bosco Dorff. This is about Dina Mraz."

Chapter 38

I started toward the phone, then stopped myself. If I didn't get over to Toluca Lake, this might all be moot. I fled out the door once more. They'd come after us, no doubt, but maybe not tonight.

The drizzle increased to steady rain, and by the time I got to the deserted parking lot of the Bionic Sushi, it was a monsoon.

Victoria drove up in a not-quite new but immaculately kept Volvo wagon.

"You'd better drive," I said. "I'll navigate." In case we did have to involve the police later, I figured it was just as well I wasn't driving what was essentially a stolen car, belonging to the guy I was supposed, under certain theories, to have killed.

"Address says Toluca Lake, but I'm guessing it's really North Hollywood." I squinted at the map book.

We wound briefly through a lovely neighborhood of huge homes, wrought-iron gates, fifteen-foot hedges, lights in the distance—you get the picture. Then we wound back to Cahuenga somehow and passed a Subaru dealership and a Korean BBQ. We made a few wrong turns, and it seemed like it took forever to find the right street.

As each minute ticked by, I thought that might be the minute that Belinda shoved something really sharp and bad into a vulnerable part of Bosco.

I didn't say it, but I was profoundly grateful to VJ. And not just for "being there." The point is to be there and do something.

VJ had good night vision, and a decent car. Her reflexes were quick, too, as she navigated through the hell of Angelenos driving hysterically in the rain. Southern California drivers, many of whom have learned to drive on the streets of Damascus, Hanoi or Mexico City, always go too fast in the rain, hoping to hurry home before they have an accident.

But sometimes, just to keep you guessing, they will unexpectedly slow down to a near stop, apparently not realizing that their brake lights went out weeks ago.

Eventually we turned onto Cypress Court (not Cypress Lane, or Cypress Terrace). Three-story apartment buildings of various eras, from shabby to merely depressing, lined both sides of the street.

"That's it!" we both said at the same time. One of the better buildings, maybe even post-Northridge Quake. The Navajo white stucco had only begun to crack, and the yellow and dark-green trim was mostly still attached.

The approach was defined for us in the dark and the mist by multi-colored begonias in raised concrete beds, illuminated by accent lights, leading to a central security door. It was difficult to see how to get in without buzzing someone. Victoria suggested we try a back door, but we immediately encountered high fences stretching from our building to the one next door on either side. Guess they'd thought of that.

We stood on the sidewalk and debated buzzing a number, any number. I was feeling more and more panicked and inclined to pound on the door until I woke everyone up and someone called the cops, but Victoria prevailed.

"Look," she said, "this woman doesn't know me. Let me talk to her."

VJ and I walked across the wet grass to the front door. She, of course, had thought to wear LL Bean overshoes.

I hadn't, and picked my way across, trying not to soak my Converse All-stars.

I caught up with her just as Belinda answered the buzzer. I heard Victoria say, "Yes, Ms. Barrett? My name is Victoria Smith and I'm looking for Bosco Dorff." She got no further when I heard Belinda let out a bellow of rage.

"That bastard!" she screeched.

"I beg your pardon?"

"That bastard!" shrieked Belinda again, apparently under the impression that this was sufficiently explanatory. And under normal circumstances I would have agreed.

Belinda yelled, "You come up here. RIGHT NOW," and then hung up.

The heavy glass door clicked. VJ grabbed at it and pulled it toward her.

"Now what?" I asked.

"Perhaps Bosco has foiled her little plan to eliminate him. And she thinks that all she has to do is command me to appear at her door and she can eliminate me instead," VJ reasoned. "I'm not really all that inclined to oblige."

"No, it isn't your job," I hung my head. "The worst thing your brother ever did was to TP the principal's house and blame you. It's better if I go up, anyway, then she'll know there are two of us."

"Do you have a gun?" VJ asked, without much hope. I didn't bother to answer and headed to the elevator, and punched in the second floor.

I found the apartment easily enough. It was a back unit, immediately to the right of the elevator. I knocked and the door flew open. Belinda stood there, her generous figure enveloped in a flowing lilac polyester ensemble. Maybe she didn't poison Bosco. Maybe she just scared him to death with her wardrobe.

She slammed both hands on her hips, and her eyes were definitely wild. It was rather comical to see her expression freeze and then change to bewilderment. Except I wasn't in a comical mood.

"But you're...his sister," she gasped. Then she slapped herself in the forehead. "Oh, of course, how stupid can I be? The old 'sister' routine." She slumped away from the door, and I hustled in.

"Hey, what are you saying? Of course I'm his sister."

The apartment was essentially a living room with a dining alcove off to the left separated from the kitchenette by hanging beads. A narrow hallway on the right lead off to what I presume was the single bedroom. The one window in the main room was off-center on the far wall; a grubby ecru drape covered what was, no doubt, a view of the side of the building next door.

Belinda shuffled over to an ugly overstuffed flower print sofa and sat down heavily. Since I don't have any furniture, maybe I shouldn't criticize other people's. But really.

A glass of something amber sat on the glass-topped coffee table.

Belinda picked it up and swallowed. "So, who is that woman downstairs?"

"A plain-clothes police officer," I answered. I figured it was illegal to impersonate a police officer, but it wasn't illegal to say that someone else is a police officer. Or maybe it was. In any event, the effect on Belinda was satisfactory. Her jaw dropped. Her eyes bulged. She spluttered.

"A police officer? Since when is being stood up a crime? Though," she said more thoughtfully, her eyes narrowing, "maybe it should be."

"OK. Uh, what are you talking about?" I asked glancing around the undersized living room filled with oversized furniture trying to see where Bosco might be. "Where's Bosco?"

She looked at me spitefully. "Excellent question. Where is Bosco? And where is Ted? And where is Billy Bonino? And where is Chris Horton? And where is Michael O'Reilly? And where is Bruce Lefsky?" Her voice rose higher and higher. I realized these must all be men she had killed. I edged back toward the door.

Chapter 39

"Yeah," she said, finally finishing the roll call, as she thrust herself between me and the door. "They're not here. That's where they are." She started to cry.

"So Bosco's not here?" I asked in a tiny voice.

"No," Belinda sniffed once last sniff, calmed down and suddenly sobered up, as though a tornado had touched down and whipped away again. "Bosco is not here. We had a great date, we did a little shopping, had a nice meal at a bistro near the center. He'd forgotten his card, so I had to pay, but he said he'd pay me back," she crossed her arms. "Then we came back here, and just when things got interesting, he got an 'emergency' telephone call on his cell phone and had to leave 'right away.' He borrowed my car, for God's sake."

"He borrowed your car? He could be anywhere!" I would have berated her for her stupendous bad judgment in lending Bosco her car, but she was so obviously well aware of it.

"What was I thinking? What is the matter with me? What am I doing wrong?"

I could have told her. I could have said you are drinking way too much, and you need to buy some clothes for this decade, and that figure, and besides, you're sleeping with way too many men, way too many of whom are married.

But I sensed the questions were rhetorical. Besides, the important part of what she had said required comment.

"Bosco doesn't have a cell phone."

Belinda looked up "He certainly does. Unless," she paused, "it wasn't even a real cell phone. I suppose that could happen. He could have a phony little cell phone that rings when he needs to make an emergency exit from ugly, desperate, older women." She was choking up again. I wasn't getting anywhere.

"Belinda, did you kill Ted?"

She blinked and sat down heavily. "No."

"Are you sure?" I asked gently.

"Yes, I am sure, you jerk! Why would I kill Ted? I liked Ted. Ted was fun. Ted, unlike other people, bought me nice presents." She stuck her left wrist out and waggled it about. The light caught a lower-end bracelet of semi-precious stones.

"But he wasn't going to marry you," I suggested. "Maybe that made you kind of mad?"

Belinda gave me a disgusted look. "If I killed all the men who didn't marry me, there would be bodies from here to Santa Fe."

Not betraying that this was, in fact, my precise fear, I realized that I was starting to kind of believe this woman. She was sincerely in self-disgust mode. Wouldn't a successful killer have an element of smugness? I sighed. "So, do you have the number of this cell phone?"

"No. Apparently I am not a worthy recipient of the cell phone number," she replied, dashing my hopes.

I sat down on the adjacent arm chair and tried to think. Now, right now, it was really important that I solve this mystery. But irrelevant thoughts kept intruding. How would Bosco get a cell phone? Would he really buy a cell phone when he didn't have the money for a TV? How much do cell phones cost? Don't they give them away free if you promise to sign up for some ridiculously onerous plan that consigned you to a life of overtime and double shifts?

I looked around, my efforts to think not at all aided by the washed-out pastels, shabby-chic slipcovers and cheaply framed Impressionist prints. An image of Ted relaxing here, with a drink in his hand, came to me, followed quickly by the answer to the cell phone puzzle.

We had cleaned out Ted's apartment together, hadn't we? Would Bosco really steal a cell phone? From a dead man? If he would steal a car from a dead man, why not a cell phone?

"Do you have Ted's cell phone number?" I asked.

Belinda looked at me bewildered, and more than a little frightened. "Ted?" she repeated nervously, glancing away and then back to me. "Uh, Fifi," she said in a shaky soothing tone, as if I was the dangerous lunatic who needed placating, "um, Ted can't come to the phone right now."

I closed my eyes. "Yes, Belinda, I am aware that Ted can't come to the phone. However, it's possible that Bosco may— never mind. Do you have the number that used to be Ted's cell phone number?"

Yes, she admitted, and gave it to me. I got up and found her phone, and asked her to give the number to me again, slowly, as I punched it in.

One ring, two rings, three rings. In the middle of the fourth ring someone picked up. Silence. I waited a half second, and before I could think of what to say, a voice whispered, "Hello?"

"Bosco?" I blurted out, realizing as soon as I said it that this wasn't Bosco. I was instantly disconnected, and it took me another half second after that to recognize the voice. I don't think I really recognized the voice, looking back. It was just everything adding up.

Chapter 40

"I gotta go," I gasped.

"Wait, where are you going?" Belinda jumped up and followed me to the door.

"Look, I don't really have time to explain, I gotta find Bosco, he's in trouble, bad trouble." I stopped when I realized I didn't know how to get where I wanted to go. "You gotta come, too."

"I don't want to."

"Don't argue with me!" I grabbed her by the arm and propelled her out the door. She threw on a clear plastic raincoat on the way out, encasing the purple lingerie.

"You look like a bunch of grapes in bubble wrap," I told her. "You have got to rethink your fashion identity."

Victoria was waiting in the car. I dragged Belinda over and opened the passenger side door.

"Are you the police officer?" Belinda asked, timidly.

"No," said Victoria at the same time I said, "Yes."

Victoria stared at me

"She's an officer of the court," I explained.

"Doesn't that just mean you're a lawyer?" Belinda needed a little shove from behind to get her in.

I climbed in the back, ignored her question and explained where we needed to go. As we turned left out of the parking area, I noticed a white Audi parked in front. It had a bumper sticker, "My Ex-wife's Other Car is a Broom."

Belinda directed us toward the Hollywood Freeway. We merged in, and there was that same white Audi behind us. Would a professional hit man have a white car with a stupid bumper sticker? I hoped not. Anyway, if I was right, we were on our way to the killer now.

The Audi stayed with us as we transitioned off the freeway to Laurel Canyon. We wound up the hill, and then down, going at a pretty fast clip in the dark. I started to feel queasy.

There is no good way to get to the west side from the Valley, I thought, as had millions and millions before me. I think we would have been better off taking the 101 to downtown to the 10. But maybe not.

We criss-crossed through Hollywood and finally pulled up in front of the nondescript, brand new, sixteen-unit complex on a quiet side street almost in Brentwood.

"Which one is it?" I asked Belinda.

"Second floor, left."

The building was a four-story rectangle of dark faux-brick facing over concrete, gated parking below.

I stared out at the downpour for a second. Then I bolted out of the car into the unrelenting sheet of water and slogged up to the entryway. The heavy glass door was locked and, although there was a phone, I had a feeling I wouldn't be buzzed up this time. I did get the condominium number of the party I was looking for, though, number Five. I peered into the hallway.

Number One was the first condo to my left, and number Four was the nearest condo to my right. That meant number Five was the front upstairs left-hand unit. My heart beat faster as I backed away into the torrent of water cascading down from the roof. I was soaked. Even my hair lay flat.

Each front unit had a concrete balcony, maybe three feet by seven, surrounded by a wooden rail. If I stood on top of the rail of the downstairs unit, I thought I could reach the concrete floor of number Five. If I had any athletic skill at all,

I could then pull myself up to the balcony of number Five. Of course, I had no athletic skill.

I turned and went back to the car. "VJ, you have to hoist me up," I told her.

"I really don't want to do that, Feef. I don't think it's an awfully good idea. I think we should call the police, if you really believe..."

A muffled crash interrupted VJ's lecture. Coming from number Five. As we looked up, a light went off in the window to the far left. Had to be the bedroom. I looked at VJ. She looked at me and got out of the car. I don't know why she was so annoyed. She had a raincoat.

We squished over the meager lawn to the left-hand downstairs balcony. VJ gave me a boost up onto the railing of number One, about five feet off the ground. I rapped gently on the window, trying to get someone's attention without alerting the killer upstairs. But no one was home.

I looked despairingly at Victoria, then hauled myself up onto the balcony rail. I teetered until I was standing up. Not great, but could be worse. Then I reached for the concrete floor of the balcony above. I could reach it, but I couldn't pull myself up. I'm not very strong.

Wordlessly, VJ swung herself up and landed on the balcony. She braced herself against the wall with two hands. I flailed around until my feet landed on her shoulders, which gave me more than enough height. The rain continued to pour down. I could only hope it was making the ground nice and soft for when I fell.

Slowly, awkwardly, standing on VJ's shoulders, I grabbed the bottom part of the rail support of the upstairs balcony. I tried holding on to the slab itself, but it was not only wet, it was slimy.

"No can do," I whispered to VJ, who made a sound like "Pphhh."

I jerked my foot out a few times but couldn't connect. VJ threatened to break my leg if I kicked her. One more time. With my last erg of energy, I got my right foot up.

Struggling, I managed to achieve a crouching position on the outside of the upstairs railing, panting and exhausted, my bottom hanging over the side. Jesus. I would have to start working out.

I took about forty seconds to catch my breath, then I carefully eased myself over the rail and onto the balcony proper. The lights were on in the living room, but the drapes were closed. I stayed to the left of the sliding glass window, against the wall, and tried to look into the darkened bedroom, where I thought the big thump had come from. The Levelor blinds were not quite closed. As I peered through the slats, I saw a shape on the floor. It could have been a big dog. But it was Bosco.

The door to the bedroom opened, and the light from the living room shone in. A much larger shape, silhouetted against the rectangle of yellow, bent over and grasped Bosco by the ankles, and started pulling him into the living room. He wasn't moving. I whimpered softly.

I shifted from leaning left to leaning right and tried to see around the edges of the drapes into the living room. The living room, unlike the bedroom, was brightly lit.

Goddam rain. I shook the water out of my eyes. The big lug pulling on Bosco's ankles backed into the room and looked up.

Turns out the drapes were more of a decorator touch than an effective screen. In less than a second the sliding door was jerked open, and I was yanked inside. Before I could even gurgle, Karen punched me—punched me!—right on the jaw.

Chapter 41

I crashed to the floor. The rain whipped into the room through the open door. Karen lumbered over and slammed it shut. She had some kind of a small gun trained on me.

I knew VJ and Belinda were right outside. VJ couldn't have seen what happened from the balcony below, but surely Belinda had been watching. She would call the cops.

Meanwhile, I gaped up at Karen, unable to think of anything to say. She eased the social tension by viciously kicking Bosco in the gut. Actually, I was glad. At least if she still wanted to hurt him, he wasn't dead.

Karen must have read my face. She seated herself in an upholstered chair facing the window and said, "Rohypnol."

"Rohypnol?" I squeaked. "The date-rape drug? You date-rape drugged my brother? That's humiliating!"

Karen stared at me. "I won't tell anyone if you won't."

"Right," I muttered and tried to stand. Karen ordered me back to a seated position. I scootched up closer to the couch so I could lean against it. I felt like I was going to puke. I hadn't been feeling great since we'd gone caroming over Laurel Canyon, and being punched didn't make me feel better. We sat there for maybe thirty seconds, just looking at each other. Karen obviously wished I wasn't there. I felt the same.

"Just to be clear," I said, breaking the silence. "You killed Ted?"

Karen nodded.

"But why, Karen? You said he was good to you."

Karen's eyes blazed. "Good to me! He was ripping off my clients. After all my hard work. He jeopardized everything."

"The premium-financing scheme?"

"Pocketing the premium money and then taking out loans to get the policies. Warren, of all people, found out. By peeking at Ted's files. He made copies of the loan documentation, all signed by Ted as broker of record. Pretty good work for a senile old fool. I think it was his last lucid moment."

"So Warren got the proof? And then what?"

Karen shifted in the seat. All the furniture in her apartment was sturdy, browns and greens, kind of depressing. But maybe that was just my mood.

"Then he showed it to me," she responded.

"Why? What did he want to do about it?" I asked. "Fire Ted?"

"No, we thought we could keep it hushed up. We were hoping we could convince Ted to pay off the finance companies—you know, put the money back. Of course, Warren would hold it over Ted's head for the rest of his life. Ted wouldn't be able to leave the firm then."

I snuck a peek over at Bosco to make sure he was still breathing.

"I confronted Ted that Wednesday. Gave him a copy of Warren's file, which is what I needed to get from his apartment, by the way—thanks a lot for butting in on that," Karen said with heavy sarcasm. "I told Chloe I would clean everything out for her."

"You got it anyway. At the Taco Bell," I replied.

"Yeah, well you made it a lot harder," Karen grumped.

"What did Ted say when you confronted him?"

"He said he just needed the money short term. He was

so stupid. He had put all this money into some dumb new teen magazine. 'Sex sells,' he tells me. Oh God. He mortgaged everything, his house, his boat, his car. He laid out all his cash. He thought the magazine would take off, he could sell out, and pay everything back. He thought he could be a big player."

New teen magazine. I had recently heard about a new teen magazine.

"But the magazine didn't take off," Karen continued. "A lot of stores were scared off from even selling it by some over-zealous vice cop who made closing it down his mission in life. It was supposed to be for teens, but this vice cop made sure the only place it could be sold was adult book shops. Without circulation, they couldn't get advertising. They couldn't even cover the cost of the second printing. Ted either came up with an extra $270,000 or the whole thing would fold, and he would be out all that money and still have to pay back the loans."

"Well, that's real sad, Karen. Say the clients found out, they wouldn't kill Ted. They would just switch brokers."

"You don't understand," said Karen, stating the obvious. "Switching brokers is what I was trying to prevent. What I had to prevent. How long do you think I would last in this business if Ted lost all my clients?"

"But why would Ted even think to invest in such a thing?"

"The magazine was started by the money guy behind SXYFX."

"So SXYFX got Ted to invest?"

"Yeah. If Ted had known anything, he would have seen that very little SXYFX funds were in the deal. It was risky. I mean, pornography is becoming more and more acceptable every day, but not child porn. People still draw the line."

"This money guy," I ventured, "Would his name be Herbie Dobbins?"

For the first time, Karen looked concerned. "Hey, how do you know that? He needs to keep that low key. The man's a pillar of the community. He supports a lot of politicians, you know. Guys who are in favor of Christian values."

I spared a moment of pity for Lloyd, who was probably inking the deal on a large campaign contribution right now. When this all came out, that deal would bite him in the ass and Mother wasn't going to be happy.

Chapter 42

"So what did you do?" I asked, stalling for time. Jeezus, how long would it take VJ and Belinda to figure out I was not okay?

"I knew our only hope was the key-man insurance. I got Warren to increase the limits."

"Made him think it was *his* idea?"

Karen looked smug, confirming my guess.

"Hey, I'm just curious here, did you switch parking cards with Schlefly?"

Karen frowned. "Yeah, it wasn't that hard. I just asked Ted for his card, told him they were issuing new ones. Then I turned the heat way up in Schlefly's office, to make sure he took his coat off before he went to the bathroom, like he does regular as clockwork at 10:00 AM. I nipped in and got his keys, ran down, got his card from his glove compartment. Everyone knows he keeps it there, and he always take a long time in the bathroom. He was still there when I got back."

"Very clever," I murmured. Karen smiled her old sweet smile.

"I switched Schlef's card with Ted's. So when Ted went home to have dinner that night and change, it looked like Schlefly leaving. Then when Ted came back that evening, it looked like he had never left and Schlefly was coming back to kill him."

"Wait a minute," I said, struggling to keep Karen talking. "The parking card register would that show Ted left on Friday afternoon. Because Schlefly left then, and he must have had Ted's card, if Ted had his card. But it didn't."

"I gave Schlefly my card, so when he left at 4:30, it looked like I was leaving. Triple switch. But when Belinda and I drove down to Laguna, we both went in her car. I told you that."

"But how did you get Ted to stay?"

"I told Ted that Stan Gastukian wanted to see him about buying his shares. Ted understood why that had to be top, top secret."

Ah, Stan Gastukian. The "S" in "8:00 appt. w/ S" noted in Ted's calendar. "And it worked?"

"Sure, he was thrilled. It was exactly what he wanted to hear."

"But Ted wasn't killed Friday night, was he? Not really."

Karen nodded. "I can't believe you guys figured that out. It was all going so well. It was easy to get Leah to take credit for my idea. Although, I practically had to put that torn birthday banner on a silver platter and tie it with a big red bow to get Eddie to notice it. All that was just, if you'll pardon the expression, insurance. I really thought everyone would think Ted died of a heart attack. It would have worked perfectly if Eddie hadn't been so greedy and stupid."

"And then?" I prodded.

"Then I used a pay phone from the bar in the hotel to call Ted on his cell phone. I told him there had been a change of plans, we had to have the meeting on Saturday night. He went home." Karen looked away for a moment. I held my breath. VJ and Belinda must be calling the cops by now, right? Right? I opened my mouth to ask another question, but I didn't have to say a word.

"On Saturday," continued Karen, "Belinda drove me back to work so I could get my car and she could meet Leah and put up the banner." Karen started to chuckle. "That's when I stole Belinda's card. Nobody could use Ted's card again, obviously. So that left my car inside without a card to get out. I knew Belinda would think she had lost it, and I knew she would sweet talk the attendant into letting her out. They're supposed to charge you ten bucks for losing your card, but girls like Belinda, they don't get charged. Neither one of them would ever say anything, either. 'Cause he'd get in trouble."

Karen was reveling in the story. It was all very ingenious, but my powers of concentration were not so good.

"Then what happened Saturday night?"

"Ted and I came back for the 'meeting.' I had it timed for when the guard at the front desk was on a break, but Ted insisted on signing in. I was so mad, I could have just killed him," Karen spat out.

I kept still.

"After the situation had resolved itself I switched his card back into his pocket, and dropped Belinda's card in her office, where she found it on Monday. On Monday morning, I got my card back from Schlefly and slipped him back his card."

"But anyone could have seen Ted on Saturday. He could have talked to somebody. How did you convince him to stay in hiding for twenty-four hours?"

"I told him that a process server was looking for him to serve him with a wage garnishment in the Mraz case."

"And you took the sign-in book?"

"Yeah, I heard from Lydia at the funeral that Eddie was hiring a private investigator. She was pretty upset with him for stranding her up at the funeral. I offered to take her home."

I recalled the picture from the funeral. Lydia punching Eddie, walking away with Karen. Seemed like a hundred years ago. When Eddie said he hadn't told anyone about hiring me, he hadn't included his wife. Who had blabbed to Karen. Which explained why the sign-in book was taken the next day.

"Ms. Ng?"

"She knew about the connection between SXYFX and Dobbins. All this stuff with the teen 'zine hits the papers. She asked me about it, so I pushed her under a bus. Don't pretend you're sorry. She was old."

"What about Dina?" I asked. "She wasn't old. Let me guess. She was blackmailing you? She called Ted on Friday. They were talking weren't they? Maybe she called him on Saturday, too?"

"That little bitch. She was trying to get Ted to get her a job as a model in that stupid magazine. Ted strung her along because he thought he could talk her into calling off the process server. What an idiot."

"She knew he was alive on Saturday."

"Worse. Ted happened to mention that he had just talked to me. So Dina not only knew Ted was alive on Saturday, she knew I knew he was alive on Saturday. When the papers all reported he died on Friday night, and she realized that I hadn't corrected the time of death, she figured something was wrong. She called me the day after the funeral. Said she wanted ten thousand dollars for 'expenses.' She already was going to get over a million dollar judgment. How greedy can you get?"

"Yeah, some people!" I exclaimed. "So Eddie? Why did you kill Eddie?"

"I didn't kill Eddie. I couldn't have killed Eddie. You know that. I was in New York when Eddie was shot."

Of course I knew that. That was the thing that had eliminated Karen from the suspect list.

"SXYFX killed Eddie." She glared at me. "It was your fault."

This was not the direction I had hoped the conversation would go. "I didn't know anything about this. How could it be my fault?" I tried to say this in a non-confrontational way, but Karen had gotten defensive at the mention of Eddie's death.

"You tipped them off that something was wrong by going there."

I considered the chronology for a moment. It was possible. Disturbingly possible.

"Once they were on to it, I had to have a fall guy, and you were perfect. I told them you were working for Eddie, and Eddie was trying to rip them off. Anything. The important thing was that they didn't find out it was Ted who'd borrowed the money. They considered Ted and me partners." Karen said this with bitterness. "But Eddie, he had nothing to do with me. And they were grateful I supplied the proof."

"You supplied the proof? Against Eddie?"

She nodded. "Yeah, faked up some documents."

"So maybe Eddie's death wasn't entirely my fault?" I ventured. She didn't respond, but she looked very satisfied. I studied her face. "It isn't just for money though is it? You like killing people."

"Why do you say that?" she asked, amused.

"Because it's too many people. One person, you might kill for money, but this many people, it's got to be about something else. Who else have you killed? A lot of people?"

"People who need it."

"Like who?" I asked, but certainty struck me with hurricane force. "Oh no, the babies. The AIDS babies. You actually killed babies, you actually..." I couldn't finish and sat there, my eyes filling up.

"They were sick. They wanted to go to heaven. The doctor said they were getting better, but that was a lie. I knew what was best for them. They were mine." Karen's voice was cracking.

I had kicked a stone and started a mental avalanche. "What about the car bomb, Karen? You could have killed anybody on that street."

The corners of her mouth had crusted over with saliva. "That was SXYFX, not me. But don't worry," she gestured with the gun, "I fully intend to pick up where they left off."

"I don't think so, big girl. People know I'm here. Belinda and a friend of mine are right outside."

Karen didn't look impressed. "Belinda's a drunk, and I doubt you have friends. You don't seem very friendly. But," Karen squared her already very square jaw, "you're right. We've got to get this over with."

"That's not what I meant," I protested. Karen moved over to a small, white end table and opened the drawer. My mouth went dry at the sight of the hypodermic syringe.

"What's that?"

"Same thing I gave Ted," Karen answered, "It's what they give you when you have an operation and they stop your breathing, and then while you're under, they intubate and breathe for you. It's like a paralyzing agent. It's called succinyl choline, if you're interested."

"I'm kind of interested," I managed to reply. "But the autopsy report was negative for any kind of drugs. I can see how you juked the time of death, but not the drug report."

"That's the beauty of this stuff. It paralyzes your nervous system but won't show up on a routine autopsy. You learn a lot hanging around hospitals. Stole it out of a closet when a new orderly got flustered."

"How did you manage to make Ted sit still for that?"

"I gave it to him in the neck. He never even knew what happened. Just walked up behind him. He never paid a lot of attention to me." Karen added viciously, "I guess he should have."

Where the hell were VJ and Belinda? What was taking them so long? My stomach heaved.

And then I puked. Karen leaped back. The smell was pretty awful. Lasagna. Everything was awful all the way around. Except it slowed Karen down. She didn't want to get near me. That was not awful.

As she stood there, gun in one had, hypodermic in the other, there was a noise at the front door. Thank God, VJ! I thought. I heard the lock being picked and door handle being turned, and I was very impressed with my old friend. I was wholly unaware that she knew how to pick a lock.

Chapter 43

I was less impressed when VJ and Belinda came in together, slowly, carefully—followed by a guy with a gun.

"Jesus, what's that smell?" yelped Stan, as he slammed the door shut behind him. Stan the pornographer. Of course. Driving the Audi that kept us so carefully in sight.

"She puked," Karen barked back. "What are you doing here?"

Stan surveyed the scene with narrowed eyes. "Some information recently came into my possession that I needed to ask you about, and I came across these jerks trying to get in the front door of the building. What the hell is going on here?"

"We had a little misunderstanding." Karen shot me a quick look to warn me to be quiet. I took my cue and started babbling.

"It wasn't Eddie. It was her and Ted," I gasped. "Eddie found out, that's what he hired me and Bosco to do, to investigate irregularities. Also, she killed Ted."

Stan's expression didn't change as he stood with his back against the door, his slick, black raincoat dripping onto the carpet. "Is this true, Karen?" he asked gently.

"Of course it isn't true. She was in it with Eddie, just like you thought. Nobody killed Ted. He just died."

"So what's going on here?" Stan asked again. VJ and Belinda edged toward the little kitchenette. I think both had the same idea to duck behind the counter if the shooting started. Good idea. I wished I could join them.

Karen's circuits were visibly overloading. She blurted out. "They know."

"Know what, Karen?" asked Stan, still in that gentle voice.

Karen darted a glance at me. I wiped my chin on my shoulder and wondered what was coming next.

"About Dobbins," she lowered her voice as if she could prevent VJ and Belinda from hearing.

I didn't like this one bit. It was obvious that Stan thought people shouldn't know about Dobbins, and I certainly didn't want to know about Dobbins.

Karen was perspiring heavily. I was sweating right with her.

VJ reached the counter and slid behind it. Belinda was sliding behind VJ. Bosco stayed unconscious.

Stan looked around at us. I could tell he was counting the bodies.

"Where is your Expedition parked?" Stan asked Karen.

"It's in my space, in the parking garage," Karen eagerly replied

"Keys," Stan demanded. Karen rushed over to the kitchen counter where her stolid black leather purse had been slung down. I tried to eyebrow Morse code to VJ to grab Karen, knock her gun away, use her as a human shield, rush Stan and grab his gun. She didn't get it.

I wanted to puke again, but there wasn't any lasagna left.

Through a daze I heard Stan say something about moving his Maserati around back and gesturing with the gun. I realized, as no doubt Stan and Karen did, that they probably couldn't shoot us all there. The walls of the complex were thin. You could hear Conan O'Brien from next door, as if it were in the next room. And it would be hard to shoot people without leaving any blood evidence.

Stan was barking at Karen to get rope, which she didn't

have, or duct tape, which she also didn't have. She did have a lot of electrical appliances and a pair of scissors. Stan instructed her to cut the cords off the coffeemaker and two lamps.

"Don't do it," I rasped out. "Karen, he's going to kill you, too."

Without responding, she cut through the cords to all her appliances, gathered them up and came at me. I tottered to my feet and circled her warily, keeping one eye on Stan with the gun.

"Karen, listen to me," I wheezed. "He knows that it was Ted who financed the premium. That's why he's here. That folder on Ted that Warren made up. You made a copy of it for Ted, but Warren's folder was still in his office. That's what Eddie had that night, the night they shot him. He must have gotten it out of Warren's office. I told you, he had keys to all the offices."

Her eyes bulged.

"Karen, I'm telling you, Eddie got that folder. He was going to give it to me, but he got shot, and it was taken. By his goon," I tilted my head toward Stan. "Was that the same guy who busted in my windshield?"

Stan nodded, unconcerned. "Yeah, he'd like to be here tonight but I sent him to Costa Rica for a little while. Vacation."

"Karen, if the goon took Warren's folder and gave it to Stan, then Stan knows. And if he knows, he's going to kill you, too." My jaw was swelling and seizing up from where Karen's fist had landed, so it came out more like "E gung kiw oo doo." But she knew what I meant.

"You told me Eddie had the sign-in book." Karen's breathing was shallow as she maneuvered to my right, trying to get another punch in. "You said that's what was taken. And you were right, it's gone. I had it hidden in my bottom drawer, and it's gone."

"Well..." I tried to think. "Eddie probably had that, too. He was a sneaky little prick. But that couldn't be all he had on him that night, because the SXYFX goon wouldn't have bothered to take the sign-in book off of Eddie's body. It wouldn't have meant anything to him. Something that mentioned SXYFX, though, that would catch his attention."

I ran out of breath. There was no way I could take Karen in a fair fight. But she had to hold me down to tie me up, and that was harder than just killing me.

It was a Mexican standoff, or in these enlightened times, a situation of power parity which immobilizes further activity. Or it was until Stan got tired of watching us circle each other and came up behind me and smacked me on the head with the butt of the gun.

I dropped, a field of purple filled my eyes, points of light swirled around. I didn't quite lose consciousness. I heard Belinda scream, but not a real good scream that makes the neighbors call the police. She could take pointers from Gursky, I thought.

Karen was pushing my face into the floor and putting her meaty knee in the small of my back. My head really hurt.

As blackness engulfed me, I remembered Stan's remark about "moving the Maserati." If Stan had come in a Maserati, then who was driving the white Audi?

Chapter 44

I came to just as red and blue lights burst upon the window. Kind of like a bomb, as I can now say from actual experience. I could hear the slamming of car doors over the rain. Big, heavy, official car doors.

For that split second, I was too startled for relief to hit. Which was just as well because before anyone in the room could react, the police loudspeaker boomed out: "Fifi Cutter. This is the police. We know you're in there. Come out with your hands up."

My hands were securely tied behind my back with electrical cord. Coming out with my hands up was nothing but a sweet, distant dream.

"Son of a goddamn bitch," Stan swore. His eyes seemed to glow yellow as he pointed the gun at me and Karen, who was still kneeling down next to me on the carpet. I knew he was going to shoot.

I squealed and tried to roll as he pulled the trigger. I felt the force of Karen's body as it was thrown back. Warm liquid splashed over me. I retched as I heard VJ's roar and Belinda's shriek.

Then the window really did explode. Out of the corner of my eye, from my awkwardly prone position, I saw Stan fall, arms and legs splayed across the shag carpeting. His face was gone. I passed out.

When I regained consciousness, a SWAT officer was

bending over what was left of Stan, making sure he was dead. He stood up and opened the door to a swarm of people—paramedics, officers, plain clothes.

And Keith Gursky. They were trying to keep him out, but he was yelling that he had a right to come in because he was the one who had called the police.

It occurred to me, through a groggy haze, that Keith had an ex-wife, whose other car probably was a broom. Keith had been spying on Belinda. He must have seen Bosco go in to her apartment and then come out. He must have seen me and VJ go in and Belinda leave, in her nightie, with us.

I don't know if he believed we were abducting her or doing something kinky, but he followed us. Then he saw Stan take VJ and Belinda at gunpoint, and—finally—called the cops.

I owed my life to the world's dorkiest stalker.

I soon found myself in a police car. VJ had tried to tell them that she was my lawyer, and that I couldn't be questioned without her, but they didn't believe she was a lawyer, or, giving the LAPD the benefit of the doubt, they believed she was a lawyer, but they didn't care.

As interrogations go, this one was mild. No latte, but since the SWAT guy confirmed that I had been on the floor, bound with electrical cord, and Bosco had clearly been in a coma, Detective Sweet was inclined to believe my story.

Especially since I told them the story. Every bit of it. What they really wanted was for me to back them up on their story that shooting Stan was necessary and justified, which I was delighted to do.

I asked the cops to take me to the hospital. I didn't feel like asking them to drive me back to Bionic Sushi to pick up Eddie's car, because that might lead to more—well—explanations. Anyway, I really didn't feel so good.

In the moderately crowded waiting room I met up with VJ and Belinda, both of whom had been treated for shock. Keith was there, too, looking so pleased with himself that it took all my restraint not to slap him. He verified what I had deduced, only the way he told it, he wasn't a jealous weirdo, he was an omniscient action hero.

VJ told me that Bosco was still out. They weren't letting us see him because it wasn't visiting hours.

I went to sign in at the emergency room desk. Uninsured, it took fifty-seven minutes, trying to convince the Nazi behind the bulletproof glass to call my stepfather to guarantee payment.

Much to my surprise and dismay, VJ told me that Karen was not dead. She had been shot through the lung, but the bullet had missed the heart. They were working on her right now to save her life.

Well, she certainly had insurance, I thought.

It only took another hour and fourteen minutes to see a doctor. Doctor, my ass; this guy wasn't any older than I was, and if he'd gotten into medical school, then I should have been up for a Pulitzer Prize. He said the huge purple lump on my jaw would go away in time and that I didn't have a concussion.

I went back out to the waiting room and became convinced that I must have had a concussion after all. It was dawn, the light was pink and gold, and Lloyd, as cardboard as ever, was standing there in his grey Brooks Brothers suit and tan raincoat.

"What are you doing here?" I asked Lloyd. "Is someone hurt?"

Lloyd looked puzzled, "Yeah, you and Bosco," he replied. "The hospital called. I came as quickly as I could."

"Why?" None of this was making any sense.

"To make sure you were okay," said Lloyd. "You're my stepchildren."

I was touched. Until I saw him look guiltily at a smiley-faced white guy in a lighter-grey Brooks brothers suit and an equally tan raincoat, standing respectfully about five feet away.

"If you don't mind sitting down for just a little bit, Fifi, there are going to be some reporters. My people," Lloyd shrugged toward the smiley-faced guy. "My people, well, your Mother thinks it would be much better for us to get our story out first. With the election coming up, and all. We could even turn this into a plus."

I sat down. I still didn't know what he was talking about.

*   *   *

It didn't get quite the coverage Lloyd had hoped for, only the briefest TV spot on local news, but there was a picture on the front page of the Valley section of the *Times* the next day of Lloyd (with a statesman-like smile) and me (with an enormous chipmunk cheek, looking more bi-species than bi-racial).

The caption described me as Lloyd's "adopted daughter" and subtly implied that he had lifted me, as the merest baby, out of a rat-infested ghetto and away from my drug-addicted mother to a better life in suburbia.

The accompanying story explained how Lloyd had refused to bow down to pressure applied by the local porno industry, which had first tried to bribe him with $125,000 in illegal campaign donations. Then, when he righteously refused to accept such dirty money, they acted just like you would expect your typical pornographer to act and tried to have Lloyd's brave and loving family killed in retaliation.

Herbert Dobbins, notorious behind-the-scenes owner of several adult film companies, including SXYFX, and the infamous new teen 'zine, was named. The paper ran a sidebar story about SXYFX that, while deploring the growth of this unsavory industry, was nonetheless illustrated with a large color photo of SXYFX star Suzie Double-Q.

Chapter 45

Two days later, I was asleep on my raft when I was awakened by the phone beeping. It was St. Vincent's. They wanted me to come get Bosco. I completely understood their desire to be rid of him, I explained, but I had no desire to re-acquire him. They insisted someone had to come get him.

He didn't look that great. He was pasty, I mean even more than usual, and his clothes were rumpled. I should have thought and brought him fresh clothes. He had a copy of the *Times* under his arm.

"So this was all about protecting the porn industry?" Bosco marveled.

"No, dog breath, none of this had anything to do with protecting the porn industry. Don't you get it? That's all just Mother's spin."

"Mom? What's she got to do with it?" Bosco was searching the story for a reference to Mother.

"Everything. This story is her way of covering up the fact that she's been chasing Dobbins for money like a hyena in heat."

"But why would Dobbins kill Ted?"

"He didn't kill Ted. Karen killed Ted. She almost killed you. Remember? And if it is of any interest at all, she almost killed me."

"But listen, Fifi, why did they kidnap you to get to Lloyd?"

Bosco persisted. "I don't understand. I mean, Lloyd doesn't even really know you."

"Stop talking, you retard. No one kidnapped me. I went over to Karen's apartment of my own free, if misguided, will."

"Why would you do that? If you knew she killed Ted?"

"Because she was going to kill you. By the way, how did she get you to leave the fair Belinda at what I have to assume was a very critical moment?"

"Oh," Bosco gulped. "Well, Karen called and, you know, told me some made-up story."

"What story?" I demanded.

"Oh nothing," Bosco shrugged. I waited. "It's just," he mumbled, "that she said, you know, she told me that you were missing and, you know, maybe you were in danger..." I hurried to change the subject.

"But why would she kill you? What did you say to her?"

Bosco didn't have an answer. He shook his head gloomily. "It wasn't anything I said. She offered me the doctored drink right away, so she knew before I got there that she was going to put me out."

I puzzled on this as we inched past the banks of Echo Park Lake, dotted with a few intrepid picnickers. The sky was grey where it was visible through the canopy of sagging telephone lines. I could see a car with its hood up blocking the left lane up ahead. I should have taken the freeway.

"So she called you on the cell phone. But wait a minute," I paused. "She must have known it was Ted's cell phone."

Bosco eyes widened. "What do you mean?"

"You idiot. She probably called Ted on that phone a million times. She didn't ask you what you were doing with Ted's cell phone?"

Bosco shook his head. "No, she did say something about paying the bill for the cell phone. I didn't really pay attention, you know, 'cause I wasn't going to pay the bill."

"Yeah, but she must have thought Chloe gave you the

phone and that you would get the bill. If you saw the bill, you'd figure it out. Ted's calls would be on the bill."

"So?'

"So, the bill would show that he talked to Dina and Karen when he was supposed to be dead. The bill would prove Karen knew Ted was alive Saturday night."

"Seems like a stupid reason to kill me."

"She likes killing. She's been doing it a long time. She may have even started with that Ollie guy, the one you thought Warren Obermeyer killed, all those years ago."

"Well, they'll never get her for Ted's death," Bosco said. "They couldn't even prove it was murder."

"What the hell do you mean?" I demanded. "I told the police about her confession."

"I know, but nobody else heard it. The cops talked to her this morning. The nurse told me that Karen was well enough to give a brief statement. Karen's story matches Mother's. You were kidnapped by Stan, brought up to the apartment before he caught VJ and Belinda. Karen said Stan smacked you really hard on the head, so you probably don't remember exactly what happened."

"For God's sake, that's not going to work!" I squealed.

"It might. After all, Ted was a heart attack, Dina was an overdose, and Ms. Ng was a bus accident. She didn't kill Eddie, which is the only murder the cops have on the books."

"What about drugging you? What about the syringe?"

Bosco waggled his hand in the maybe gesture. "If she has to, Karen will just say I brought the Rohypnol with me, and make out like I'm some druggie."

With a sudden chill, I recalled that Bosco had been expelled from Lehigh University for selling marijuana to the Resident Advisor. Turned out it was really oregano, but that didn't help.

Bosco offered small comfort. "Maybe she'll die anyway, Feef. I heard they had her back on the respirator just as I was leaving. Her lung collapsed." Bosco reached in his pocket. "Here," he said kindly, "this will make you feel better. I swiped it off the end table as Karen was getting ice for my drink."

I glanced over at the huge diamond ring glittering in the palm in his hand. We exchanged smiles.

Chapter 46

When we got home, I put Bosco to bed and told him to rest up. I called the hospital for a report on Karen's condition, which they wouldn't give me.

I brooded. About Bosco and the AIDS babies, those that were gone and those that didn't even have a slim chance if Karen got well. And Chloe, really sad about her Dad. Even Lydia and Eddie Jr., sad about Eddie. Ms. Ng who came to America, worked hard, and got tossed under an RTD bus. And I thought about having my face pushed into a puke-soiled carpet.

Bosco woke up around noon. I fed him some soup in bed. Well, in futon.

"You gonna be okay for a while?" I asked.

"I think so. I have a head ache but I'm mostly just tired. Why?"

"I gotta go back to the hospital. I need to have it out with her."

"Fifi, are you crazy? Leave it alone. There's nothing more you can do."

"She's killed so many people. And she almost killed us, Bosco. Besides. I want her stay away from those AIDS babies. Maybe she won't be prosecuted for what she did in the past, but she's got to know someone's paying attention now."

I left Bosco slurping his soup thoughtfully. Deep in my closet, I found an old pair of overalls. I put my hair up in a red scarf and grabbed a mop and pail. Little dark people can make themselves invisible so easily.

I sailed right in the back door. No one so much as glanced at me. I made my way to Karen's room and pretend-mopped around that general area until the foot traffic cleared. I bumped the door with my butt and spun in. Karen was lying on the bed, almost unrecognizable under white sheets, tubes criss crossed over her like telephone wires in East LA. A plastic mask obscured her face. It was attached to a machine. A machine that was breathing for her.

I started toward her but slammed to a halt when a figure in green scrubs suddenly rose from the side of the bed. We both gasped in surprise. At first I didn't recognize her. Every time I'd seen her she had been so beautifully dressed, the Manolo Blahniks, the St. John's knits.

"Corazon. What are you doing here?"

At first, she looked right through me. When she spoke her voice was thick and her accent more pronounced. "Oh, iss you. The grief girl."

"Yeah. Uh. Sorry. I didn't realize you and Karen were tight."

"Tight? What do you mean tight? You mean like friends? You think we were friends, this big, fat maggot and I? Oh no, no, no. We are not friends." Her hands spasmodically gripped the cord she was holding, a cord that was attached to a plug in the wall at one end and to the breathing machine on the other.

"You can't do it, Corazon."

"Why not?"

"Because, you just can't."

"But I can." Her black eyes flicked back in focus, losing the dazed look. The naked grief was much worse. "I heard from Belinda how you said she killed the babies. If she killed the babies, I can kill her."

"Corazon, nobody believes me about that."

"I believe you."

It took me a few mental steps but I worked it out. "The

baby who was christened the night Ted died. His name was Miguel. And in the hospice, one of the babies who died was Miguel. Was he your nephew too?"

Corazon nodded. Her eyes sparkled with tears. "The first Miguel. He was the son of my brother Tomas. Tomas was always getting into trouble, but he had a good heart. That girlfriend, though. She was bad. Into drugs. Needles. Many men. All those things. We told Tomas to leave her but he didn't listen. And then the baby came, and the girlfriend was the one who left." She wiped her eyes. "I said they could live with me, Tomas and Miguel. I had to. They were family, you know?"

I knew.

"And they did live with me but Miguel was diagnosed with this terrible disease at seven months. By then, I already loved him." Corazon's face twisted with pain. "He didn't have a mother, so I was his mother. I was going to teach him to read. Miguel would do very good in school, you could tell. Smart. He was going to go to college."

Behind her, Karen stirred, rustling the sheets, a softly ominous sound.

"They put him in the hospice. To treat him. They said some babies live. They go into remission and they live. Everyday I went to work and I worked hard. But also every day I prayed."

"And Karen?"

Corazon grasped at her perfect hair and her tears were falling freely. "I beg God to forgive me. I was the one who asked her to come with me and help. To hold the babies. I brought her there. I was the one."

"Corazon, please, you couldn't know. No one could blame you."

"Blame and guilt. Not the same thing." She wiped her nose with the back of her hand. We both stared at the plug.

"You still can't do it," I said. She opened her mouth to argue, but I pointed to red button on the side of the machine.

"There's an alarm. If you don't turn it off, it'll blast as soon as the plug is disconnected."

She looked at me. I left.

When the paper reported Karen's death the next day, nothing was said about a cord having been unplugged. Of course, the first nurse to find her would certainly make sure that cord was right back where it was supposed to be before reporting that the patient had expired.

I paid my property taxes and my Visa bill, got the roof fixed, and had $27.34 left over.

My brother Joe got promoted. Turns out, he was the "pesky vice cop" who had been keeping the pressure on Ted's teen 'zine. He called to see how I was doing the other day.

Belinda and Keith got married. Robert and Dolly got divorced.

D'Metree left Party All-night and opened his own party supply store.

The SXYFX goon was killed in a Costa Rican prison awaiting extradition.

Lloyd's election chances are looking good. The publicity from my rescue gave him both the minority and the Christian values vote. Mother was so pleased, she bought me a television. A huge flat screen high definition television.

Bosco is still here. His dad is paying me $1,000.00 a month to keep him. Like I said before, Mr. Dorff is very fond of his only son.

THE END

After clerkships with the CIA, and the Dade County Attorney's Office, Gwen Freeman graduated from the University of Virginia Law School, and joined a law firm in Los Angeles, where she specialized in insurance law. More recently, she has represented death row inmates, and was successful in obtaining relief for the longest resident of California's Death Row.

An artist of note, Gwen shows her work in galleries nationwide and has a loyal cult following. Her work has been featured on the sets of Frasier; The O.C.; The Sweetest Thing: American Pie II; and Daddy Day Care.

Gwen presently lives with her husband, daughter, two dogs, five cats, 217 birds and a raccoon in a 100 year old restoration project, one hill over from Dodger stadium.